Dear Readers,

There's nothing like curling up with a good book on a crisp fall evening, and this month we present four new Bouquet romances that are sure to warm your heart.

With Thanksgiving only weeks away, Adrienne Basso's **Sweet Sensations** is a perfect first course in a month full of captivating stories. Adrienne's heroine is a pastry chef who finds that only one man will complete her recipe for love. Next, Zebra and Avon author Jane Kidder serves up a second chance at love in **Heart Song,** when a pianist with a previous secret must face the man she once loved . . . and lost.

Of course, once Thanksgiving draws to a close, Christmas is just around the corner—and this month our authors are inspired by the spirit of the season. Longtime Zebra and Harlequin author Patricia Werner offers the charming tale of a woman in charge of a retirement home who rediscovers her Christmas cheer—with the help of a resident's handsome son—in **Jenny's Star.** And in **A Christmas Bouquet,** three of our favorite authors spread holiday joy. In **"Amy's Gift"** by Suzanne Barrett, a young widow whose child is looking for Santa meets a bachelor who just may fit the bill. Then a Christmas decorating enthusiast and her bah-humbug neighbor clash—passionately—in Kate Holmes's **"Merry and Her Gentleman."** Last, in Vella Munn's **"Silver Christmas,"** a small-town shopkeeper with contemporary flair meets the handsome, if old-fashioned, man of her dreams.

So build a fire, make a pot of tea, and get ready for the kind of smart, sexy love stories we know you adore.

The Editors

ROMANCE

SWEET REUNION

"I can't remember the last time I had lobster."

Alexei smiled and his dark eyes took on a faraway look. "Do you remember the time we rented a car and drove all the way to Gloucestor because you were so hungry for lobster?"

Natalie laughed in fond remembrance. "Yes. We went to a lobster shack right on the wharf. As I remember, it was absolutely wonderful."

Slowly, Alexei reached across the table and covered Natalie's hand with his. "As I remember, that whole day was wonderful."

Natalie gazed down at their clasped hands and all the long, lonely years spent apart seemed to melt away. "After we ate, we took a walk," she said softly. "We climbed up a hill and stood looking down at the bay . . ." Slowly, she raised her eyes to meet Alexei's. ". . . And you kissed me."

He nodded, his eyes drifting closed as the tender memory flooded his mind. "I remember that kiss—and everything that happened afterward." He opened his eyes and lifted Natalie's hand to his lips. "It was always wonderful between us, Tasha."

Natalie nodded, biting her lip as she fought back tears. "I'm sorry for the pain I know I must have caused you. Are you still angry with me?"

"I was never angry with you. I was hurt, I was confused, but I was never really angry. And whether you want to hear this or not, I never stopped loving you."

"Oh, Alex," she moaned. "I never stopped loving you either. You are the—"

She never finished her sentence for the next thing she knew, she was being pulled up against Alexei's body and his lips were covering hers. . . .

HEART
SONG

JANE KIDDER

Zebra Books
Kensington Publishing Corp.

http://www.zebrabooks.com

ZEBRA BOOKS are published by

Kensington Publishing Corp.
850 Third Avenue
New York, NY 10022

Copyright © 1999 by Jane Kidder

Zebra and the Z logo Reg. U.S. Pat. & TM Off.

First Printing: November, 1999
10 9 8 7 6 5 4 3 2 1

Printed in the United States of America

To Marion Gorton Edwards, who for more than thirty years has been my dearest friend.

This one is for you—and for Triscuit and Alouette, who started it all.

ONE

There he was. Alexei Romanov. The Russian genius, the greatest pianist in the world . . . and the only man Natalie Worthington Saxon had ever loved. It had been more than eight years since she had last seen him, but as she sat in the fifth row of Boston's Symphony Hall and stared at him, standing so proud and erect on the stage as he accepted the accolades of the enthralled audience, she realized that he hadn't changed at all. He was still just as tall, just as handsome, just as dangerously seductive as he'd been when he was a visiting professor at the Juilliard School and she'd been his twenty-two-year-old student.

Natalie closed her eyes for a moment, shocked by the emotions coursing through her. "Let's go," she said suddenly, leaning toward her friend, Susan Bedford, and giving her sleeve an urgent tug.

Susan's hands stopped in midclap. "Go! Why would you want to go? The concert's not over yet. I'm sure he'll play another encore."

"He's not going to play another encore," Natalie said. "He never plays more than one. Anyway, if we leave now, we can beat the traffic out of the parking lot."

"Oh, for heaven's sake, who cares about the traffic? Besides, we can't go yet. When I spoke to his publicist this afternoon about interviewing Romanov, he told me to come back to his dressing room after the concert to set up a time." She threw

Natalie a teasing look. "Come on, Nat. Wouldn't you like to go with me and say hi?"

Natalie gaped at Susan, appalled. "Absolutely not! I barely knew the man and, besides, it was a long time ago. I certainly have no desire to burst into his dressing room like some groupie hoping he'll remember me."

Susan shrugged. "If you don't want to renew old acquaintances, that's up to you, but I'm not going to miss the opportunity to meet him and set up an interview."

"All right. I'll just wait outside while you make your appointment."

Susan frowned, wondering what was bothering her usually adventurous friend. Come to think of it, Natalie had been acting strange all evening.

As the two women turned back to the stage, Alexei Romanov turned to bow in their direction but stopped short as his eyes settled on Natalie.

"Oh, my God, he's spotted you!" Susan squealed, reaching over and giving Natalie's hand an excited squeeze. "Look, Nat, he's staring right at you—and you thought he wouldn't remember you."

Natalie gasped with alarm as she realized that, indeed, Alexei Romanov's gaze was riveted on her. Abruptly, she pulled her hand out of Susan's grasp and picked up her opera glasses, holding them in front of her face like a shield. She quickly turned her head, gazing off through the glasses as if fascinated by something on the other side of the auditorium.

"This is so unbelievable!" Susan continued. "Everyone in the whole hall has noticed him looking at you." Susan threw her friend a quick glance, then frowned. "Natalie, put those stupid glasses down and wave at him or something. What is wrong with you tonight?"

Reluctantly, Natalie set the tiny gold binoculars back in her lap, but still she refused to look at the man on stage. Finally, Alexei pulled his gaze away and with a practiced flip of his tuxedo tails, reseated himself at the Steinway.

"There, you see?" Susan said. "He *is* going to play again." Throwing Natalie an I-told-you-so look, she settled back in her seat.

Natalie looked around surreptitiously, relieved to see that the audience had again directed its attention to the stage. *I can handle this,* she told herself silently. *It's almost over.*

But when the first rippled chord of Beethoven's *Moonlight Sonata* filled the auditorium, she almost bolted and ran. Oh, God, she thought desperately, not the sonata.

Suddenly, in her mind's eye, Natalie could see herself seated at a piano in a stuffy little practice room at Juilliard, struggling with the third movement of Beethoven's famous piece as Alexei sat patiently beside her, his deep, heavily accented voice intoning, "You must feel the music, Tasha, darling. Remember, Beethoven wrote this sonata for his lover. Try to *feel* his passion and everything else will follow."

Natalie squeezed her eyes shut, trying hard to block out the bittersweet memories as Beethoven's great love song continued to flow over her. Finally, when she felt like she was again in control of her emotions, she opened her eyes only to find that Alexei was not truly concentrating on his playing, but rather, kept throwing quick sideward glances in her direction. *Susan's right,* she thought desperately, *he* does *recognize me. Lord, I wish I could get out of here!*

After what seemed like an interminable length of time, the sonata and the concert finally ended and the crowd began to move toward the exits. "Come on," Susan said, standing up and gathering her coat and purse. "Let's go backstage before every well-wisher in Boston gets there ahead of us."

"You go ahead, Sue. Like I said, I'll wait for you outside."

Susan turned around, looking at Natalie aghast. "You can't be serious! You have to go with me. Romanov saw us sitting together, and if I go back to his dressing room alone, he's sure to ask me where you are. What am I supposed to say? That an old friend refused to show him the common courtesy of saying hello?"

"That sounds reasonable to me."

"Well, not to me! Nat, I don't know what's wrong with you tonight, but this interview is very important to my career, and you know how temperamental these artist types can be. Please don't put me in an awkward position with Romanov. He might get mad and cancel the interview altogether, and then what would I tell my editor?"

Natalie sighed in resignation. "All right, I'll go with you. But I want you to promise me that we're not going to hang around, that you'll just set up your interview and then we'll leave."

Susan shot her friend another bewildered look. "Okay, I promise. Let's just get back there before the crowd in his dressing room gets so big that we have to wait all night to see him."

Quickly, the two women made their way backstage, winding through a confusing labyrinth of corridors until they finally came upon an open door outside of which stood a large knot of people.

Tall and slender with dark eyes, short dark hair, and the no-nonsense attitude of a seasoned reporter, Susan maneuvered through the crowd, dragging the mortified Natalie behind her.

"Mr. Romanov," she said loudly as she reached the front of the throng, "I'm Susan Bedford of the *Boston Morning News*. I spoke to Mr. Svetlanov this afternoon about setting up an interview with you."

Alexei turned toward the aggressive woman, opening his mouth to direct her to where his publicist, Sergei Svetlanov, was making appointments, but his words died in his throat. Standing slightly behind the demanding reporter was the blond woman he'd seen in the fifth row, the same blond woman he'd seen every night in his dreams for the past eight years.

"Tasha," he whispered. "My God, it *is* you." Completely oblivious to the startled, offended faces of the people waiting to see him, Alexei reached out and pulled Natalie into his dressing room, unceremoniously slamming the door in the crowd's faces. "I thought I saw you in the audience tonight."

Natalie stared at Alexei, speechless for a moment. She could hardly believe that the man whom she had loved so passionately, the man whose handsome face and dark, brooding eyes she had seen so often in her dreams was actually standing before her, holding her hand and staring back at her.

"Alex," she croaked, quickly clearing her throat to cover the tremor in her voice, "you're looking well."

Her stilted words belied the turmoil going on in her mind. He had called her Tasha—the affectionate Russian nickname for Natalie. He was the only person who had ever called her that, and after all these years, she had never thought to hear it from him again.

Alexei stepped toward her, hardly able to believe that the hand he was pressing to his cheek was really Natalie's. Oh, there were changes in her, to be sure. She was nearly thirty now, and her face was a little older and her figure a little curvier. The long blond hair that he had once loved to brush was now shorter, cut in a sleek style that just brushed her shoulders when she turned her head. She looked more sophisticated, more elegant, although he was glad to see that the color of her hair was still just as golden, her sea-blue eyes just as bright.

But, despite the changes the years had brought, the beautiful woman standing before him was definitely still his Tasha—and she had called him Alex. No one else had ever called him that, and hearing it from her lips was a balm to his spirit after all the long, lonely years he'd spent without her. "I can't believe it," he breathed. "What are you doing here? Do you live in Boston now?"

Natalie nodded and pulled her hand away. "Yes. I moved back here from New York after I finished school."

Alexei's dark eyes continued to search hers, making her uneasy as she realized that he still seemed to have the power to see into her very soul. "I teach," she added, taking a step back.

"At the Boston Conservatory of Music. Classical piano. To college students." Her voice trailed off as she realized how inane her chatter must sound.

But Alex only smiled—that devastating smile that softened his sculpted lips and crinkled the tight, bronze skin around his eyes. Natalie nervously wet her lips with her tongue, unnerved by the effect his smile still had on her.

"Your concert was wonderful tonight, Alex. I enjoyed it very much."

Alexei nodded his thanks, then picked up her hand again, staring down at it as he rubbed his thumb across its smooth surface. "Why did you stop writing to me, Tasha?"

"Oh, Alex, please." Natalie laughed, trying to make light of his unexpected question. "That's ancient history."

He raised his eyes, his expression somber as he stared at her. "After all we shared, did you truly not care enough to even answer my letters?"

Natalie again pulled her hand from his warm grasp. "Alex, really, now is not the time or place to discuss this." Throwing her arm wide, she gestured toward the door. "There are about a hundred people waiting out there to see you. They must think it's very rude that we're in here . . ."

She never completed her sentence. Without warning, Alex pulled her close and lowered his lips to hers, kissing her with a passion that made her head reel. For a long moment, she allowed herself to revel in the sheer, sensual pleasure of his kiss, knowing in that moment that no other man could ever evoke the feelings in her that this man did.

Alexei felt Natalie's lips part beneath his and held her closer, erotically tangling his tongue with hers as the long-smoldering flames of their desire flared back to life.

From somewhere far away, Natalie heard him groan and felt his long, tapered fingers brush against her breast. His intimate caress brought her careening back to reality, and with a little cry, she pushed herself out of his arms. "I have to go now," she gasped, lunging toward the dressing room door.

"Tasha, please!" He followed her to the door, turning her toward him. "I'm sorry. I shouldn't have done that."

"No, you shouldn't have."

"I apologize. It won't happen again. Please tell me that I can see you while I'm here. Lunch maybe, or dinner."

Natalie shook her head adamantly. "I don't think that would be a good idea, Alex. What was between us was over a long time ago. Let's just leave it at that."

Alexei stepped back, looking at her as if she'd struck him. "It really meant that little to you?"

Natalie's gaze dropped to the floor, unable to meet his eyes. "I have to go now."

With a curt nod, Alex reached behind him, opening the door, then stepped aside to let Natalie pass. "It was nice to see you, Miss Worthington," he said loudly enough that the people still standing outside the door could hear.

Natalie was startled by his use of her maiden name. Instinctively she opened her mouth to correct him; then, thinking better of it, she simply nodded and left the room, pushing her way heedlessly through the gaping crowd of fans.

When she finally reached the edge of the crowd, she broke into a run and did not stop until she reached the sidewalk outside Symphony Hall.

It was there that Susan found her, leaning against a street lamp and breathing hard.

"Are you all right?" Susan asked.

"Yes, I'm fine."

"What happened in there?"

Natalie turned away, unable to face the probing eyes of her friend. "Nothing. Please, let's just go."

"All right. If you don't want to talk, you don't want to talk. Let's go get some coffee."

"Not tonight, Sue," Natalie pleaded. "I'm really tired."

"Nonsense. It's obvious you've just been through some major life crisis, and if you think I'm going to let you go home without telling me about it, then you're crazy. Now, come on. A nice mocha latté is just what you need."

Reluctantly, Natalie nodded, and the two women headed for the parking lot.

"You know, you should have brought Jenna with you tonight," Susan remarked as they buckled themselves into her car.

Natalie threw her a grateful smile, silently thanking her for changing the subject. "She's too young," she answered, "and, besides, tonight's a school night."

Susan shrugged. "So what? It would have been worth letting her skip school tomorrow to have the experience of hearing Alexei Romanov play."

"Spoken like a true childless woman," Natalie retorted. "The idea that its okay to skip school tomorrow to stay out late tonight is not a message I want to convey."

"Oh, come on." Susan laughed, wheeling her car into the coffee house parking lot. "Jenna is hardly your average seven-year-old. Personally, I think it would be a lot more valuable for a musical prodigy of Jenna's caliber to hear Alexei Romanov play than to get her daily dose of Dick and Jane tomorrow."

"Well, that's where our philosophies differ, Sue. Musical prodigy or not, Jenna *is* only seven years old, and her daily dose of Dick and Jane, as you call it, is very important."

"Okay," Susan conceded, unsnapping her seat belt. "You're the mommy."

It wasn't until the women were seated at a small table at the back of the coffee shop that Susan finally asked the question that was plaguing her. "So, what's the deal with you and Alexei Romanov? What happened tonight—and don't tell me nothing, because I know something did."

Natalie looked up from her latté, her expression guarded. "I don't know what you're talking about. Nothing happened. We just spoke for a few minutes, and then I left."

"Right. And I could tell by the way you calmly sauntered out of his dressing room that you had a lovely time reminiscing about the good old college days in New York."

"That's exactly right. No wonder you're such a great journalist, Sue. You have an uncanny knack for gleaning the facts of a situation."

Susan threw her a withering look. "Quit ducking the issue. Are those rumors I heard about you and that handsome Russian true or not?"

"I don't know what you're talking about. I didn't even know you when I was in college, so how could you have heard any rumors about me?"

Susan chuckled knowingly. "Oh, I heard plenty from your old roommates that time they came to visit." She paused, waiting for a response, but when Natalie remained silent, she plunged on. "They told me that you and Alexei were quite an item for the entire semester he was teaching at Juilliard, and then he went back to Russia and you suddenly upped and married Tom Saxon."

Susan abruptly stopped talking as she saw Natalie's eyes fill with tears. "My God," she whispered, reaching out and taking Natalie's icy hand. "Nat, sweetie, I'm sorry. I didn't know. Really, I didn't. I thought it was just some flirty thing. Please forgive me. I never would have teased you if I'd known there really had been something serious between you and Romanov."

Natalie closed her eyes and pressed trembling fingers to her lips. "It *was* serious," she mumbled, her words muffled against her hand, but I thought I was over it. It was so long ago. But tonight when I saw him . . . well . . . it just brought everything back. The pain of breaking up with him . . . the loneliness after he was gone . . . Jenna . . ."

Susan sucked in a startled breath. "Jenna! My God, Natalie, are you saying that Jenna . . ."

Natalie nodded and bit her lower lip in an attempt to stem the flood of tears that threatened.

"Come on," Susan said, rising. "Let's get out of here. You

need something a lot stronger than latté, and I have some really good wine at my apartment."

Natalie nodded and allowed Susan to herd her out of the restaurant. They rode in silence for the short distance to Susan's apartment. It wasn't until they were settled on her plush sofa, wineglasses in hand and a box of tissues sitting between them, that their conversation continued.

"So, where does Tom fit into all this?" Susan asked.

Natalie leaned her head back against the sofa cushion. "Tom Saxon," she whispered in a voice choked with bittersweet emotion. "My savior."

"Your savior?"

Natalie nodded. "Without Tom, I most certainly would have disgraced the fine old family name."

"Ah, yes." Susan smiled. "The Worthingtons of Beacon Hill."

"And the Wellesleys of Louisburg Square," Natalie added. "Let's not forget them."

"That's right. I always forget that you're the illustrious Stuart Wellesley's great, great, great-granddaughter."

"How could you forget? I live in his house."

"I know, but coming from plain old Midwestern farm stock like I do, pedigree just isn't something you think about."

Natalie took a sip of her wine and sighed. "Well, when your grandfather is Benjamin Worthington and your grandmother is Cynthia Wellesley, no one lets you forget. And that's why Tom was such a savior to me. Without him, all of Boston society would have known that Malcolm and Sarah Worthington's daughter had gotten herself into trouble in New York, and they would never have let my parents live it down."

"But, Natalie," Susan protested, "this is the nineties. Nobody cares about those old taboos anymore. Single women have babies all the time. Just look at all the movie stars!"

"Oh, Susan, surely you know that Boston and Hollywood are two very different places."

Susan held up her hands in defeat. "You're right, I do know

that. So Tom saved your good name by marrying you when you were carrying another man's child."

Natalie nodded.

"And he knew right from the beginning that you were pregnant and who the father was?"

Another nod.

"Then why did he marry you? Were you two that much in love?"

"No, we weren't in love at all."

As Susan's eyebrows shot up in surprise, Natalie rushed on. "Oh, don't get me wrong. I loved Tom dearly. The whole time I was at Juilliard, he was my closest friend. When he found out what had happened with Alex, he offered to marry me and give the baby his name."

"And you immediately said yes, even though you didn't love him."

"Of course not! I said no the first ten times he asked me, but we finally came to an agreement that worked out for both of us."

"And that agreement was . . ." Susan prodded.

Natalie paused a moment, then said, "The agreement was that Tom would marry me, we would stay married for a year or so after the baby was born, then we would get quietly divorced."

Susan looked at her in bewilderment. "And he was willing to do this . . . to make this commitment to a woman who wasn't in love with him . . . just because he was a nice guy?"

Natalie smiled and gazed at Susan with tear-glazed eyes. "Yes. Just because he was a nice guy. Tom didn't want anything in return, but I wouldn't accept his offer on those terms. In the end, we agreed on a quarter of a million dollars."

"*What?* Are you telling me that you paid Tom Saxon two hundred and fifty thousand dollars to marry you?"

Natalie nodded. "It was the only way I would agree."

Susan shook her head in disbelief. "No wonder they say the rich are different."

Natalie smiled at her friend's astonishment. "Susan, it was a business arrangement. Tom was sacrificing a great deal to help me, and I felt that he deserved to be compensated for it. He was a brilliant violinist. Brilliant and penniless. He'd gone to Juilliard on a full scholarship, but I knew that once he got out of school, he'd have no choice but to spend the rest of his life conducting some high school orchestra somewhere. He wanted to be a performer, and the money allowed him to pursue that. It was the least I could do to repay him for what he did for me." Her voice had started to quaver and she looked down. "Poor Tom."

Susan cleared her threat. "I know that Tom is dead, but you never said how it happened."

The tears that Natalie had been trying so hard to hold back began to slip unheeded down her cheeks. "He was killed in a car accident less than a year after we divorced. He had won a position playing violin with the Pittsburgh Symphony. From what I was told, he was on his way to a concert one evening. There was one of those terrible ice storms that Pittsburgh sometimes has. The roads were slippery . . . he was driving too fast. He hit a semi head-on and was killed instantly." Natalie's voice caught on a sob. "He was such a wonderful man. I'll never stop missing him."

"Oh, Nat," Susan moaned, leaning forward and picking up her friend's icy hand. "When I think of all you've been through . . ."

Natalie plucked a tissue out of the box Susan had set between them. "It was a long time ago, but I still break down every time I think about him."

Susan nodded sympathetically and waited a moment while Natalie wiped her eyes and blew her nose. "And what about Alexei? He doesn't know anything about any of this?"

"No," Natalie answered, "and he's never going to."

"But why? From what you've told me tonight, it sounds like you loved him. Didn't you think he deserved to know you were going to have his baby?"

"It wasn't that at all. You have to remember, all of this happened while the Communists were fighting to stay in power. Alex was a product of the Russian system, and in order to be successful, he had to live within those confines. . . . He had to follow their rules."

Susan nodded in understanding. "And their rules didn't include a pregnant American girlfriend."

Natalie looked down at her lap, shaking her head. "No, they didn't."

"So, he just left you and went back to Russia?"

Natalie looked up, and when she spoke, her voice held a definite trace of anger. "It's not like he abandoned me, Susan. He wanted me to go back with him."

"Why didn't you?"

Natalie jumped up and paced over to the window. "I just couldn't. It was so complicated. I wanted to finish my education, my grandmother was dying and I didn't want to leave her and, most of all . . ." She turned, looking at Susan with beseeching eyes. "Most of all, I knew that my life would be in the control of a government I didn't understand. Alex was scheduled to spend the next year touring Russia and Eastern Europe, and there was no guarantee they'd let me go with him. What if I wound up spending all those months alone in a country where I didn't even speak the language? I know it probably sounds selfish, but I just didn't have the courage to make that kind of move."

"Oh, Natalie," Susan said, walking across the room to put her arms around her friend, "you weren't being selfish. At twenty-two, and under those circumstances, I would have made exactly the same decision you did."

Together, the women walked back to the sofa and sat down again. "So," Susan asked quietly, "did you ever hear from him after he left?"

"Yes, I heard from him. In fact, I received a letter practically every week, begging me to reconsider and join him in Russia."

"Did you answer his letters?"

"At first. But, after awhile, there didn't seem to be much point."

"And he finally gave up?"

"Yes. But not until . . . He wrote me one last time and asked me to marry him. By then, I knew for sure that I was pregnant, and Tom and I had made our arrangement, so I wrote back and told him that I was getting married. After that, I never heard from him again."

She paused, staring out the window of Susan's apartment for a long moment and shaking her head. "It took me so long to get over it and then, when I saw Alex tonight, it all came rushing back." Again, tears began to course down Natalie's cheeks and, with a small cry, she threw herself against Susan, giving vent to all the pain she'd repressed for so long.

When her sobs finally subsided, Susan gently pushed her away and handed her another fistful of tissues. "Natalie, I just have one more question, and then we won't talk about this anymore if you don't want to."

Natalie looked at her friend through tear-glazed eyes. "What?"

"Tonight, when you were actually with him again, was your reaction to each other really as casual as you said it was in the coffee shop?"

Natalie glanced at Susan with a slightly guilty look on her face. "Well, not quite as casual as I said."

"Oh, Natalie, for heaven's sake, tell me what really happened."

Natalie swallowed hard, fighting back another wave of tears. "He kissed me, Susan. He kissed me and asked me why I didn't answer his letters. Then he asked to see me while he's in town."

"My Lord." Susan sighed. She leaned back and thoughtfully tapped a fingernail against her front teeth. "So, how did it feel?"

Natalie looked up at her through teary eyes. "How did what feel?"

Susan threw her an exasperated look. "The kiss, Natalie, the kiss! Did you feel anything when he kissed you?"

Natalie closed her eyes and nodded. "Yes. It was . . . wonderful. And terrible."

"Terrible?"

"Yes. Terrible that after all this time, he could still make me feel like I was going to faint just by kissing me."

Susan groaned. "I should have such problems."

Natalie sniffed and shot her friend a baleful look. "Well, you may think this is all very amusing, but, trust me, it's not."

"I know it's not, sweetie. But now that you two have seen each other again and you know that at least some of the old feelings are still there, what are you going to do?"

"Nothing."

"Natalie, you can't just do nothing! It's too late for that. Do you want to know what I think?"

"Probably not, but you're going to tell me anyway, aren't you?"

"Of course. If what you've said about how you felt tonight is true, then I think you should see Alexei while he's here."

Natalie looked at Susan incredulously. "Why? What good would it do after all these years? We don't even know each other anymore."

Susan ignored the interruption and rushed on. "I think you should see him, and I think you should tell him about Jenna."

To Susan's surprise, the pain in Natalie's eyes disappeared, to be replaced by a look of blazing indignation. "I'm going home now," she announced, grabbing her coat off a nearby chair. "I don't want to talk about this anymore."

"But, Natalie," Susan argued, "she has his gift. He deserves to know about her."

"No, he doesn't! If he knew, he might insist on being involved in her life, and it's far too late for that."

"It's never too late, Natalie. Jenna has never known what it's like to have a father. Don't you think you owe it to both of them to let them get to know each other, so they can decide what they want their relationship to be?"

"No," Natalie answered bluntly. "I don't think that at all."

TWO

"Marvelous concert tonight, Alexei. I have not heard you play with such feeling in a very long time."

Alexei handed his coat to his valet, Yuri Domovich, and entered the sumptuous hotel suite. "Thank you. I was pleased that the audience seemed to enjoy it. They were very receptive."

"And well they should be. It has been many years since they had the privilege of hearing you play." Quickly, the valet walked over to a bar in the corner of the sitting room and poured his employer a snifter of brandy. Alexei nodded his thanks and sank down tiredly on a plush sofa.

"I was surprised, though, that you chose *Moonlight Sonata* as your encore," Yuri said casually as he hung up Alexei's coat.

Alexei looked up from a stack of telegrams he was disinterestedly perusing. "Oh? Why is that?"

Yuri walked toward him, carefully maintaining his air of nonchalance. "I don't know. It's just such a common piece. So traditional."

Alexei gave up on the telegrams and threw them down on the table. "Actually, I was going to play a Chopin nocturne, but I changed my mind at the last minute."

Yuri nodded knowingly. He had been in the service of the great pianist for over ten years and their relationship was more like that of a younger and older brother than employer and employee. Yuri had seen everything that had passed between Alexei and the blond woman in the audience that night, and he knew exactly why his boss had decided to play the Beethoven piece. Still, he continued his charade, hoping that Alexei would confide in him voluntarily. "Were you too tired to attempt the nocturne?"

"No, not at all. In fact, the audience's reception was so enthusiastic that I still felt fresh, even at the end of the concert." Alexei paused, slowly swirling the brandy in the snifter as he stared off into space. "Actually, I saw a woman in the audience who made me think of the *Moonlight Sonata.* Somehow, it just seemed right to play it tonight."

Yuri's lips tightened imperceptibly. "I know, Alexei. I saw Miss Worthington in the audience too."

Alexei's head snapped around in surprise. "You saw her?" The valet nodded.

Alexei sank back against the sofa cushions, his voice taking on a soft, melancholy quality. "She's still beautiful, isn't she? In fact, I think she's even prettier now than she was as a girl."

"Beautiful," Yuri agreed curtly. As beautiful and as cruel as ever, he added silently.

Natalie Worthington. Yuri hated even the sound of her name. The American girl whom Alexei had loved with such a passion that when she had ultimately rejected him, her betrayal had nearly ended his career. And now, even after all these years, it was obvious that Alexei was still not over her, that just seeing her sitting in an audience could bring that haunted look back into his eyes.

"Did you speak to her?" Yuri asked quietly.

"Why do you ask that?"

"Because I saw her and the friend she was with heading back toward your dressing room. I assumed she wanted to talk to you."

Alexei shook his head. "It was her friend who wanted to talk to me. She's a reporter for the *Boston Morning News,* and she wanted to set up an interview."

"So you didn't speak to Miss Worthington?"

"Yes, I did," Alexei admitted. *And I kissed her too. And*

after that one kiss, my world is turned upside down again, just like it was eight years ago.

Yuri sat down on the sofa opposite Alexei and looked at his boss closely. "Did you have a pleasant conversation?"

Alexei set his brandy snifter down with an angry bang. "We had a very short conversation, Yuri, and to answer the question I know you're dying to ask, no, we are not going to see each other again. Are you happy now?"

Yuri winced, knowing that the only time his boss became this surly was when he was truly distraught about something. "It is your happiness that is important, Alexei, not mine."

"And you don't think Natalie Worthington made me happy?"

"I know for a fact that she made you very unhappy."

Alexei erupted in a sharp, cynical laugh. "That's ancient history, Yuri. She said so herself, tonight. She also made it perfectly clear that she has no interest in resurrecting any part of our relationship."

Yuri nodded in acknowledgment, careful not to let the profound relief he was feeling show on his face. Picking up a small notebook from the coffee table, he said, "Do you want to review your schedule before you retire?"

Alexei shrugged disinterestedly. "I guess so."

Yuri opened the notebook, then pulled a wrinkled pile of telephone call slips out of his pocket, spreading them on the table in front of him. "First, a producer from the "Today Show" in New York called. They want to interview you the day after tomorrow."

Alexei looked up, surprised. "The day after tomorrow? Why don't they just wait until we get to New York next week?"

"Since Boston is the first stop of your tour, I think they want to interview you from here, before one of the other morning news programs gets to you."

"It's all right with me. Set it up."

Yuri made a note in his book, then continued. "Also, there are several local television shows here in Boston who want to talk to you, and the music reviewer at the *Boston Morning News* would like an interview so she can write a special column about your return to America. Oh, that must be the woman you talked to tonight."

"Yes, it must be. What's her name?"

Yuri squinted at the scrap of paper in front of him. "Susan Bedford."

Yuri nodded. "Yes, that was she. Actually, I think she set up a time with Sergei. You might want to check with him so that I don't end up having two appointments with her."

Yuri nodded and made an additional notation in his book. "I think that's all for now."

"Except the little girl," Alexei reminded him. "I want you to find some time tomorrow for me to see her."

Yuri looked at him blankly. "The little girl?"

Alexei threw his valet an annoyed look. "Yes, the little girl. The prodigy I've been reading so much about lately. She lives here in Boston."

"Oh yes. Yuri nodded, "Now I remember. She was written up in *Piano Masters Magazine*. I read the article on the plane."

"Right, Alexei agreed. "What was her name?"

Yuri picked up a magazine from the coffee table and began flipping through it. "Here she is," he said, pointing to a picture of a young child seated at a piano. "Her name is . . ." His finger ran along the text until he found what he was looking for. "Jenna Saxon."

Alexei took the magazine from Yuri and looked at the picture. "That's right, Jenna Saxon. Anyway, I want to see her. Actually, I want to hear her play. If she's as brilliant as the press is saying, then I cannot miss this opportunity to witness her talent firsthand."

"I don't remember if there is anything in that article that says how one might get in touch with her," Yuri commented.

Alexei ran his finger down the page. "Not really. It says here that she takes lessons at the Schumann Piano School and that her teacher's name is Penelope Pendergast. I'm sure you could call the school. Either that, or you could get in touch directly with the child's mother."

"Does the article give the mother's first name?"

"Ah . . . yes. Here it is. Natalie. Natalie Saxon."

A sudden hush fell over both men, broken finally by a nervous chuckle from Yuri. "Is every woman in America named Natalie?"

Alexei tossed the magazine down. "I think it's a relatively common name in this country, just as it is in ours. Now, make the appointment, Yuri. Talk to the teacher, talk to the mother, talk to someone. I'd like to see the child tomorrow afternoon, if possible."

Yuri made one final notation, then closed his book and yawned expansively. "If there's nothing else, Alexei, I'd like to retire."

Alexei glanced at the clock on the fireplace mantel and nodded. "By all means. It's very late. Is Anya back yet?"

Anya Romanov was Alexei's younger sister. A talented pianist in her own right, she had foregone a summer tour of the Baltic countries to accompany her brother to America.

"No," Yuri said. "She said she was going out with some people for a late supper after the concert and she has not returned."

Alexei frowned. "I don't like her being out alone so late."

His words caused Yuri to smile. "I don't think you need to worry. I'm sure she'll be here at any moment."

Alexei nodded, but Yuri could tell that he was still uneasy. Anya was ten years younger than her brother and had lived with him in their Moscow apartment since their parents' deaths six years before. Although she was now twenty-three, Alexei still felt responsible for her and, in Yuri's opinion, often treated her as if she were a schoolgirl. Yuri did not feel it was his place to say anything about the siblings' relationship, however, and he kept these thoughts to himself. "Is there anything more I can get you?" he asked solicitously.

Alexei shook his head. "No. I think I'll just stay up a while longer and finish my brandy."

After he heard Yuri's bedroom door close, Alexei strolled over to the window of the penthouse suite and gazed out at the harbor below.

Yuri was right about one thing: Natalie Worthington had caused him more pain than anyone he'd ever known. And yet, when he'd seen her tonight, when he'd taken her into his arms and kissed her, all the pain, all the loneliness and despair he had felt when she had rejected him had disappeared. All that mattered at that moment was that she was back in his arms.

He also knew that Yuri was right when he said that Natalie was the one woman he would never get over. Natalie, with her blond hair, her blue eyes and her porcelain skin. Even as a very young woman, her beauty had been dazzling, but there had been many beautiful girls in Alexei's life and it had not just been her looks that had captured his heart. Rather, it was the other, more subtle aspects of her character that had truly attracted him. Her intelligence, her gift for conversation and, most of all, her wicked sense of humor.

She was the only woman he'd ever truly loved. The only one he'd ever asked to marry him. But she had turned him down.

Alexei ran his fingers across his forehead, as if trying to rub out the memories enshrouding him. He had loved Natalie with a consuming passion and had thought that love was returned. And yet, when he'd asked her to go back to Russia with him, she had refused. Even after he'd returned to his homeland, he'd written to her, begging her to reconsider and join him, but after a few stilted responses, she'd stopping answering his letters altogether.

Finally, when he realized that all the fame and glory being heaped on him meant nothing without her to share it with him, he'd written her one more time, taking the ultimate step and asking her to marry him.

This time she had written back, but her answer had been

brief and devastating. She'd told him she remembered that he'd always said he didn't believe artists and performers made suitable husbands and therefore, she was very flattered that he cared enough for her to ask her to marry him. But, in her next sentence, she added that she couldn't consider his proposal because she was engaged to marry another man.

Alexei had been furious. After all they had shared, how could she have found someone else so quickly? They had only been apart for three months, but already she had replaced him.

Her betrayal was like a neverending ache in his heart—one that he tried desperately to assuage with a long string of meaningless love affairs. He had thought that if he became involved with enough women, surely he would find one who could take Natalie's place, one who could erase all the torturous memories that plagued him far into the night and rendered him sleepless more times than he could count.

His plan had not worked, although, God knew, it was not for lack of trying. With his good looks, fame, and ever-growing fortune, Alexei could have just about any woman he cast his eyes upon, and he had sampled the delights of dozens of willing lovers on three continents. But he could find no one to suit him. The only woman he cared about was Natalie, and she was the one woman he couldn't have.

Finally, Alexei gave up his fruitless quest and threw himself into his work. He spent endless hours practicing until he proved that his early promise had matured into lifelong brilliance. He taught, he performed, he even tried his hand at composing. And gradually, as the years passed and his notoriety grew, the memory of Natalie's long blond hair brushing seductively across his chest and her soft voice whispering words of love to him in the cold darkness of a late December night finally faded.

Until tonight. Tonight, when he'd stood on that stage and his eyes had settled on her seated so properly in the fifth row, all the memories of their lost love had come crashing down on him again. And in that moment, all he could think about was how she had loved the *Moonlight Sonata*.

And so he had played it. Played it with a yearning and passion that had enthralled the audience and brought them to their feet in an explosion of applause. But their accolades hadn't mattered. Nothing had mattered except that Natalie had heard it and had known that he was playing it for her.

Then, when he'd opened the door of his dressing room and seen her standing there staring at him, it was like a dream come true. At least until she'd told him that what had once been between them was over—that it was ancient history and that she had no interest in seeing him again. Then the pain had come rushing back—as blinding in its intensity as it had been all those years before.

Still, despite their sad reunion, he was glad that he had played the *Moonlight Sonata*. It was their special piece, and somehow it seemed fitting that he had played it and she had heard it one last time.

For Alexei knew that, after tonight, he would never play it again.

THREE

"Miss Pendergast, you have a telephone call."

The prim, middle-aged woman seated on the folding chair next to the piano looked up in surprise. "A call for me?"

Llynwen Osborne, the pretty, dark-haired secretary at the Schumann Music School nodded.

"Did you tell the caller that I am in the middle of a lesson?"

Again the secretary nodded. "I did, but he was most insistent that he speak to you immediately."

Penelope Pendergast's pencil-thin eyebrows rose nearly to her hairline. It was almost unheard of for her to receive telephone calls at the music school, and the few times she had, it was nearly always a student's mother advising her that little Matthew or Heather was ill and wouldn't be in for their lesson that day. "You say it's a gentleman on the line?" she asked, trying hard to act as though having men call her was an everyday occurrence.

"Yes," Llynwen confirmed, trying equally hard to suppress the smile that threatened.

"Did he give you his name?"

"No, he merely asked for you and told me it was very important. He had a foreign accent."

"A foreign accent!" Penelope's interest was, by now, thoroughly piqued, and for the first time since Llynwen had appeared in the doorway of her studio, her pencil ceased its rhythmic tapping against the edge of the worn keyboard. "You may stop playing for a moment," she directed her nine-year-old student. "Apparently, there is a phone call that I must take, but I will return directly."

With hurried footsteps, Penelope walked down the hall to the office, picking up the phone and saying breathlessly, "This is Miss Pendergast. May I help you?"

"Yes, I hope so," came the deep, heavily accented reply. "My name is Yuri Domovich and I am calling on behalf of Mr. Alexei Romanov."

Llynwen, who had followed Penelope back to the office, now looked at her with interest as the older woman's eyes widened in disbelief.

"Ye . . . yes, Mr. Domovich," Penelope stammered. "What may I do for you?"

"I understand that you have a student named Jenna Saxon."

"Yes, I do."

"Good. Then I have reached the right person. Mr. Romanov has read about young Miss Saxon and he has an interest in hearing her play. I am calling to see if this is possible and, if so, to set a time."

Penelope drew in an astonished breath and reached up to pat her already perfect bun. "I . . . I am sure it is possible, sir. What day would be convenient for Mr. Romanov?"

Hearing Alexei's name, Llynwen unconsciously took a step closer to Penelope.

"Sometime this afternoon would be good."

"Today?" Penelope gasped.

"Yes. Is that a problem?"

"Ah, no," Penelope answered quickly. "Jenna has a lesson at three o'clock, so that should work out very nicely. Of course, I must ask her mother's permission, but I am sure there will be no problem."

"I should think not," said Yuri arrogantly. "As I'm sure you are aware, Mr. Romanov receives thousands of requests every year from parents all over the world, asking that he listen to their children play. Many have even offered him large sums of money just for the privilege of receiving his opinion on their child's potential."

"Oh, yes, sir," Penelope jumped in. "I am very aware of what an honor it is that Mr. Romanov wishes to hear Jenna. Just let me call her mother, and then I will get back to you immediately to confirm."

"Fine," said Yuri. "I will wait for your call."

They hung up. Then Penelope whirled around, grabbing Llynwen by the arms and shrieking, "Did you hear that? Alexei Romanov wants to hear Jenna Saxon play. Imagine! Alexei Romanov wanting to hear *my* student. Oh, I feel positively faint at the prospect of even being in the same room with such a great master!"

Llynwen stared aghast at the usually reserved Penelope. "It's very exciting, Miss Pendergast," she agreed.

"Oh, I have so much to do," Penelope fussed. "I have to dust the piano, polish the brass on the pedals, wash the windows in my studio . . ."

"Don't you think you should call Mrs. Saxon?" Llynwen suggested. "After all, you don't want to keep Mr. Romanov waiting."

"Oh, you're right, of course! Whatever am I thinking of? I must call Mrs. Saxon immediately." Fumbling for the phone, Penelope grabbed the receiver, then suddenly turned back to Llynwen in dismay. "Oh, my word! I have no idea what Mrs. Saxon's number is, and I left my student roster at home this morning. What *am* I going to do? This is a disaster!" With trembling hands, Penelope dropped the receiver back onto its cradle.

"Relax, Miss Pendergast," Llynwen soothed, walking over to a bank of files and pulling a drawer open. "The number is right here in Jenna's file."

"Thank the Lord!" Penelope exclaimed, flipping open the file and running her finger down Jenna's admission form. "Ah, yes, here it is." She picked up the receiver again, babbling nearly incoherently as she punched in the numbers. "Of course, this call is merely for form's sake. What parent in her right mind wouldn't want Alexei Romanov to evaluate their child? I'm sure Mrs. Saxon will be just as thrilled as we are. There's not a chance in the world that she would say no."

"No."

Penelope Pendergast's jaw dropped in disbelief. "Did you say no, Mrs. Saxon?"

"Yes, Miss Pendergast, I said no."

"But, but . . . " Penelope sputtered, "but Mrs. Saxon! This is Alexei Romanov we're talking about. And he wants to hear your daughter play!"

Natalie drew in a shuddering breath, trying desperately not to let the prissy old spinster on the other end of the line hear how shaken she was. "I know who we're talking about, Miss Pendergast, but I simply feel that Jenna is too young to be put under the pressure of being evaluated by someone of Mr. Romanov's stature."

Behind her half glasses, Penelope's eyes blinked several times as she racked her mind for another argument. "Mrs. Saxon, please reconsider. Surely you must be aware that Mr. Romanov receives thousands of requests from parents all over the world, asking him to listen to their children play." Penelope paused, then felt encouraged when Natalie remained silent on the other end of the line. "In fact," she added, continuing to repeat Yuri Domovich's words, "I have been told that many of these parents even offer Mr. Romanov large sums of money to do so."

"I'm sure that's true," Natalie answered, wondering if Miss Pendergast could hear her heart pounding over the phone line, "but the fact still remains, I do not want him to listen to Jenna. Please tell his representative that although I am honored by Mr. Romanov's interest in my daughter, I must decline his request."

"Oh, Mrs. Saxon . . ." Penelope moaned. "I just don't know

how I'm going to tell him that. Perhaps you should call him yourself. Perhaps if you explained your feelings to him directly . . ."

"No!" Natalie blurted. "I mean, I'm sorry, Miss Pendergast, but I can't do that. I have a full schedule today and I'm keeping a roomful of students waiting even now. So, please, just do as I ask and give Mr. Romanov my answer. Good day, Miss Pendergast."

As Penelope opened her mouth to voice another protest, she suddenly heard the dial tone buzzing in her ear. Slowly, she replaced the receiver, then braced her hands on the desk and shook her head.

"What did Mrs. Saxon say?" asked Llynwen, her curiosity rampant after hearing Penelope's side of the conversation.

"She said no," Penelope answered. She raised her eyes to Llynwen, her expression stupefied. "She said no! Now, what in the world am I going to tell Mr. Domovich?"

Llynwen shrugged philosophically. "I guess you're going to tell him no."

Natalie put down the telephone receiver and raised her hands to cover her mouth. Alexei wanted to see Jenna. She couldn't believe it. Could he have somehow found out that Jenna was her daughter? No, that was impossible. He could have no way of linking a child named Jenna Saxon to her.

Natalie had deliberately not mentioned Tom's name when she had written to Alexei, telling him of her plans to marry. She was also quite sure that Alexei hadn't been in the United States in the past eight years, and that the friends he had made when he lived in America were all in New York.

No, there was no way that Alexei could possibly know that she and Jenna were related. He must simply have read one of the many articles that had been written about Jenna in the trade journals over the years and decided to take advantage of his time in Boston to see for himself if all the press about the child was true.

Still, it was not a chance she was willing to take. Although Jenna did not really look like her father, instead favoring Natalie with her blond hair and fair skin, she did have his dark brown eyes. And, although Natalie doubted that Alexei would notice the resemblance, if, in talking with the obviously awestruck Miss Pendergast, he happened to learn that she was Jenna's mother, he might become suspicious.

Natalie nodded, having convinced herself that she had made the right decision in refusing to allow Alexei to meet her daughter. The less Alexei knew about Jenna, the better Natalie's chances of keeping her great secret exactly that—a secret. And nothing was more important than that.

"What do you mean, the mother refused to let me hear the child play?"

Yuri winced and mentally braced himself. Over the years, he had witnessed Alexei's volatile temper more times than he cared to remember, and he was not looking forward to the explosion he feared was coming.

"I don't know what else to say, Alexei. The child's piano mistress seemed very willing to accommodate your request, but she said she would have to get the mother's permission. Then, when she called me back, she said the mother had refused to give it."

"That's ludicrous!" Alexei barked. "Does the lady not realize that people all over the world beg me to listen to their children play?"

"I did mention that," Yuri noted quietly.

"And yet, now," Alexei continued as if he hadn't heard Yuri speak, "when I actually *want* to hear a child play, her mother refuses to allow it? It's incredible! Why would she refuse?"

"I don't know," Yuri answered honestly. "The teacher said something about the mother feeling that the child was too young to be put through the stress of having someone of your stature—I think that's the term she used—evaluate her."

"Evaluate her! I don't want to evaluate her. I just want to listen to her—to see if she's everything the papers say she is. Certainly she's not too young to play in front of an audience of one. How old is she? Seven? Why, when I was that age, I was already performing in concert halls before hundreds of people. That argument makes no sense." Restlessly, Alexei paced over to the window and stared out. "Maybe I should talk to the mother myself. You know, to assure her that I have no intention of passing judgment. If she realizes that I just want to listen to her daughter, how could she disapprove?"

"I don't see how she could," Yuri agreed.

Alexei thought for a moment, then snapped his fingers. "No, I have an even better idea. Why don't I talk to the child's father? He might be less emotional about the girl and more likely to listen to reason."

Yuri shook his head doubtfully. "I don't think there is a father."

"You mean, the mother is a widow?"

"I'm not sure. I just assumed she's probably divorced. At any rate, there was nothing in the article I read about a father."

Alexei chuckled. "If the mother is as unreasonable as she appears to be, I wouldn't be surprised if she's divorced. Well, if there is no father, then I shall go back to my original plan and call the mother. Do you have her number?"

Yuri was so grateful that Alexei hadn't lost his temper over the unprecedented insult Natalie Saxon had dealt him that he nearly dove onto the sofa to get his notes. "Here it is," he said, thrusting a scrap of paper at his boss. "When Miss Pendergast called me back, I managed to wangle it out of her."

Alexei grinned. "Good work, Yuri. As always, you're one step ahead of my every thought."

Yuri smiled at the rare compliment, then discreetly left the room while Alexei made his call. He was delighted that Alexei had decided to handle this matter himself. Being well acquainted with his boss's charismatic effect on women, he had no doubt that once Alexei turned his devastating charm on the unsuspecting Mrs. Saxon, there would be no question who would come out the winner. No question at all.

"Mrs. Saxon, you have an urgent phone call."

Natalie looked up in alarm from the notes spread on the podium in front of her.

"Excuse me for a moment," she said to the forty students seated before her.

She walked quickly over to the secretary standing in the doorway of her classroom. "Is it my daughter's school?"

"Oh, no, it's nothing like that," the secretary assured her. "In fact"—she lowered her voice conspiratorially—"it's very exciting."

Natalie frowned. "What are you talking about, Marie?"

"Well, you're probably not going to believe this, but it's Alexei Romanov on the phone, and he says he would like to speak to you immediately."

Natalie was so shocked to hear that it was Alexei on the phone that she grabbed the door frame for support. Why was he calling her, and how had he found her?

"Mrs. Saxon, are you all right?"

Natalie forced her eyes back to the worried secretary. "Yes, I'm . . . fine. Do you have any idea what Mr. Romanov wants?"

"He was a little vague, but I think it has something to do with his wanting to meet Jenna."

Natalie exhaled a long sigh of relief. So, he wasn't really calling *her*. He was simply calling Jenna Saxon's mother. Quickly regaining her composure, she said, "Please tell Mr. Romanov that I am in class and cannot speak with him."

"What?" Marie gasped. "You're joking, right?"

"No, I am not joking," Natalie assured her. "Also, please tell Mr. Romanov that if he is calling to ask me the same question he posed to Miss Pendergast this morning, my answer is still no."

For a long moment, Marie just stared at Natalie in horrified disbelief. Finally, she said, "Let me be sure I have this straight. You want me to tell Alexei Romanov that you won't come to the phone, and if he wants to talk to you regarding the same thing he talked to Miss Pendergast about, the answer is still no."

"Exactly," Natalie affirmed. Turning, she stepped back up onto the dais and returned to her podium.

Alexei slammed down the phone, and this time Yuri knew that he was not going to escape a display of his boss's temper.

"This Natalie Saxon," Alexei thundered, "is without a doubt the rudest woman I have ever had the misfortune to encounter!" Pivoting on his heel, he threw Yuri a furious glare. "She wouldn't take my call. Can you believe it?"

Yuri's expression was genuinely shocked. "Wouldn't take your call?"

"No. And, what's more, she told her secretary to give me a message that if I was calling to ask to hear her daughter play, her answer was still no! Never, ever, have I *ever* had anyone treat me so rudely. I am . . . offended!"

Yuri almost smiled. It was not often that he saw his boss at a loss for words. "So, is that the end of it, then?"

"Absolutely not! I *will* hear this child play—with or without her mother's permission."

"But, Alexei . . ."

"Don't bother arguing with me, Yuri. I have made up my mind. Now, what time did the teacher say the girl takes her lesson?"

"Three o'clock."

Alexei glanced at his watch. "It's already after two. Get my coat for me, please. I'm not going to take the chance of missing a single minute of that lesson. I am going to hear every note the child plays. Every single note."

FOUR

"Excuse me. I wonder if you could help me."

Llynwen Osborne looked up from the letter she was typing, her eyes widening as she stared at the handsome man standing on the other side of the office counter.

Good Lord, it's him! she thought excitedly as she rose from her chair. Hurrying over to the counter, she flashed the man a blazing smile. "Certainly, sir. What can I do for you?"

Alexei answered Llynwen's smile with one of his own, causing the young secretary's heart to take a leap into her throat. "I'm looking for . . . " He paused, digging a scrap of paper out of his pocket and peering down at it. "Miss Penelope Pendergast's studio. Could you point the way, please?"

"I can do better than that," Llynwen answered, stepping around the end of the counter. "I'll escort you there myself."

Alexei threw her another smile. "I'd appreciate that very much."

Together, they walked out of the office and proceeded down a long corridor. "You're Alexei Romanov, aren't you?" Llynwen asked unnecessarily.

Alexei looked over at her, not at all surprised that she recognized him. "Yes, I am. And you are . . ."

"Llynwen Osborne. I'm the secretary . . . um, administrative assistant to Mr. Kingston, the head of the school."

"I'm very pleased to meet you, Miss Osborne."

"And I'm thrilled to meet you, Mr. Romanov. I attended your concert last night. It was magnificent."

Alexei nodded graciously. "Thank you. I'm glad you enjoyed it."

"Oh, I did!" Llynwen gushed. "I particularly enjoyed hearing the *Moonlight Sonata*. It's always been one of my favorites, and you don't hear it played very often in concert." She had been gazing up at Alexei as she talked and now, after mentioning the *Moonlight Sonata*, she was surprised to see his smile fade, replaced by a rather melancholy expression.

"It's always been one of my favorites too," he said quietly.

Llynwen found herself at a loss for words at Alexei's sudden change of mood and was almost relieved when they arrived at Penelope's studio. "Here we are," she said brightly. With a sharp rap, she flung the door open. "Miss Pendergast, there's someone here to see you."

Penelope, who was leaning over a table covered with sheet music, nearly jumped out of her skin at Llynwen's unexpected entrance, but as she turned to reprove the secretary for her rude interruption, her words died in her throat.

"Mr. Romanov," she gasped, her hand unconsciously lifting to her hair, "this is such an honor!" Quickly, she moved forward to greet Alexei, her hand extended. "I didn't expect . . ."

"I know you didn't," Alexei apologized. Taking Penelope's hand, he nearly caused the old woman to faint as he bent his head and lightly grazed the back of her fingers with his lips. "I hope you will forgive my breach of manners in arriving uninvited."

Penelope giggled like a schoolgirl and with a quick jerk, pulled her hand back, embarrassed but thrilled by Alexei's display of continental charm. "Of course," she trilled. "Won't you come in?" With a fluttering gesture, she motioned for him to sit down on her folding chair, then turned to address Llynwen. "Thank you for escorting Mr. Romanov, Miss Osborne. You may return to the office now."

Llynwen frowned at Penelope, offended by her obvious dismissal, then looked over at Alexei. "It was wonderful to meet you, Mr. Romanov. If there's *anything* else I can do for you, just let me know."

Alexei smiled at the pretty girl, fully comprehending her meaning. "The pleasure was all mine, Miss Osborne. Thank you for your assistance."

Llynwen cast him one last smile, then glared angrily at Penelope as the door closed in her face.

Turning back to Alexei, Penelope clasped her hands in front of her. "Now, to what do I owe this honor?" But before Alexei could answer, an alarmed look came over her face. "Oh, dear, you *did* get the message that Mrs. Saxon would not give permission for you to evaluate her daughter, didn't you? Your Mr. Domovich assured me that he would tell you. . . ." Her voice trailed off.

"Yes, he told me," Alexei assured her, feeling suddenly guilty that he was causing the poor woman such obvious distress. "But, Miss Pendergast, I have a favor to ask of you in that respect."

Penelope looked at him warily. "A favor?"

Rising from the hard little chair, Alexei took a step toward the piano teacher. "I don't mean to put you in an awkward position with Mrs. Saxon, but I simply must hear Jenna play."

"Oh, Mr. Romanov," Penelope protested, "I don't know. Mrs. Saxon was quite adamant in her refusal."

"I know. I even tried calling her myself to see if I couldn't change her mind, but she wouldn't speak to me."

Penelope was clearly surprised at this bit of information. "She wouldn't?"

"No. It is very regrettable because I think if we had spoken, we could have come to an agreement. You see, from what you told Mr. Domovich, I believe that Mrs. Saxon's problem with my hearing Jenna play is that she doesn't want her daughter intimidated by feeling that her talent is being evaluated by me. Am I right?"

Penelope nodded dumbly.

"I thought so. What I wanted to tell Mrs. Saxon is that I

have no desire to evaluate Jenna. I only want to listen to her. I have read so much about her that I can't pass up the opportunity to witness this kind of talent firsthand."

"She is extraordinary," Penelope agreed. "I have taught many gifted students over the years, but never have I come across one with a natural talent to equal Jenna's. I truly believe she's destined for greatness."

Alexei nodded encouragingly. "Then you understand why I am so anxious to hear her play."

"Well, yes, of course. But you must understand my position. Mrs. Saxon is, to some extent, my employer when it comes to Jenna, and she has the final say as to what she will and will not allow regarding her daughter."

"I do understand," Alexei said, "and the last thing I wish to do is upset the little girl in any way. But, Miss Pendergast, surely there must be some way that I could hear Jenna play without her being aware of my presence. If she doesn't know I'm here, then what could be the harm?"

Penelope couldn't argue with this logic. After all, what *could* it hurt to let the great master listen to Jenna take her lesson if the child didn't even know he was there? "Perhaps we could leave that door ajar and you could stand on the other side," she said thoughtfully.

"That door?" Alexei asked, pointing to a door set into the studio's side wall.

"Yes. It's a connecting door to Mr. Fowler's studio, but he is not here this week, so I suppose there wouldn't be any harm . . ."

"Oh, Miss Pendergast, thank you!"

Penelope closed her eyes in sheer delight as Alexei picked up her hand and gave it a warm squeeze. Just wait until the girls in her bridge club heard that the great Alexei Romanov had kissed her and held her hand! They'd never believe it. Oh, what she wouldn't give for a video camera at this very moment.

"Now, Mr. Romanov," she said, trying desperately to compose herself, "you must promise me that you will not make your presence known to Jenna. She cannot even *suspect* that you're in the next room."

Alexei held up his hand, as if taking an oath. "You have my word, madam. I will be as quiet as a mouse."

Penelope smiled at his earnestness. "All right, then." Walking over to the narrow door, she pushed it ajar and gestured Alexei through. When he had disappeared into the adjoining studio, she called, "Is there a chair in there for you to sit on?"

"Yes, I'm fine," Alexei assured her, knowing that if the child was anywhere near as brilliant as the trade magazines touted her to be, he'd probably do very little sitting.

Penelope glanced at her watch. "It's three o'clock right now," she said in a loud stage whisper, "and I believe I hear Jenna coming down the hall. Remember, quiet, please!"

Alexei rolled his eyes at this last admonishment but obediently whispered back, "Not a sound, Miss Pendergast. I promise."

Just then, there was a light knock on the door; then Alexei heard a child's voice say, "Hi, Miss Pendergast. I'm here."

"Come in, dear, come in. I've been waiting for you."

"I'm sorry I'm late," Jenna said, throwing down her book bag and seating herself on the piano bench. "Mommy let me join the croquet club and we had our first meeting today after school.

"Croquet!" Penelope cried. "Are you sure that's wise? What if you injure your hands?"

Jenna giggled. "You can't hurt yourself playing croquet, Miss Pendergast. It's not like football or field hockey or something."

"Well, if your mother says it's all right, then I suppose it is. Just be very careful, please."

"Yes, ma'am," Jenna promised.

"Now, open your books and let's warm up with some scales. Did you practice your Chopin?"

"Yes, and my Bach and my Mozart."

Alexei smiled as the proper pronunciation of the great composers' names tripped easily off the little girl's tongue.

"Good, then let's get started."

For the next five minutes, Alexei paced silently around the tiny studio as Jenna played her scales. There was nothing more boring than listening to someone run scales, and nothing more important to a pianist than warming up by playing them. His boredom vanished, however, when Miss Pendergast told her to start with her Chopin piece and Jenna Saxon began to play.

She was everything the magazines and newspapers said she was, and more. Never, in all his years at the Central Music School in Moscow or later at the Moscow Conservatory, had he heard a child her age play with such natural flow and grace. Her style was that of the classical romantics, and as her tiny fingers flew over the keys and her child's voice asked questions regarding technique, Alexei knew he was, indeed, witnessing the birth of greatness.

By the end of the lesson, Alexei could stand it no longer. He had to see this child, had to speak to her.

Realizing that he was undoubtedly going to bring the wrath of Miss Pendergast down on his head, he nevertheless pushed through the door into her studio and squatted down, holding out his hands to the astonishingly beautiful blond child. "You, my pretty little lady, are one of the greatest pianists I have ever had the pleasure of hearing."

Jenna turned fascinated eyes on the tall, dark man before her, then hopped off the bench and approached him. "Thank you." She giggled, taking his hand and shaking it. "Did you hear me play just now?"

"Indeed I did." Alexei grinned. "And a rare privilege it was."

"You're Mr. Romanov, aren't you?" Jenna questioned. "I saw your picture in the newspaper this morning while I was eating breakfast."

"Yes, I am," Alexei acknowledged.

"The newspaper said that *you're* the greatest pianist in the world."

Alexei smiled and ran a long, tapered hand over Jenna's golden hair. "Maybe for today, little one, but I am afraid after hearing you that I might not be considered so for long."

The smiling man's rather formal statement was somewhat lost on Jenna, but Penelope beamed, thrilled by his words. To hear the great Alexei Romanov heaping such praise on *her* student was the most exciting moment of her very sheltered life. How she wished her colleagues at the Schumann School could hear him!

Standing up, Alexei took Jenna's hand and led her back to the piano, seating himself on the bench and her next to him. "So, tell me, Jenna . . ."

"How do you know my name?" she interrupted.

"Everyone knows your name," Alexei answered. "I've read about you in the newspapers too."

"Just like I read about you?"

"Yes."

"It's fun to see your name in the newspaper, isn't it?"

For the first time, Alexei laughed out loud. "Yes, little one, it is fun. Now, tell me: Who are your favorite composers? Who do you like to play the most?"

Jenna pursed her little lips and thought for a moment. "I like Mozart because when he was seven he was writing music, and now that I'm seven, I'm playing it. And I like Beethoven 'cause everybody likes Beethoven."

"How about Chopin?" Alexei questioned.

Jenna nodded. "Him too. Oh, and I also like John Lennon and Paul McCartney. You know, the Beatles?"

"Yes, I know the Beatles"—Alexei chuckled—"but why do you like them?"

"Because I play their songs and my mommy sings along. She knows all the words and she sings them real loud. It's a lot of fun."

"I'm sure it is." Somehow, after his exposure to the difficult

Mrs. Saxon, Alexei could not imagine her belting out a chorus of "I Want to Hold Your Hand." But it did his heart good to know that she obviously wasn't as icy with her daughter as she had been with him.

"And how about your father? Does he like to sing Beatles' songs too?" Alexei didn't even know why he asked this question, but he truly hoped that this precious little girl had a loving father in her life.

"I don't have a father," Jenna responded. "It's just Mommy and me."

Alexei digested this information, wondering if, perhaps, Jenna might be the product of a love affair rather than a marriage.

"Maybe if you come back tomorrow, we could play together," Jenna suggested, quickly changing the subject away from her nonexistent and, therefore, uninteresting father. "I like to play four-handed."

Miss Pendergast suddenly cleared her throat uncomfortably. "Come on now, Jenna, get your coat on. It's after four and your mother is going to be here any minute." She threw a meaningful glance at Alexei, who nodded and got to his feet.

As Jenna gathered up her coat and book bag, he pulled Penelope aside and said quietly, "You don't need to worry about me coming again, Miss Pendergast. I have plans tomorrow. But, as I'm sure you're aware, my sister, Anya, is traveling with me. I would very much like for her to have the opportunity to hear Jenna also. Do you suppose it would be possible for her to come tomorrow if she stays in the other room as I did today?"

Penelope knew she should say no, that allowing Miss Romanov to come tomorrow was taking another chance that Natalie Saxon might discover her deceit, but, somehow, looking into Alexei's hopeful brown eyes, she couldn't deny him. "I suppose so." She sighed resignedly. "If she promises to stay out of sight . . . for the *entire* lesson."

Alexei did not miss her meaning. "I'll make sure she understands." He smiled. "And thank you, Miss Pendergast, for today. I can't tell you what a memorable experience this has been. You are to be congratulated on the work you're doing with this student."

Penelope's good mood was instantly restored by Alexei's compliment. "You're most welcome, Mr. Romanov."

Turning back to Jenna, Alexei took her hand. "It was a pleasure to meet you, Miss Saxon. I hope we'll see each other again sometime." Then, bowing, he planted the same type of light kiss on her knuckles that he'd given Miss Pendergast.

Jenna let out a little squeal at the unexpected kiss from the strange man and yanked her hand out of his. "You're funny." She giggled.

Just then, the door to the hall opened and a woman's voice said, "Who's funny?"

Alexei froze, his back to the door, knowing his indiscretion had just been discovered by the one woman he'd hoped to avoid. He shot a quick look at Penelope, but she was staring at the woman behind him, her expression just as horrified as he knew his must be. Taking a deep breath, he slowly turned, mentally rehearsing what he might say to extricate himself from this impossible situation. But none of the excuses running through his head could have prepared him for the shock he received when he actually faced the woman standing in the doorway.

For an endless moment, he and Natalie simply stared at each other, both of them speechless with surprise. Finally, Alexei found his voice.

"Tasha," he gasped, "what are you doing here?"

Suddenly, Natalie snapped out of the trance she seemed to have fallen into. Her lips thinning ominously, she snapped, "I could ask the same of you, Alex."

"I came here to listen to Jenna Saxon play," he explained, gesturing vaguely in Jenna's direction. "And you?"

"I would think that would be obvious. I'm Jenna's mother." She turned toward Jenna. "Come on, honey, it's time to go home." Then, directing a furious glare at Penelope, she said, "I will speak to you tomorrow, Miss Pendergast."

The warning tone in Natalie's voice finally galvanized the fascinated Penelope into action. "Do you two know each other?"

"Yes," they answered simultaneously.

"A very long time ago," Natalie added.

"You didn't tell me that!" Penelope accused, throwing a shaming look at Alexei.

"I didn't know Jenna's mother was . . ."

"It doesn't matter," Natalie interrupted as she hustled Jenna toward the door. "Good-bye."

Alexei wrenched his gaze away from Penelope and tore out the door after Natalie and Jenna. "Wait! Natalie, please!" Catching up with the fleeing woman, he put a hand on her arm. "Please, don't go," he implored. "Couldn't we go somewhere and talk?"

"I know, Mommy," Jenna enthused, "let's all go have hamburgers."

"Hush, Jenna. We're not going to go have hamburgers. We're going home."

Angrily, she shook off Alexei's hand. "Let go of me. We're leaving."

"But, Tasha . . ."

"Alex, stop!" Whirling around, Natalie held up a warning hand. "I thought I had made my position perfectly clear. I want you to stay away from my daughter. Do you understand?"

Alexei's face hardened. "Perfectly, Mrs. Saxon. I understand perfectly."

Without another word, Alexei strode off down the hall, too angry to even hear Jenna's little voice as she called out a bewildered farewell to his retreating back.

FIVE

Alexei stormed down the hall in the opposite direction from the one in which Natalie and Jenna were heading. He rushed past the gaping Miss Pendergast, then suddenly stopped short, pivoting on his heel and returning to where she stood in her studio doorway.

"May I talk to you?" he asked in a surprisingly quiet voice.

"Ah . . . I suppose so."

Alexei looked up and down the hallway, noticing for the first time how many people were staring at him. "Not here. In your studio, please."

Penelope looked at Alexei warily for a moment, as if she wasn't quite sure she wanted to be alone with him; then with a curt nod, she gestured him into the small room.

Alexei walked over to the window, releasing a long, calming breath, then turned back to the piano teacher. "First of all," he said, "I want to apologize for the rather unpleasant scene you just witnessed. As I'm sure you guessed, Mrs. Saxon and I knew each other a long time ago, and I was shocked to see her here today."

"Yes, I did guess that," Penelope concurred.

Alexei looked at the earnest lady for a long moment as if considering how much to tell her; then, with a slight shrug, he continued. "Actually, Mrs. Saxon and I had, at one time, what I believe you Americans call a relationship."

Penelope's eyes widened with ill-concealed astonishment. She could hardly believe that the great Alexei Romanov was about to confide some intimate information about his private life to her, but here he was, looking for all the world as if he intended to do just that.

"Mr. Romanov, you don't owe me any explanation about—"

"I know I don't," Alexei interrupted, "but I have a few questions regarding Mrs. Saxon that I thought maybe you might be able to answer for me, and I thought that if I explained a little about . . ."

Now it was Penelope's turn to interrupt. "Oh, Mr. Romanov, I don't feel at all comfortable in spreading gossip about Mrs. Saxon. I hope you understand."

Alexei smiled at the little woman, guessing that Penelope Pendergast's pursed mouth had never spread a word of gossip in its life. "Please don't misunderstand, Miss Pendergast," he said quickly. "It is not my intention to coerce you into telling me anything you feel uncomfortable with. And," he added, "I am certainly not interested in gossip about Mrs. Saxon. I just wondered, since it has been a long time since she and I have spoken, and since you seem to be on friendly terms with her, if you might satisfy an old friend's curiosity about a few things."

Penelope thought for a moment, then sat down on the folding chair and clasped her hands in her lap. "Well, all right, Mr. Romanov, since you put it like that. But please understand if I decline to answer any questions that I do not feel are appropriate for us to discuss."

"Certainly," Alexei agreed, again thinking what a perfect diplomat Miss Pendergast would have made.

"So, what would you like to know?"

"Well, Natalie and I were acquainted before she was married. She told me that she was planning to marry, but I have heard very little since. Then, today, Jenna mentioned that she doesn't have a father. Am I correct in assuming that Mrs. Saxon is not married at this time?"

Penelope shook her head.

"Is she a widow?"

"I believe she is now."

Alexei sighed inwardly, realizing that getting this woman to divulge anything about Tasha was going to be akin to an interrogation between two hostile military forces.

"What do you mean by 'now'?"

"After her divorce from Mr. Saxon, I heard that he was killed in an automobile accident."

"How terrible," Alexei said, genuinely shocked by this piece of news. "Did you know her husband?"

"No, I never met him. Several other people around here knew him, though. He was a violinist—very talented. I heard that they met in New York and then moved back to Boston together when Mrs. Saxon took a teaching job at the Boston Conservatory of Music. As I'm sure you know, Boston is Mrs. Saxon's home."

Alexei nodded. "Were they married long?"

"No, I don't believe so. It is my understanding that they were married quite a short time."

"Do you know how long?"

Penelope cast him an appraising glance, as if judging what his motives might be in asking such a specific question. "I really don't know."

At Alexei's look of disappointment, she relented. "Actually, I did hear once that the marriage only lasted about a year and that they divorced shortly after their baby was born. It was in the papers, you know. Natalie has always been followed by the society editors, since she's part of both the Worthington and Wellesley families. It must be very difficult to have your life scrutinized so closely by the press just because of who your family is."

Alexei nodded distractedly, having stopped listening to Penelope's speech after he'd heard the words he'd been fishing for. Natalie and her husband had divorced shortly after their baby was born. *Their* baby. So that was that.

He swallowed, surprised at how painful this realization was. Ever since he had seen Natalie walk into Penelope Pendergast's studio and acknowledge that she was Jenna Saxon's mother, he had been toying with the thought that he might be Jenna's father. Although he knew the thought was probably ludicrous, he couldn't get it out of his mind. After all, he and Natalie had been lovers eight years ago, and Jenna had told him that she was seven years old. There was at least a chance Jenna might be his child.

But in his heart of hearts, he knew Jenna wasn't his. In the first place, she looked nothing like him. More importantly, he was confident that Natalie would never have kept it from him if she had been carrying his child.

No, Jenna wasn't his, and apparently Natalie never really had been either. From the last letter he'd received from her, he'd known that she planned to marry, but he'd had no idea how quickly she'd actually done so. Now, with what Miss Pendergast had told him today, he was forced to face the fact that Natalie had met, fallen in love with and married another man within a very few months of his return to Russia. No wonder she'd stopped answering his letters. It had obviously taken her no time at all to replace him—both in her bed and in her heart.

But maybe there was some good in what had happened today. Maybe now, after he dealt with the hard truths he'd just learned, he could finally forget Natalie Worthington. Put her out of his mind once and for all and get on with his life. Maybe he'd even marry Margot Petrikova, the beautiful Russian opera singer he had been seeing on and off for the past couple of years. God knew, the poor woman had waited long enough for him. Discovering that Natalie had taken her violinist to her bed and married him practically before Alexei's Moscow-bound plane had left the ground was certainly reason enough to give Margot more serious consideration.

But even as Alexei thought about this possibility, he realized that Margot was not who he wanted. Rather, she was a charming companion to take to social events and a passionate partner to warm his bed for a night when he could no longer stand the loneliness of his solitary life. Although Alexei felt a great deal of affection for Margot, he knew, deep down, that his feelings for her were not profound enough to sustain a serious relationship.

"Don't you agree, Mr. Romanov?"

Alexei blinked, startled out of his brooding thoughts and having no idea what Penelope had just said to him. "Yes, I certainly do, Miss Pendergast."

Penelope rose from her chair. "Well, if there's nothing more, I must prepare for my next student."

"Oh, yes, Miss Pendergast, please don't let me keep you any longer."

Alexei walked over to the door, turning back one last time to thank Penelope and remind her that his sister would be coming the next day to hear Jenna play.

Penelope gazed after him thoughtfully as he walked down the corridor. "I do believe there's more here than that man wants me to know," she mused aloud. "I just wish I could have met Thomas Saxon. He must have been quite something to have stolen Natalie Worthington away from a man like Alexei Romanov!"

"Hello?"

"He was at Jenna's school today when I arrived to pick her up from her lesson."

"My God, Nat, you're kidding!" Susan pushed herself up against her bed pillows and tossed aside the book she was reading.

"Don't shout," Natalie admonished. "This isn't a press conference. And, no, I'm not kidding. I don't find this situation anything to kid about."

"You mean he went to Jenna's lesson even after you expressly told him he couldn't?"

"That's right," Natalie confirmed. "It's so typical of him too. I'd forgotten how stubborn he can be once he's made up his mind about something."

"So, what did you say when you saw him there?"

"I told him to stay away from my daughter. Period."

"I bet he took that well." Susan chuckled. "What else happened?"

"Nothing. I assure you, neither of us was in the mood for a chat. He knew I was angry, and then he got angry, and we both left in a huff."

"You're certainly not cutting him any slack, are you?"

"What do you mean?"

"Well, Nat, considering that you were once lovers and that the last time you heard from him was when he wrote to ask you to marry him, don't you think he probably wonders why you're being so hostile?"

Natalie sighed wearily. "Maybe he does, but there's nothing I can do about it. The only thing that matters is that he doesn't get any further involved with Jenna."

Susan frowned and shook her head, the romantic in her disagreeing with Natalie's logic. But prudently, she kept her thoughts to herself, saying only, "What was his reaction when he found out you were Jenna's mother? Was he shocked?"

"Yes," Natalie answered, "I'd say so."

"Do you think he suspected anything?"

Natalie thought for a long time before she answered. "No. After all, he knows I was married, Jenna doesn't look anything like him and . . ."

"Except for her eyes," Susan interrupted. "She has his eyes. They're exactly the same shape and color."

"I know," Natalie conceded, "but I don't think any man would notice something as subtle as that unless it was pointed out to him."

"You're probably right," Susan agreed. "So, what happens now?"

A quizzical look came over Natalie's face. "What do you mean? Nothing happens now. He's only going to be in town for five more days, and after the altercation we had today, I doubt very much that I'm going to hear from him again."

"So you think you successfully dodged the bullet?"

"Yes."

"And you're relieved about that?"

"Very."

Susan paused for a moment, then said, "Nat, tell me something truthfully: Didn't you feel *anything* when you saw him with Jenna today?"

Natalie squeezed her eyes shut, trying desperately to block out the memory of the emotions that had rampaged through her when she had seen Jenna and Alex together. "I felt plenty," she said softly.

"Really?" Susan questioned, encouraged by the slight break in Natalie's voice. "What?"

"Guilt, mainly, and regret for what might have been, and pride that Jenna has inherited so much from him and . . . oh, God, Sue, I don't want to talk about it. It's over and that's that."

Susan smiled, a sage little grin that would have infuriated Natalie had she seen it.

"What are you thinking?" Natalie asked as the silence on the phone line lengthened.

"I thought you didn't want to talk about it anymore."

"I'm asking you, what are you thinking?"

"I'm thinking the same thing I was thinking last night. That you should go see Alex and tell him that Jenna is his daughter."

"I was afraid that was it."

"Natalie, it's the right thing to do and you know it. He deserves to know . . . and so does Jenna."

"Intellectually, Sue, I know you're probably right."

"So, are you going to take the advice of this wise and worldly friend and confess everything to the man? I guarantee, you'll feel a lot better if you do."

Natalie chuckled despite the heaviness that lay in her heart. "No, I'm not going to confess anything to the man, but I appreciate your concern for my emotional well-being."

Susan blew out a disappointed breath. "Whatever you think, Nat. But just remember, you have a perfect opportunity here to set this thing to rights. Once he's gone, he's gone, and the opportunity may never present itself again. Is that what you really want?"

"Once he's gone, everything will get back to the way it was before he appeared," Natalie insisted, "and *that's* what I really want."

Susan sighed, knowing there was nothing more she could say to change her obstinate friend's mind. "Okay, then. I guess we're at five days and counting, right?"

"Right."

Soon after, the friends hung up. Natalie rose from her French Provincial writing desk and paced absently around her bedroom, allowing her mind to stray back to what she had told Susan about seeing Alex and Jenna together.

As much as she hated to admit it, she *had* felt guilty when she had seen Alexei squatted down next to Jenna, smiling and chatting with the child. They had somehow seemed so comfortable together, so natural in the way they had talked and laughed.

You're imagining things, she told herself firmly. *Jenna's so friendly, she can talk to a brick wall, and Alex has always liked children . . . especially if they're musical. It had nothing to do with the fact that they're related. Anyway, it's over now. In five days he'll be gone, and none of us will ever see each other again.*

Slowly, she padded into the bathroom, looking at her woebegone face in the lighted mirror over her vanity. "That thought should make you feel better, stupid," she told her reflection, "so why do you look so lonely and lost?" With a melancholy sigh, Natalie snapped off the light and headed downstairs to make dinner.

It was around eight that evening, while Natalie was sitting in her study grading term papers, that she heard the doorbell ring. She threw down her pen and rose, but sat back down when she heard Moira, her housekeeper, walking across the foyer toward the front door.

She listened for a moment, trying to ascertain who might be calling at that hour on a Thursday night. She could hear nothing except Moira's soft voice speaking to someone; then the front door closed. Natalie shrugged and picked up her pen again, but before she could return to her work, Moira appeared in the doorway.

"Is someone here?" Natalie asked.

Moira shook her head and approached the desk. "Just a courier service, ma'am, delivering an envelope for you, and one for Miss Jenna."

Natalie rose and walked around the desk. "I'll take them."

The housekeeper handed her two heavy cream-colored vellum envelopes, and Natalie peered at them curiously, trying to determine who might have sent them. There was no return address on either envelope, but hers and Jenna's names were printed neatly on the front of each in a handwriting she didn't recognize.

Looking up from the intriguing letters, she asked, "Is Jenna in her room?"

Moira nodded. "She's getting ready for bed."

Natalie walked across the marble foyer and started up the staircase that led to the upper floors of the town house. As always, her eyes swept along the gallery of family portraits as she climbed, then paused at her favorite—a late-nineteenth-century oil painting of her devilishly handsome ancestor, Stuart Wellesley, and his radiant red-haired wife, Claire. The Louisburg Square town house where she lived had originally belonged to this couple, and whenever Natalie looked around the grand old home with its carved oak wainscoting and intricately patterned silk wallpapers, she always felt grateful that this particular family residence had been bequeathed to her. Not only was the town house a masterpiece of nineteenth-century elegance, but knowing that it had been the home of her great, great, great-grandparents, who had met when he was a Union army captain and she a Confederate spy, leant it an air of romance that Natalie found very appealing.

She walked down the second-floor hallway and paused at

the open doorway to Jenna's bedroom, watching in amusement as Jenna wiggled into her nightgown. When the process was finally completed, Natalie stepped into the room and held out one of the envelopes. "You've received a letter, sweetie."

"Me?" Jenna cried, rushing over to her mother and reaching up to pluck the letter out of Natalie's hand. Racing over to her bed, she sat down and unceremoniously ripped the envelope open, reaching inside and pulling out two tickets.

"It's tickets for something," she said unnecessarily, holding them up to show her mother.

"I see that," Natalie responded. A definite feeling of unease rippled through her as she walked over to the bed and sat down next to Jenna. "Is there a note with them?"

Jenna peered into the envelope again, then nodded and pulled out a single piece of stationery. Unfolding it, she looked at it for a moment, then held it out to Natalie. "I can't read it. It's grown-up handwriting."

Natalie plucked the note from Jenna's hand, scanning it quickly before she read it out loud.

Dear Jenna,

Since you were kind enough to play for me this afternoon, I would like to return the favor. Here are two tickets to my concert tomorrow night. I hope you and your mother can attend, and afterward, stop by my dressing room to say hello.

Sincerely,
Alexei Romanov

"Oh, Mommy!" Jenna squealed excitedly. "Can we go? It's a Friday night, so I don't have to get up for school. Please, Mommy? Can we?"

Natalie stared down at the brief message, seething inside.

Damn him, damn him, damn him! she thought angrily. *Why won't he give up?*

"Mommy! Please, can we go?"

Natalie looked down at Jenna's excited face and knew she had lost this battle. "Are you sure you want to, Jenna? The concert will probably be pretty long. Are you sure you won't get bored?"

"I'm not gonna get bored," Jenna said positively. "I've been to lots of concerts before. I want to go, Mommy. Please, I want to hear Mr. Romanov play."

Natalie nodded in weary resignation. "All right, then, honey, if you really want to."

Jenna grinned and scrambled under the covers. "I'm so excited! Just wait till I tell Miss Pendergast."

Natalie smiled wanly, trying hard to hide the trepidation she was feeling. Bending down, she hugged her daughter close. "Get a good night's sleep now, baby. You're going to have a late night tomorrow."

"I will, Mommy, I promise."

Natalie smiled lovingly at Jenna and quietly left the room. Slowly, she walked down the hall to her own bedroom, closing the door behind her and flopping down on the bed. She lay there for a long moment, staring at the ceiling as she tried to collect her chaotic thoughts. *This won't be so bad,* she told herself. *Just a quick hello and then we'll leave. Besides, it* will *be a wonderful experience for Jenna to hear him play.*

Feeling a little better after giving herself this pep talk, Natalie sat up and pulled the letter addressed to her out of her pocket, tapping it thoughtfully against her fingertips as she debated whether or not to open it.

Finally her curiosity got the better of her, and she tore open the envelope, holding the single sheet of stationery under the illuminating glow of her bedside lamp. For a long moment, she simply stared down at Alexei's bold handwriting, transported back eight years. At Juilliard, he'd regularly written her notes.

How exciting those hurriedly scrawled messages had been—full of declarations of love and provocative promises of ecstasy. She smiled, remembering how her roommates would literally wrench them out of her hands, sighing with envy as they read aloud his passionate words.

Natalie looked again at the letter, realizing that Alexei must have remembered how she loved to receive written messages from him. That must be why he had decided to write to her, rather than simply call and verbally extend the invitation to the concert.

Shaking off the feelings of melancholy that were stealing over her, she forced herself to focus on the words scrawled on the expensive paper.

Tasha —

> *Please don't be angry with me for inviting Jenna to the concert. I wanted to repay her for the privilege of hearing her play (she is brilliant, you know) and this was the best way I knew how.*
>
> *After the concert, won't you please have a late supper with me? We could take Jenna home and then have a few hours to spend together. Don't say no, daragaya. I just cannot leave Tuesday with the harsh words we had today being the last ones between us. No strings, Tasha, I promise. Just supper.*
>
> *Think about it and let me know tomorrow.*

> *Alex*

Natalie burst into tears. He had called her *daragaya*—the beautiful endearment that Russian men had bestowed on their lovers for centuries. She had almost forgotten the word even existed. To be called Tasha one day and *daragaya* the next was almost more than she could take.

How she would love to have dinner with him. She closed

her eyes, remembering some of the intimate meals they had shared so long ago. Picnics under the trees in Central Park, eating bread and cheese and drinking wine while the city's wealthy equestrians trotted past on the nearby bridle path. Or sitting on the floor in the living room of his tiny apartment; eating pizza and talking about inconsequential things until the hour grew too late for her to go home. Then they would climb into his soft bed and make love till dawn.

Natalie's eyes flew open. *Stop this! You're going to make yourself crazy. Those days are long over and everything is different now. You're different, he's different, and life is far more complicated than it was then.*

Springing off the bed, she began to disrobe. No, much as she might want to, she wouldn't go to dinner. There was no point to it. Being with Alex would just make her feel more guilty and remorseful than she already did and, God knew, she was wallowing deeply enough in that mire already.

Natalie pulled on a pair of silk pajamas. Then, with an exhausted sigh, she climbed into bed and turned out the light.

Oh, but wouldn't just one more supper with him be wonderful?

SIX

"I knew you would be as excited to see this child as I was, so I made an appointment with her teacher for you to hear her play today at three o'clock."

Anya Romanov looked up from the bowl of fruit yogurt she was eating and frowned at her older brother. At twenty-three, she was a beautiful young woman, tall and slim, with thick dark hair and eyes the color of aged brandy. Like her brother, she was an esteemed pianist but, unlike him, music was not her only passion in life. Rather, almost as much was written about Anya Romanov in the social and gossip pages of Russian newspapers as in the arts sections.

"I wish you had asked me before you set up this appointment," she said now. "Did it never occur to you that I might have plans this afternoon?"

Alexei looked at Anya in complete surprise. "Do you?"

"That's not the point, Alexei. The point is that you treat me as if I'm still a child you can direct. You've never accepted the fact that I am a grown woman, with a life of my own, and that I expect you to consult with me before you commit me to something."

Alexei nodded. "I know you're a grown woman, Anya, and I understand what you're saying, but this child is so special that I didn't want you to miss the opportunity to hear her. I felt it best to set the appointment with her piano mistress while I was with the lady."

Anya slapped her spoon down on the table with an annoyed

clank. "Did you stop to think, even for a moment, that maybe I don't care about seeing this child, no matter how good she is?" Seeing her brother's startled expression, she quickly amended her words. "Don't misunderstand, Alexei. Its not that I'm not interested in children. You know I am. I have every intention of teaching someday, just as you do. But this is my first trip to America, and right now there are about a thousand ways I can think of to spend my time that interest me far more than sitting in some stuffy little practice room listening to a child run scales, no matter how talented she is. Can you understand that?"

"Not really," Alexei admitted. "When you decided to accompany me this summer instead of touring the Baltic countries, I thought you were interested in assisting me with this tour, but from what I've seen since we arrived in Boston, it appears you're only interested in shopping, eating in expensive restaurants and meeting eligible American men."

"And what's wrong with that?" Anya asked, her tone again becoming defensive. "I don't think it's unusual for a woman my age to be interested in meeting eligible men. And I don't think it's strange that I enjoy shopping and eating in fine restaurants either. You seem to think I should be concerned only with mastering some obscure and impossible Liszt étude that no one understands or wants to listen to anyway."

Alexei glared at his sister for a moment, his lips pressed into a tight, angry line. When he finally spoke, his voice was icy with sarcasm. "I will call Miss Pendergast this morning and cancel the appointment. That way you won't have to worry about not making it to Saks before they run out of clothing."

"You're being very unkind, Alexei."

"You're right, I am." Alexei sighed, relenting as he usually did when Anya turned a hurt expression on him. "And I do apologize for not talking to you before I made the appointment. I was just very anxious for you to hear Jenna Saxon, especially since I discovered that I know her mother. It made the child even more interesting."

For the first time since the conversation had begun, Anya looked at her brother with a spark of interest lighting her eyes. "You know her mother? How?"

"She was a student of mine at Juilliard."

"Really? How extraordinary! How did you come to find that out?"

"Her mother came to pick her up from her lesson while I was still there."

"And you recognized each other?"

"Yes."

Anya looked at Alexei closely for a moment, curious at how guarded his answers had suddenly become. "Was she someone you knew well?"

"Actually, I knew her quite well," Alexei answered. He sat silently for a moment; then, noticing Anya's exasperated expression, he added, "She and I saw each other socially for awhile."

Anya again put down her spoon, leaning forward intently. "And the woman's name is Saxon? I don't remember you ever mentioning anyone with that name."

"Saxon is her married name. Her maiden name was Worthington."

Anya drew in an astonished breath. She might not recognize the name Saxon, but Worthington was a name she knew well. *Natalie Worthington.* The American girl who had broken her brother's heart. Even though she had only been a schoolgirl when Alexei had returned from his year in America, Anya could remember well the procession of letters that had sat on the silver salver by the front door of their Moscow apartment, waiting to be mailed to Natalie Worthington. She also remembered that it was only a few weeks before Alexei stopped receiving answers. Finally, several months after his return home, a single letter had arrived from America. Alexei never confided to her what that last letter said, but Anya was aware that after he received it, he never wrote to the American girl again.

It wasn't until much later that Yuri Domovich told her that

Alexei had asked Natalie Worthington to marry him and that she had refused.

Anya had seen firsthand the devastating change that letter had brought about in her brother's life. For months, he'd refused to even play the piano, instead spending his days staring sightlessly out the front window of their apartment with a glass of vodka in his hand.

Finally, though, Alexei had seemed to recover from the blow of losing the woman he loved and had gone back to his piano, renewing his career aspirations with a passion that virtually precluded any kind of personal life.

To this day, Yuri maintained that the heartbreak Alexei had suffered at the hands of Natalie Worthington was the reason he had never married—had never even allowed himself to become serious about another woman.

There was Margot Petrikova, of course, but Anya had never felt that Alexei was truly serious about the beautiful singer.

Anya often felt sorry for Margot. It was obvious the woman was in love with her brother, and that she worked very hard to maintain a place in Alexei's life, even if it was a minor one. Anya had no doubt that Margot would leap at the chance to marry Alexei if only he would ask her, but she was equally convinced that Alexei never would.

Pulling her wayward thoughts back to the present, Anya said, "It must have been quite a shock for you to see Natalie Worthington after all these years."

Alexei remained bent over his eggs. "Yes, it was a surprise to find out she was Jenna Saxon's mother."

Anya threw her brother a jaundiced look, knowing that he was purposely being noncommittal. "And was she equally surprised to see you?"

Alexei sighed and put down his fork, knowing his tenacious sister wouldn't relent in her interrogation until he told her what she wanted to know. "Actually, we had seen each other the night before. After the concert, she and a friend of hers came back to my dressing room for a few moments."

"She did?" Anya exclaimed. "Well, wasn't that friendly of her."

"Why do you say that?"

"Honestly, Alexei, after all the pain that woman caused you, I'm surprised she would have the courage to face you."

"That was a long time ago," Alexei muttered.

Anya studied him for a moment, convinced that he was more disturbed by Natalie Worthington's reappearance in his life than he was willing to admit. "You know, Alexei, I've changed my mind," she said suddenly. "If Jenna Saxon is as gifted as you say she is, it *would* be a mistake on my part to pass up the opportunity of hearing her play. I think I will keep the appointment this afternoon."

"Are you sure?" Alexei asked.

Anya nodded. "Absolutely."

Three o'clock found Anya seated on a chair in Horton Fowler's studio just as Alexei had been the day before.

He could have told me that this was to be a spying mission, she thought crossly to herself. *Had I known I was going to have to stay hidden behind a door, I wouldn't have come, regardless of whose child Jenna Saxon is!*

Irritably, she yanked on the hem of the cherry red wool skirt she was wearing and crossed one slim leg over the other. *Hiding in an adjoining room, for heaven's sake. What is wrong with these Americans that they're all so paranoid about everything?*

At that moment, Anya heard the sound of a child's voice in Miss Pendergast's studio, and despite the old lady's repeated admonitions to stay out of sight, she couldn't help peeking around the door to get a look at Jenna Saxon.

What a beautiful little girl, she thought, smiling to herself as she admired Jenna's cloud of blond hair. *If her mother is half as pretty as she is, it's no wonder Alexei was so taken with her.* Anya leaned a little farther around the door frame, then quickly pulled back out of sight as Jenna turned in her direction. Silently, she retreated to the chair, praying it wouldn't squeak as she sat back down.

Just as Alexei had the day before, Anya suffered through the boring ritual of listening to Jenna's warm-up scales, but the moment the little girl began to play her first piece, she forgot her initial reluctance to attend the practice session and began listening raptly, her complete attention riveted to the sounds leaking through the partially open door. "Lord in heaven, she *is* brilliant," she breathed. "Why, I bet not even Alexei could play like that at seven."

The half hour flew by as Anya listened to Jenna play Chopin, Mozart and even a bit of Beethoven. When, finally, the lesson came to an end and she heard Miss Pendergast tell Jenna to pack up her music, she could hardly contain her excitement.

Tiptoeing over to the door, Anya again risked a peek into the studio, only this time Jenna saw the movement from the corner of her eye. "Miss Pendergast," the child asked, "is Mr. Romanov in Mr. Fowler's room again?"

"Of course not," Miss Pendergast assured her, flashing a sharp look at the door.

"Well, somebody is," Jenna insisted. "I just saw them looking at us from behind the door."

Miss Pendergast immediately rose from her chair and hurried over to pull the door shut, but just as she reached for the knob, Anya stepped into her studio.

Smiling broadly at Jenna, she announced, "Mr. Romanov isn't in the next studio. I am. I'm Anya, Mr. Romanov's sister."

Jenna giggled with delight and turned toward Penelope. "Somebody new hides in there every day!"

Miss Pendergast remained silent, but she turned a furious glare on Anya, her mouth pursed so tight with anger that it almost disappeared.

With her usual aplomb, Anya ignored the disapproving old lady. "Jenna, tell me about your music," she said, seating herself happily on Miss Pendergast's chair and pulling the little girl close.

The next few minutes passed quickly as Anya and Jenna discussed composers and compositions, much as Jenna and Alexei had the day before. To Anya's surprised delight, she found Jenna to be not only friendly, but extremely intelligent, with a keen knowledge of music theory and composition that belied her years. As their conversation continued, Anya found herself becoming as enamored with the beautiful child as Alexei had been.

"You play Beethoven very well," Anya noted. "Is he one of your favorites?"

Jenna nodded. "But I can't play him as much as I'd like because of my funny thumb."

Anya's brows drew together. "Your funny thumb? What's a funny thumb?"

"Watch," Jenna said, and held up her left hand. With a quick, jerking movement, she snapped the second joint of her thumb out of position, causing the digit to stick out at a weird, forty-five-degree angle. "See?" she explained. "There's something wrong with it."

Anya let out a sharp gasp, staring at Jenna's hand incredulously. "My God," she whispered. "Has your thumb always been like that?"

Jenna nodded. "Always. Mommy said it's something I was born with."

Anya turned away for a moment, covering her mouth with trembling fingers and breathing so hard that Penelope thought she was going to faint. "Miss Romanov, are you all right?" she asked fearfully.

"Yes, I'm fine," Anya replied, turning back to Jenna. "Has your mama taken you to see a doctor about your thumb?"

Again, Jenna nodded. "The doctor says I'll probably grow out of it."

"I see."

"I hope I do too," Jenna continued, "because sometimes it

hurts when I try to reach an octave, and reaching an octave is very important."

"Yes, it is," Anya agreed distractedly. With a quick, unexpected movement, she rose from her chair and started toward the door. "It was very nice to meet you, Jenna. You, ah, play beautifully."

Turning toward the bewildered Miss Pendergast, she added, "I have to go now. Thank you for allowing me to listen to Jenna play."

And before Penelope could even open her mouth to form a response, Anya was gone.

The Romanov Curse. The child had that terrible, cursed Romanov thumb.

Anya walked along the crowded Boston street, oblivious to the many people staring at her and stepping out of her way as she mumbled to herself.

Anya knew that the official name for the condition was Romanov's Syndrome, but for the hundreds of people in her family who had suffered from it over the centuries, it was known simply as the Curse.

For hundreds of years, the Romanov family had excelled at music, producing generation after generation of pianists, violinists and cellists—except when, without warning, the Romanov Curse would hit some luckless individual.

Although generations of Romanov children had found the thumb to be a source of great amusement, the deformity in later life often caused pain and lack of mobility, ending many a promising musical career. And because the problem seemed to be limited only to people in the Romanov family, little research had ever been done to find a cause or a cure. Only recently, a doctor at a Moscow hospital had perfected a surgical procedure that, so far, was proving to be successful in correcting the deformity in children.

Anya sighed, thinking that only three children in the latest generation of her family had shown symptoms of the syndrome. And now Jenna Saxon made four. She had the curse, and that meant that she had Romanov blood running through her veins. And as Anya had realized with such stunning clarity when Jenna had demonstrated her "funny thumb," it also meant that Jenna was Alexei's daughter.

SEVEN

"Are you sure it's the Romanov Curse, Anya? Certainly there must be more than just that one hereditary defect of the thumb. Maybe it's just a coincidence."

It was early evening and Yuri and Anya were seated opposite each other in the luxurious sitting room of Alexei's hotel suite. The hours since her return from meeting Jenna at the Schumann School of Music had seemed like an eternity for Anya. Restlessly, she'd paced her bedroom, looking at her watch every few minutes as she waited anxiously for Alexei to leave for that evening's concert. The moment that she had finally heard the suite's front door close, she had flown out of her room and pounded on Yuri's bedroom door.

"It's no coincidence, Yuri. I remember seeing my grandfather's thumb when I was a child, and it popped out of the socket exactly the same way Jenna Saxon's does. I have no doubt that she has the Romanov thumb, and that means . . ."

". . . that she's Alexei's child," Yuri finished, shaking his head solemnly. "I just don't understand Natalie Worthington giving birth to Alexei's baby and not telling him about it."

"Did you know Natalie, Yuri? You were with Alexei part of the time that he was teaching in New York. You must have met her."

Yuri shrugged his heavy shoulders. "Yes, a few times."

"And did she seem like a duplicitous person?" Anya asked.

Yuri thought for a moment, then shook his head again. "I can't say that she did, Anya. She seemed like every other

American college girl that I met that winter. She was pretty, she laughed a lot and she seemed completely devoted to your brother. That's why I was so surprised when she wouldn't return to Russia with him and then wrote him that terrible letter telling him that it was over between them and that she was marrying someone else. I was never able to put that cold, unfeeling letter together with the girl I'd met. I guess now I finally understand."

"Understand what?"

Yuri threw his arms wide. "Why she married so quickly. She must have discovered that she was pregnant, so she went out and found someone to stand in as the baby's father as soon as she could."

Anya strolled thoughtfully over to a collapsible room service table, which stood in front of the hotel suite's windows. Idly, she poured herself some tea, stirring sugar and cream into the amber liquid before turning back to Alexei's valet. "You say you think she loved Alexei, but I can't agree. If she had cared about him she would have at least had the decency to tell him he was going to be a father. That way, the two of them could have decided together what to do about the baby—and their relationship. In my opinion, that's what a woman would do who truly cared about a man. She wouldn't just write him a cruel letter of rejection and then go about her life as if he'd never existed."

Yuri held up his hands defensively. "Don't misunderstand me, Anya. I have no love for Natalie Worthington. I saw what her actions did to your brother and I hated her for it, just as you do. But considering what you discovered today, I think I have a little better understanding of what a quandary she must have been in. Alexei was gone, she was single, pregnant and very young. Maybe she thought that hiding the truth about the baby's father was her only option."

Anya set her teacup down and turned on Yuri with flashing eyes. "How can you defend her? It wasn't her only option. Alexei wanted to marry her, even though he didn't know she was carrying his child. All she would have had to do is say yes to his proposal and her 'quandary,' as you call it, would have been solved."

"Anya, Anya, think about it," Yuri protested, getting up and pouring himself a glass of vodka. "Natalie Worthington was an American heiress accustomed to a life of comfort and privilege. She might have loved your brother, but that doesn't mean that she could picture herself spending the rest of her life as a Moscow housewife under a Communist regime."

"I don't care what you say," Anya said stubbornly. "If she had truly loved Alexei, she would have made whatever sacrifices were necessary for her child to be able to take her rightful place as his daughter."

Yuri chuckled. "Anya, you're speaking like a good Russian woman, but you're not listening to what I'm saying. Natalie Worthington is an American—and a rich one. You know how self-centered rich Americans are. *Sacrifice* is a word that is probably not even in her vocabulary."

Anya cast the older man a conciliatory smile. "You're right, Yuri. But I still think what the woman did was wrong."

"I agree," Yuri said, "but it is also history and cannot be changed. What you have to decide now is whether you're going to tell Alexei what you've discovered."

Anya sank back down on the sofa. "I know. I've been thinking about that all evening."

"Have you come to any decision?"

"I think so. Even though I believe Alexei deserves to know about his daughter, I have decided not to tell him—at least not now."

Yuri walked around the coffee table, sitting down next to Anya and taking her small hand in his huge one. "Why have you decided this?"

Anya stared at the floor for a long moment, then said in a quiet voice, "Because I feel that right now, Alexei doesn't need the burden this knowledge is bound to give him. I know how important this tour is to him. He hasn't performed in America for many years and he needs to be completely focused on his playing in order to make the tour successful. Knowing that Jenna Saxon is his daughter is bound to be a serious distraction. It might even cause him to cancel the tour, and that would do irreparable harm to his reputation." Slowly she lifted her eyes to meet Yuri's. "Do you agree?"

"Completely," he answered, nodding his gray head. "I saw the effect just seeing Natalie in the audience on opening night had on Alexei. He could hardly concentrate on his encore. If he knew everything we now know, I think he probably *would* cancel the tour, and we cannot let that happen. I agree completely that you should keep what you know about Jenna Saxon to yourself."

Anya looked at Yuri gratefully. "I'm glad that we're in accord on this, although I do think that at some point Alexei should be told about Jenna."

"So do I," Yuri concurred. "But not now."

Anya squeezed the loyal servant's hand. "Well, there is one thing we can take comfort in."

"What's that?"

"Since you and I are the only two who know about this situation, there is no way Alexei will find out until we decide the time is right."

"I hope you're right about that."

Anya shrugged. "How can I not be? It's likely that the only other people who know the truth about Jenna are Natalie Worthington and her husband. Natalie certainly isn't going to tell Alexei anything, and since she and her husband are divorced, it's unlikely that Alexei would meet him."

"Very unlikely," Yuri said, "since the man is dead."

Anya's eyes grew round. "Dead?"

"Yes," Yuri confirmed. "Alexei told me yesterday after he visited the child's school that her piano instructor told him that Natalie's ex-husband was killed in a car accident several years ago."

Anya shook her head. "That's a shame, but knowing that,

I feel even more confident that Alexei will not find out about Jenna."

Yuri sighed, wishing he felt as confident as Anya did. "From your lips to God's ear, my dear."

Anya rose and headed for her bedroom. "Thank you for everything, Yuri," she said gratefully. "I knew I could count on you to help me. And as long as you and I do everything in our power to see that Alexei does not have any further involvement with Natalie Saxon, our secret should remain safe."

Yuri smiled encouragingly, but as soon as Anya closed her bedroom door, he leaned back into the plush cushions of the overstuffed sofa and exhaled a weary sigh. Anya was right: She could count on him to help keep the distressing truth of Jenna Saxon's paternity from Alexei for as long as possible. But something had happened the previous afternoon that made him uneasy. He had been present when Alexei had summoned the hotel messenger to deliver the letters to Natalie and Jenna, and although Yuri did not know exactly what those letters said, he had also heard Alexei make reservations for a late-night supper. It was not a great leap to figure out that Alexei was planning on seeing Natalie and Jenna this evening.

Since it was reasonable to assume that the more time Alexei spent in Natalie and Jenna's company, the more chance there was of him learning the truth, Yuri hoped desperately that Natalie had turned down whatever invitation was contained in those messages. But as tenacious as his employer could be, even if Natalie had turned him down for tonight, Alexei might not give up.

In all the years that Yuri had worked for Alexei, he had always found him to be a reasonable man . . . except when it came to Natalie Worthington. The girl had come close to unraveling Alexei's life once before, and it had taken him over a year to get himself back on track. Now, here she was again, eight years later and, already, Alexei's behavior was worrisome.

Even if Natalie wasn't interested in renewing the relationship, Yuri knew how persuasive Alexei could be once he decided he wanted something. And there was no doubt in Yuri's mind that Alexei still wanted Natalie Worthington.

Yuri sighed and took a long swallow of his vodka, knowing there was very little he and Anya could do to prevent Alexei from pursuing Natalie, if that was what he was determined to do. At least he only had four days in which to do it.

"Four days." Yuri grunted. "Only four days."

And yet, many things could happen in four days. That worried Yuri Domovich a lot.

EIGHT

"Jenna, come on! It's past seven-thirty and if we don't leave right now, we're going to be late for the concert."

Jenna ran to the top of the stairs and looked down at her mother with beseeching eyes. "I can't find my shoes."

With a sigh, Natalie set down her purse and started up the staircase. "Which shoes?"

"My black shiny ones—my party shoes."

Natalie nodded and headed down the upstairs hall toward her daughter's room. "When did you last have them?"

"I don't know," Jenna answered. "I can't remember."

"You've looked in your closet and under your bed?"

The little girl gazed up at her mother and nodded. "Yes, and they're not there."

"Well, then, you're just going to have to wear your school shoes."

"I don't want to wear those ugly shoes!" Jenna wailed. "I want to wear my pretty ones."

Natalie did a quick search of Jenna's bedroom, then glanced at her watch and frowned. "Honey, we have to leave now, so you're just going to have to wear your school shoes." Looking down at her daughter's stricken face, she smiled encouragingly. "Don't worry; it'll be dark in the concert hall. No one will notice that you're not wearing your party shoes."

Tears welled up in Jenna's brown eyes. "Please, Mommy, can't we look for just a minute longer?"

Natalie glanced at her watch again. "One more minute; then

we have to go." She walked into the bathroom adjoining Jenna's room and gave it a cursory glance. "They don't seem to be in here."

Jenna looked around too, then ran over to the dirty clothes hamper and flipped the lid open. "Here they are!" Reaching into the hamper, she pulled out a pair of black patent leather Mary Janes and held them up, beaming.

Despite their tardiness and the bad case of nerves that Natalie had been suffering all day, she laughed. "What in the world are your shoes doing in the clothes hamper?"

Jenna shrugged and sat down on the edge of the bathtub, pulling the shoes on without unbuckling them. "I don't know. I must have thrown them in with my socks. There," she said, standing up and stamping her feet to force her heels into the shoes. "Now I'm ready."

Natalie grinned at her daughter. "Good. Now, let's go!"

"They're not coming."

Alexei stood in the wings of Symphony Hall and peeked out from behind the curtain, his eyes riveted on the two empty seats in the center of the third row.

Yuri gazed at his boss sympathetically. After his conversation with Anya, he had been so restless that he had decided to go to the concert hall to help Alexei dress. In the course of the preparations, Alexei had confessed what Yuri had already suspected—that he had sent tickets to Natalie and Jenna to attend that evening's performance. "Did you really think they'd come?" he now asked quietly.

"When she didn't respond to my message, I had my doubts," Alexei admitted, "but I was still hoping. . . ."

Yuri clenched his teeth together in an effort to prevent Alexei from seeing how furious he was that Natalie Worthington was again causing him such pain. "You must not let it bother you, Alexei. The only thing that's important right now is the concert.

Natalie Worthington may not be here, but hundreds of people are, and it is them you have to think of."

"I know that," Alexei flared angrily. "And don't worry, they'll get their money's worth."

"Of course they will," Yuri soothed. "I just don't want you to let this situation upset you. You said yourself that Natalie told you it was over between you and had been for a long time. I'm not surprised that she didn't show up tonight."

Alexei sighed heavily. "I guess I'm not either, really. I just thought that maybe she could put aside her personal feelings toward me long enough to let her daughter attend the concert."

Her daughter, Yuri thought. *Your daughter.* Thank God he didn't know that.

"It's time, Alexei," he said now, as the house lights dimmed and the audience quieted. "Go and be brilliant."

Alexei nodded curtly and, with a dignity that belied the turmoil raging within him, walked out onto the stage.

He had just completed the second piece on his program when he noticed Natalie and Jenna hurrying down the aisle and taking their seats. His eyes locked with Jenna's, and as she waved gaily at him, a rare smile crossed his face, causing many a female heart in the audience to thump in dazzled appreciation of his handsomeness.

Natalie was getting settled in her seat and missed the exchange between Jenna and Alexei, but she looked up in surprise as she heard an audible sigh from the middle-aged woman seated next to her.

"Do you know Mr. Romanov?" the lady asked, leaning toward Natalie.

A flash of alarm sprang into Natalie's eyes. "Excuse me?"

"Well, he seems to be looking at you and smiling. I just thought maybe you two were acquainted."

Natalie shot a quick look at Alexei, but he had already turned away and was returning to the piano. "I think he was smiling at my daughter," she whispered. "She met him yesterday during her piano lesson."

Her words caused the corpulent lady to lean forward and peer at Jenna. With a little gasp of surprise, she refocused her attention on Natalie. "Why, that's Jenna Saxon, isn't it? And you must be her mother."

"Yes, I am," answered Natalie shortly. Then, with a dismissive smile, she turned her attention back to the stage, hoping the woman would take the hint and cease her conversation.

Alexei reseated himself at the piano and began a Chopin Polonaise, playing the difficult and intricate piece with a mastery that stunned even the most discriminating of attendees. Natalie closed her eyes for a moment, swept away by the lyrical beauty of the music, then slowly opened them, allowing herself for the first time to really study Alexei.

That profile, she thought. Has there ever been another man with such a perfect profile? The aquiline nose, the sculpted lips, the strong, almost arrogant chin. Natalie smiled, thinking that if Alexei had been alive during Roman times, they probably would have put his profile on a coin.

Her gaze dropped to his hands. He had the touch of a true artist, his long, finely boned fingers caressing the keys of his instrument with a finesse that brought back unsettling memories as she remembered those same exquisite hands rapturously caressing her.

She pictured herself lying in his soft bed, sighing with pleasure as his tapered fingers toyed provocatively with her breasts, then slowly moved downward, trailing across her soft belly as they made their erotic journey toward the hot, moist core of her femininity.

Natalie shivered, jerking herself back to reality. Shocked and embarrassed by her wayward thoughts, she looked around, praying that she had not made any audible sounds during her lusty ruminations and greatly relieved when she saw that neither Jenna nor the nosy woman on her other side were paying any attention to her. She put a discreet hand up to her neck, mortified to feel telltale heat emanating from her body and grateful that the dark auditorium hid the flush she knew must be visible.

She drew a long, calming breath and looked again at Jenna. The little girl was staring at the stage, transfixed by the beauty of her father's playing. Out of the corner of her eye, Jenna noticed Natalie watching her and whispered, "Oh, Mommy, isn't he amazing? Will I ever be able to play like that?"

"Of course you will, darling," Natalie assured her, stroking Jenna's soft blond hair. "Maybe, someday, you'll even be better than he is."

"No one could be better than he is," Jenna whispered back. She returned her attention to the stage, a look of focused concentration on her piquant little face as she studied Alexei's technique.

No one except maybe his child, Natalie thought. She pulled her eyes away from her daughter and looked again at Alexei, startled by how similar his expression of concentration was to his daughter's.

Quit thinking about it, Natalie silently commanded herself. *Just sit back and enjoy the music.*

But, despite her resolve, Natalie could not stop herself from glancing surreptitiously back and forth between Alexei and Jenna, and each time she did, the striking similarities between father and daughter increased her feelings of guilt over the choices she'd made so long ago.

She's much more like him than I ever realized, she thought. *I just hope he doesn't notice.*

Natalie so dreaded tonight's meeting with Alexei in his dressing room that she wished the concert would never end. When, inevitably, he finished the last piece listed in the program, she felt a real sense of panic.

Up to that point, she hadn't thought he had noticed her sitting in the audience, but now as he rose to take his final bow, he looked directly at her and smiled, as though the two of them shared an intimate secret.

Natalie could not imagine what the meaning of that smile

was until he again sat down at the piano and began to play his encore.

What happened next was to become the subject of fascinated speculation and heated arguments among Boston's music mavens for years to come. For Alexei Romanov, the greatest classical pianist of his time, did not finish his concert with Chopin or Beethoven or Rachmaninoff. Instead, he played a medley of hits by Lennon and McCartney, beginning with the hypnotic, repetitive strains of "Hey Jude" and building to a raucous finish with "Back in the USSR," a choice that brought most of the audience to its feet, clapping and stomping their feet like the teenagers they'd all once been.

Not everyone in the audience was receptive, however, and Alexei could tell from the expressions of those who remained seated that he had probably lost a few fans for life. But he didn't care, because the two people for whom he was truly playing were on their feet, and their obvious delight in his choice brought a feeling of joy to his heart that he had not known in many years.

When the last crashing chord finally faded, the audience went crazy, their applause and cheers bouncing off the vaults of the high ceilings until the staid old concert hall sounded more like a rock venue than the site of a classical piano recital.

Alexei drank in the adulation for a moment, then with a last look cast directly at Natalie, calmly walked off the stage.

The extraordinary concert was over.

"Oh, Mommy, wasn't that last song the best thing you ever heard?"

Natalie looked over at Jenna as she picked up her coat, her expression still reflecting the laughter and excitement she and her daughter had just shared. "It was pretty incredible, wasn't it?" she agreed. "I've never heard anything like it at a piano concert."

Jenna grinned. "I know why he played those Beatles songs."

Natalie was pulling on her coat as Jenna made this announcement, but she paused, staring at her daughter curiously, her coat hanging off one shoulder. "You do? Why?"

"Because," Jenna said, drawing the word out dramatically, "I told him how much I love to play Beatles songs and how you sing along and everything, so I think he played them for me." She paused a moment, then added, "And for you."

Natalie felt an unexpected rush of pleasure course through her but carefully tamped down her exultation before she spoke again. "There are many people who like the Beatles' music, Jenna. Mr. Romanov didn't necessarily play those songs just because of us."

"Yes, he did," Jenna said positively. "I saw him look at us and smile right before he played them. I know he did it because of what I said."

Natalie stared at her daughter for a long moment, knowing the child was probably right. "Well, if you really think Mr. Romanov played those songs especially for you, then you must be sure to thank him when we see him."

"I will," Jenna promised. "Let's go do that now." Reaching up, she grabbed Natalie's hand and began pulling her toward the center aisle.

Reluctantly, Natalie let herself be herded along, again joining the crowd headed for Alexei's dressing room, just as she had with Susan two nights before.

Tonight was different, though. Where, with Susan, she had merely felt embarrassed and a little wary about seeing Alexei, so much had happened in the ensuing two days that tonight she felt sheer, unadulterated dread. Despite the fact that she had seen the man twice in the past forty-eight hours, they had not shared so much as a single civil word, and the last time, when they had parted at Jenna's music school, they had both been extremely angry. She had purposely not responded to his invitation for dinner, hoping that her silence would give him her answer without any more hurtful words being exchanged between them.

But now she had to face him again—and this time, their meeting would be in front of Jenna. For her daughter's sake, she must maintain her poise, regardless of how disquieting it was to be in Alexei's company.

"Do you think he'll sign my program?" Jenna asked as they followed the crowd through the concert hall's backstage maze.

"I'm sure he will if you ask him, but right after we say hello and he signs your program, we have to leave. It's very late, and there will be a lot of people wanting to see him, so we can't take up too much of his time."

Jenna looked disappointed, but she nodded her understanding.

Finally they reached Alexei's dressing room. He was standing in the hallway, responding distractedly to a barrage of questions while looking over the crowd's heads for signs of their arrival.

Natalie paused at the edge of the crush of reporters and was standing on tiptoe, trying to make eye contact with him, when she suddenly felt a hand clamp down on her upper arm and a heavily accented voice demand, "Young woman, where is your press pass?"

She whirled around to find a tall, heavyset woman glaring down at her, but before she could regain her composure enough to identify herself, Sergei Svetlanov, Alexei's publicist, came to her rescue.

"Sophie!" he cried, rushing over and peeling the glowering woman's hand off Natalie's arm. "This is Mrs. Saxon and her daughter, Jenna. Alexei is expecting them."

"Oh!" Sophie said, her voice suddenly chagrined. "I . . . I'm sorry."

Turning to Natalie, Sergei said, "Please excuse my wife. She didn't know who you were."

Natalie graciously accepted the embarrassed man's apology, then smiled, amused to finally be meeting the famous Sophie Svetlanova, Sergei's wife.

Suddenly, she had a vision of herself seated on a large pillow on the floor in Alexei's tiny New York apartment as he regaled her with hilarious stories about his travels. According to Alexei, Sophie, who always accompanied her husband when he toured with Alexei, had two defining characteristics: a propensity for wearing babushkas regardless of the weather and an insatiable appetite for whatever expensive items were to be found in Alexei's hotel room honor bar. Looking at the corpulent woman now, Natalie could see that Alexei's stories of Sophie's excesses had not been exaggerated.

"Alexei has told us about your daughter," Sophie said in an obvious attempt to make up for her previous gaffe. "He says she is very talented. Of course, I could not offer an opinion myself since I have not heard her play."

Natalie's eyes widened at this left-handed compliment, but she was saved from having to respond when she suddenly heard Alexei calling her name.

Turning toward his voice, she watched as he pushed aside the microphone a local reporter had just shoved in his face and made his way through the crowd, ignoring the many pens and programs being pushed at him by hopeful autograph collectors.

"I'm so glad you came." He smiled when he finally reached her. "If we can get through this throng and into my dressing room, we can have some privacy."

"Oh, that isn't necessary," Natalie blurted. "Jenna and I can't stay, anyway. We just wanted to thank you for the tickets, and Jenna was hoping that you would sign her program."

Alexei looked down at Jenna and grinned. "Of course I'll sign your program, little one." Squatting, he took the wrinkled program and pen Jenna thrust at him and scrawled an indecipherable message followed by his signature across the front. Handing the paper back to the little girl, he said, "How did you like my encore? I played it just for you because of what you told me yesterday."

Jenna looked up at Natalie in beaming triumph. "See, Mommy? I told you he played it for me!"

Natalie smiled at Jenna, then watched as Alexei straightened up and cast her a knowing look. "And how did you like the encore, Mrs. Saxon?"

"It was . . . very interesting," Natalie stammered, unsettled by his use of her married name, "and very unexpected. I didn't know you were such a Beatles fan . . . Mr. Romanov."

Alexei looked at her for a long moment, wondering how long they were would play this little name game before one of them cracked. "Actually, I'm not." Lowering his voice, he leaned closer, his next words for her alone. "*You* were the Beatles fan, *daragaya*—and now your daughter is. That was reason enough for me to play it tonight."

Natalie took a quick step back, unnerved by the sensation of Alexei's warm breath so near her ear. "Jenna and I both enjoyed your encore very much, but I'm afraid some of the critics might have a different opinion."

Alexei waved a dismissive hand. "Critics, bah! Who cares what they think?" Reaching down, he gave Jenna's shoulder an affectionate little pat. "As long as you enjoyed it, then I am happy."

Natalie reached down and caught Jenna's hand in hers. "Well, thank you again, Mr. Romanov. Now, we really must go. There are a lot of people waiting to see you and we don't want . . ."

"Never mind those other people," Alexei interrupted, suddenly realizing that Natalie was preparing to leave. "You are the only ones who have been invited here so, please, do not feel that you have to go."

"Oh, but we must," Natalie insisted. "It is late and Jenna has to go to bed."

Alexei studied Natalie for a moment, as if trying to weigh the truth of her words, then stepped toward her again. "And our supper, Tasha? What about that? You didn't respond to my invitation."

"I know," Natalie said quickly, wishing desperately that her heart wouldn't leap every time he called her Tasha, "and it was very rude of me not to call."

"Never mind that. Will you go to supper with me?"

"I can't."

Alexei's eyes narrowed. "Can't, or won't?"

"Please don't ask me that. I really do have to get Jenna home now."

Alexei looked over at Jenna, who was staring at the adults with interest. "Your mama says it's time for you to go home and go to bed."

"I know." Jenna sighed. "She always says that."

Alexei laughed, a deep, rich sound that made goose bumps rise all over Natalie's arms. Again he squatted down in front of Jenna, pulling her to him and kissing her lightly on both cheeks. "Thank you for coming to my concert."

Jenna giggled and rubbed her cheeks with her knuckles. "Thank you for having me . . . and thanks for playing the Beatles for me."

"Anytime, Jenna," Alexei replied softly. "Someday, maybe we'll play their music together."

"Duets," Jenna trilled. "I love duets."

Alexei rose and turned toward Natalie. "She's wonderful, Natalie. You must be very proud."

Natalie nodded, too overwhelmed by the warmth and kindness Alexei had shown Jenna to trust herself to speak.

"When will I see you again?" he asked quietly.

"I don't think you will."

Alexei shook his head, refusing to accept her answer. "Yes, I will. I cannot leave until we have had a chance to spend at least a few hours together."

"Alexei, I'm very busy and so are you," Natalie began.

"Neither of us is that busy," he interrupted. "Look at your schedule and call me tomorrow."

"But . . ."

"Please, Tasha. Call me."

Natalie looked at the man whom she had once loved so

deeply and knew that despite the distance and the years between them, she still could not deny him. "All right, Alex. I'll call you tomorrow."

Alexei smiled. "Do you promise?"

Natalie nodded.

"Good. Now, go home and put your daughter to bed."

Natalie again took Jenna's hand and headed down the hallway toward the stage, thinking to herself what she had not had the courage to say aloud. *I'm going, Alex. Home to put our daughter to bed.*

NINE

"I just don't know what to do."

Susan Bedford frowned into her telephone receiver and leaned across her desk to close her office door, effectively shutting out the noisy din from the city room beyond. It was early Saturday morning, and although Natalie was still comfortably ensconced in her huge four-poster bed, Susan was at work, preparing her column for the Sunday edition. "I don't see that you have any choice, Natalie," she said, slumping back into her desk chair. "You told him you'd call him today. You can't go back on your word."

"But he's going to want me to go out with him."

"So, when he asks, you say, 'Yes' or 'No.' It's as simple as that. If you want to go, go. If you don't, don't."

Susan waited through a long silence on Natalie's end of the line; then a smile slowly spread across her face. "You want to go, don't you?"

"Yes, I guess so, but . . ."

Susan straightened up in her chair, focusing all her attention on her friend's voice. "You're scared."

"Oh, all right, yes! I'm scared. In fact, I'm terrified."

By now, Susan was sitting bolt upright and grinning. "Why? Are you afraid you won't be able to control yourself once you're alone with your handsome Russian again?"

"Something like that," Natalie admitted.

Susan flopped back in the chair and let out a long, envious breath. "Then, by all means, go, girl!"

"That's easy for you to say."

"Natalie Saxon, you listen to me. By the time a woman gets to be our age . . ."

"What do you mean, 'our age'?" Natalie blustered. "I'm not even thirty yet."

"All right," Susan amended impatiently, "by the time a woman gets to be close to thirty, she doesn't have too many chances left to be swept off her feet. It's obvious that you've been in love with this guy forever and . . ."

"Susan . . ."

"Don't interrupt me, Nat. I've been thinking a lot about this in the past few days and I'm going to say my piece. I've known you for five years and in that time you must have gone out with fifty different men."

"Oh, please. I hardly think it's been fifty," Natalie scoffed.

"Never mind. It's been a bunch. But you've never allowed yourself to get involved with any of them, and I always wondered why. At first I thought maybe you were still in love with your ex-husband, but it wasn't the memory of Tom Saxon that was holding you back. All this time you've been in love with Alexei Romanov, and you still are. The amazing thing is that fate has delivered him back into your hands and given you a second chance."

"Susan, you sound like a romantic teenager." Natalie laughed.

"Maybe, but I know that what I'm saying is true. What I don't understand is why you're fighting it."

"I've explained all this to you." Natalie sighed. "I can't get involved with Alex again. What if he found out about Jenna?"

Susan pressed her lips together in frustration. "Natalie, he's only here for four more days. How is he going to find out about Jenna unless you tell him? That doesn't mean that you shouldn't see him."

"What's the point?" Natalie asked, her voice rising. "As you said, in four more days he'll be gone. So why should I go out with him and let myself . . ."

"What, Natalie? Let yourself what? Remember how happy he made you? Remember how much you loved him? Is that what you're scared of? That being with Alex will make you *feel* something again?"

"Yes!" Natalie wailed. "That's exactly what I'm afraid of. That I'll feel all that same, crazy wonderfulness that I felt before, and then he'll go back to Russia and I'll be alone again. I don't think I could stand going through that a second time."

"But you don't know that any of that would happen," Susan protested. "You're both older and more mature. Things could work out very differently this time. All I'm saying is that you'll never know if you won't allow yourself to see him and find out."

"Nothing would be different," Natalie insisted. "He's still Russian and I'm still American. He doesn't want to live here and I don't want to live in Russia."

"Natalie, for heaven's sake, it's been eight years! How do you know he doesn't want to live here? Russia is very different now than it was back then, and his feelings could have changed a great deal."

"I doubt that. He's very patriotic. He must have told me a hundred times that he owed all his success to the Russian educational system. Regardless of how much the government has changed, I'm sure his feelings of obligation haven't. And besides, even if we could work out the logistics, there is far more to consider here than just what Alex and I might want. I have to think about what's right for Jenna."

"Have you ever considered that what might be right for Jenna is to have her father in her life?"

"Of course I've considered it! In fact, for the last three days I've thought about almost nothing else."

"And yet you still don't think that he and she deserve to know about each other?"

"I don't know what I think," Natalie admitted. "It seems like the more I think, the more confused I become. Oh, God, Susan, why did he have to come back? I've been perfectly happy with my life and now he's turning my world upside down just like he did eight years ago."

"Oh, come on, Nat!" Susan snorted. "You haven't been perfectly happy with your life and you know it. You've just been coasting, that's all. Your life is easy, comfortable, familiar. But if it was as happy as you say it is, then you wouldn't be lying awake nights thinking about Alex. You would have gone to his concert, said hello to him in his dressing room and that would have been the end of it. Well, that didn't happen. What that says to me is that there's still something there between you, and I think you owe it to yourself and your daughter to find out what it is."

"I don't know," Natalie said hesitantly. "Maybe you're right."

"I know I'm right. Now, promise me you'll call him."

Natalie exhaled a long, shuddering breath. "All right, I'll call him. I guess I owe him that much."

Susan threw her head back and indulged in a silent shout of triumph. "Good. Now, I've got to go. Some of us have to work on the weekends, you know. Call me tomorrow and tell me everything. Or"—she chuckled—"if things go *really* well, don't tell me everything. I'll settle for the non-X-rated stuff."

"Oh, Susan, you're terrible!"

"I know . . . and it's such fun. 'Bye!"

"Alexei, you have a telephone call."

Alexei's head jerked up from the sheet music he was perusing. "Is it a woman?"

Anya nodded curtly. "Yes. An American woman."

A smile spread across Alexei's handsome features as he rose from the piano and headed across the suite. "Thank you, Anya. I'll take it in my bedroom."

An intense frown darkened Anya's features, causing Yuri to look at her curiously as he walked into the room. "What's wrong?" he asked. "Your face is as black as a thundercloud."

"She's on the telephone," Anya replied angrily. "Alexei is talking to her now . . . in his bedroom."

Yuri did not have to ask who *she* was. It was obvious from Anya's expression that the caller could only be Natalie Saxon. "He took her call in the bedroom?"

Anya nodded. "Apparently, he did not want you and me to hear what he was going to say."

"You know what he's going to say, Anya. He's going to ask to see her." Casually, Yuri picked up two cups from the coffee table and set them on the table in the suite's raised dining room.

"Well, you certainly seem unconcerned," Anya accused. "Doesn't it bother you that Alexei has spent the entire morning sitting at the piano and staring at a piece of music without so much as playing a note?"

Yuri shrugged. "Your brother doesn't have a performance tonight, so skipping a morning practice isn't going to harm him. I'm sure he'll make up for it tomorrow."

"It's not really the missed practice I'm worried about," Anya said. "It's the fact that that woman is distracting him from his routine. Why, when I told him that he had a phone call from a woman with an American accent, he nearly tipped the piano bench over in his haste to answer it."

She paused, thinking for a moment, then added, "No, I take back what I just said. *I am* worried about him skipping practice because the only other time he ever did that was the year after that same woman rejected him. Now it's starting all over again. She comes back into his life, and within three days, he's not practicing. I'm telling you, Yuri, Alexei is heading for disaster, and we have to do something to put a stop to it."

Yuri gazed at the young woman sympathetically. "Anya, Anya, you must stop upsetting yourself over this. Alexei is a grown man, and there is nothing either you or I can do if he is determined to see the woman."

"Determined to ruin his life again, you mean," Anya said bitterly.

"He's a grown man," Yuri repeated.

Anya turned on the valet, her lips pressed together in fury. "I'm sorry that I can't share your nonchalance, Yuri, but I care about my brother. Apparently, far more than you do."

"I care about your brother too, Anya, don't ever doubt it, but I also realize that there are limits to what you and I can do. We cannot live Alexei's life for him. In the end, regardless of what we do, he will live it as he sees fit."

Anya gave her head a vehement shake. "I cannot accept that. I cannot just sit by and watch him destroy himself a second time over that woman."

"Be careful," Yuri warned. "Do not force your brother to make a choice between you and the woman he loves or you might find yourself the loser."

"Then that's just a chance I'll have to take."

Yuri sighed heavily, wishing there was something he could say to make Anya change her mind but knowing it was futile to try. He would give a great deal to be able to reroute the emotional collision course on which the siblings were headed, but with the experience of a man who had seen much of life's turmoil, he was aware that there was little he could do except sit back and watch the drama unfold.

Alexei sat on the edge of the bed, the telephone clutched in his hand. "I thought we could have dinner at Aujourd'hui here in the hotel tonight. How does that sound?"

On the other end of the line, Natalie's eyes widened at this suggestion. Aujourd'hui was considered to be one of the finest restaurants in Boston and had long been one of her favorites, but the thought of sharing an intimate dinner with Alexei was not what she had in mind for this meeting.

"I don't think I could do that."

"Oh?" Alex responded. "Do you not like that restaurant? We could go somewhere else if you prefer."

"It's not that," Natalie said quickly. "Aujourd'hui is a wonderful restaurant. I just thought that we could meet someplace this afternoon. I . . . haven't made any provisions for a baby-sitter tonight, so going out for the evening could be difficult." Natalie hoped that Alexei wouldn't detect the lie in her voice. She knew that Susan would be more than happy to stay with Jenna, but she was too unsure of her feelings to commit to such a romantic encounter. "How about taking a walk on the Common?" she suggested. "It's a lovely day, and it would give you an opportunity to get out of your hotel and get some fresh air. The tulips are beginning to bloom in the Public Gardens, and it's a very pretty sight."

Alexei took a moment to form his answer, determined not to let his voice betray his disappointment. A walk in a city park filled with tourists snapping photographs of budding tulips was certainly not what he'd had in mind for this reunion, but at least it was a start. And, if the afternoon went as he hoped, they would find a way to have their dinner. Maybe Anya would look after Jenna, or perhaps he could even coerce Yuri into baby-sitting duty. The important thing was that he and Natalie have some time alone, and a walk through the Boston Common was better than nothing.

"All right," he said agreeably. "A stroll through the Common it is."

"I can't stay long," Natalie warned. "I have to pick Jenna up from her gymnastics class at three."

Alexei sighed inwardly. If the limitations Natalie was putting on their meeting became any more confining, they might as well just wave at each other from passing cars. "Tasha, if today is not good for you . . ."

"No, today is okay," Natalie assured him. "I'm just very busy." She grimaced, realizing how disinterested she must sound. Forcing a lightness into her voice that she was far from feeling, she added, "Really, Alex, today is fine. It's just that with a full-time job and a young daughter, I don't have much time to indulge myself in leisurely afternoon strolls, even on the weekends. I always seem to have something more important that I have to do."

"Indulging oneself occasionally *is* important," Alexei countered wryly.

Natalie ignored his innuendo, saying quickly, "What time should we meet?"

After they set the time and place of their rendezvous, their conversation ended quickly. Alexei set down the telephone receiver, frowning at the instrument as if it was at fault for his disappointing conversation. Then a smile lit his face and he rose, walking over to the dresser and sifting through the pile of telephone call slips lying on it. Finding the one he sought, he returned to the telephone, calling the number on it and saying, "Miss Susan Bedford, please. Alexei Romanov calling."

Natalie saw him before he saw her. Dressed in dark brown corduroy slacks and an ivory sweater that fit his tall, muscular body perfectly, he was standing on the path next to the lagoon, looking out over the still water with a contemplative expression on his face. Natalie paused, her heart taking a now familiar bound as she surreptitiously watched him. She had always thought that Alexei was the most handsome man she had ever known, and time had not changed that. If anything, the mature self-assurance in his posture made him even more attractive than he'd been eight years earlier.

For one incredible moment, Natalie felt a nearly uncontrollable desire to run up to him and throw herself into his arms. Instead, she took a deep breath and strolled over to where he stood, planting what she hoped was a friendly but slightly impersonal smile on her face.

"Hello, Alexei," she said brightly.

He turned toward her, his dark, moody eyes sweeping over her with a look of unguarded masculine appreciation. She looked gorgeous, dressed in a pair of black wool, pleated pants and a cherry red sweater. Her blond hair was pushed back, caught by a pair of barrettes that kept it off her face but still allowed it to swing free around her shoulders. The early spring breeze had painted her cheeks with a pink tinge and her blue eyes sparkled with aquamarine lights as the afternoon sun shone into them. "Tasha." He smiled. Without a moment's hesitation, he stepped forward, placing his hands on her arms and giving her a warm kiss on the cheek. "You look beautiful," he said, dropping his hands from her stiff shoulders and moving back a step.

"Thank you," she answered, cursing herself for her breathy voice and the telltale flush she could feel creeping up her neck and into her cheeks. "Isn't it a lovely day?"

He nodded, his eyes never leaving hers. "It's a perfect day."

Nervously, Natalie looked away. "Shall we walk?"

"By all means."

As they turned, Alexei's arm brushed against the side of Natalie's breast, causing her to take a quick step to the side to put some space between their bodies. They strolled together in silence for a moment, careful to stay on the path so as not to step on the new season's fragile green shoots, which were just beginning to pop up.

"So, tell me," Natalie said when she again felt she could trust herself to speak, "how are you enjoying Boston?"

"Far more than I thought I would," Alexei answered, throwing her a meaningful look.

She ignored it. "Have you ever been here before? I don't remember if you ever mentioned visiting here the last time you were in America." Her voice trailed off as she silently berated herself for the unthinking comment, knowing her words had brought their past relationship to both their minds.

"I've never been here, but it's a beautiful city." He looked around appreciatively at the perfectly laid-out flower beds, the immaculately manicured lawns and the small lagoon that was the centerpiece of the famous park. "It even smells fresh."

Natalie smiled, gazing about as she tried to see the familiar gardens through a stranger's eyes. "The Commons and the Public Gardens are among Boston's most popular attractions," she said. As if to prove her point, she gestured at the many groups of meandering tourists, most of them laden with cameras and picnic baskets. "But," she added, "the city has a lot of other interesting places to see too. As you probably know, it's very rich in American history. You should try to take a tour while you're here. There are a lot of good walking tours offered by various organizations. Some of them even have guides." Natalie noticed the curious glance Alexei shot at her and squeezed her eyes shut in embarrassment. *Good Lord, I sound like the Chamber of Commerce!*

"I particularly like the parks and the beautiful old cobblestoned streets," Alexei said, graciously filling the sudden, awkward silence that had risen between them. "It reminds me a little of parts of Europe I've visited."

Natalie nodded. "I love the parks too. The house where I live is built on a square, and in the center of it there's a wonderful little private park that was built purely for the enjoyment of the street's residents."

"How nice," Alexei responded; then he began to laugh.

Natalie looked at him curiously. "What's so funny?"

"You are, *daragaya,*" he answered, looking down at her with a soft smile.

"Me? Why?"

Alexei stopped walking and picked up Natalie's hand, lifting it to his lips and kissing it softly. "Because you're talking to me like I'm a complete stranger. I'm not some Russian dignitary come to visit your conservatory, you know, and you haven't been assigned by your employers to give me a tour of Boston." Turning her to face him, he placed a finger under her chin and lifted her eyes to meet his. "It's me, Tasha. It's Alex, and we're far from being strangers, no matter how long it's been since we've been together."

The gentleness of his words made Natalie feel like she was going to cry, and when she answered, her voice quavered. "I'm sorry, Alex. I don't mean to sound so impersonal. I don't know what's wrong with me. I'm just nervous, I guess."

With a casualness that neither of them were feeling, Alexei looped Natalie's arm through his and they began walking again. "Let's start over," he said. "How have you been, Tasha? Are you happy? Do you like your work? Why did you stop answering my letters? Why did you marry someone else when you knew how I loved you?"

These last two questions were blurted with such wrenching emotion that Natalie stopped short and looked up at him incredulously. "My word, Alex, you don't waste any time, do you?"

"You are the one who said you had limited time," he reminded her. "If we waste all of it talking about what a lovely day it is and then part without any of my questions being answered, I think I just might go mad."

"Let's go sit down," Natalie suggested. "There's a bench right over there."

They settled themselves on a bench under a tree, and a long silent moment passed as Natalie tried desperately to think of how she could answer Alexei's blunt questions without giving away what she didn't want him to know.

"I enjoy teaching at the conservatory very much," she started, still playing for time as she answered his most innocuous question first. "I teach theory, method and history classes in the mornings and then work with individual students in the afternoons."

Alexei nodded. "That schedule sounds similar to the schools in Russia. Are you working with anyone with real promise?"

Natalie thought for a moment. "I have some very talented students, but I can't say that I think any of them is going to take the music world by storm."

"Except Jenna," Alexei said quietly. "She's going to."

Natalie laughed, a nervous little titter that betrayed how uncomfortable she was talking about her daughter. "Jenna's not my student."

"I wondered about that. Why aren't you teaching her yourself?"

"Because I couldn't be objective," Natalie explained truthfully. "And regardless of how great her talent is, I felt that she needed an objective instructor to guide her. Besides, I didn't want to get the reputation of being an obnoxious stage mother, so I decided to stay as detached from her lessons as possible."

"I don't believe you could ever be obnoxious," Alexei said, "but even if you believe you could, you don't allow Jenna to perform, so how would you get that reputation?"

Natalie bristled slightly at his barb. "It's not that she's never going to perform. Of course she will, if she wants to. I just don't think it's necessary to trot a seven-year-old onto a stage just for the personal gratification of watching the world ooh and ahh over her."

"I don't think 'personal gratification' has anything to do with it," Alexei argued. "Talent the caliber of Jenna's should be shared with the world, no matter what her age. The fact that she is only seven just makes her that much more awe-inspiring."

"That's easy for you to say," Natalie said defensively. "You're not . . ." She stopped short, realizing that she was about to say, "You're not her parent." Even though Alexei believed that to be true, she could not bring herself to voice such a bald-faced lie.

"Not what?" Alexei asked, looking at her sharply.

"Not . . . responsible for her well-being and happiness," Natalie finished, successfully covering her gaffe. "And what about you, Alex?" she asked hurriedly, determined to veer the subject away from Jenna. "What have you been doing since you were last in America? Have you spent all these years performing?"

"Not all of them," Alexei answered, a trace of bitterness creeping into his voice as he thought about the year he'd spent drinking and brooding over the woman sitting next to him. "But for most of the time I have been. I've also done some composing and quite a bit of lecturing, although I haven't taken any kind of permanent teaching position as you have. I'm on tour too often to do that."

"Do you really enjoy all that traveling?"

"I don't mind it. Why do you ask?"

Natalie shrugged. "I would think that by the time one gets to be our age, being constantly on the road would become tiresome and you would want to settle down. Don't you ever wish you could stay in one place, live in your own home instead of constantly being in hotels?"

Alexei looked at her pointedly for a moment. "It's been a very long time since I've met someone with whom I wanted to settle down, so staying in one place hasn't seemed very important."

Natalie swallowed hard, realizing that she was suddenly treading on dangerous ground. Desperately, she cast about in her mind for another subject, finally saying, "Where do you go after you leave Boston?"

Alexei frowned, having been aware of the conflict of emotions his blunt words had caused her and hoping that it would introduce the topic he so desperately wanted to discuss. "I go to New York for a week, and then . . . Oh, God, Tasha, please tell me what happened with you after I left. I have to know. Why did you marry another man when I'd been gone only three months?"

Natalie dropped her eyes, knowing that he was not going to allow her to avoid his questions any longer. She looked at her watch hopefully, but it was not yet time to pick up Jenna. "Alex, please, do we have to discuss this?" she asked, raising her eyes and looking at him beseechingly. "Couldn't we just spend the rest of the time we have together chatting and then part like the old friends we are?"

"We're not just 'old friends,' " Alexei gritted, frustration rampant on his handsome face. "We were never just 'friends' and well you know it. We were lovers. We were mad about each other in a way no two people who are just friends could ever be. That last night before I had to go back to Russia . . . my God! Don't you remember? The things we said to each other, the lovemaking we shared, the promises we made. And then, nothing. You stopping answering my letters, you wouldn't take my telephone calls. It was as if once my plane took off for Moscow, I was out of your life and forgotten."

"That's not true!" Natalie cried. "I loved you as much as you loved me. You must know that!"

Alexei grabbed Natalie's hands, holding them tightly in his as his eyes bored into hers. "Then why, Tasha? Why did you abandon me and marry someone else? *Why?*"

Natalie wrenched her hands out of his and buried her face in them. "I don't want to discuss this! It was all so long ago. What is the point of dredging it up now?" Again, she looked at her watch. "I have to go," she said, jumping up from the bench. "It's almost time to pick up Jenna."

"You don't have to pick up Jenna," Alexei said, rising also and following her down the sidewalk. "I called your friend, Susan Bedford, and asked her to do it."

At his words, Natalie immediately halted her headlong flight and whirled around to face him, her expression furious. "You did *what*? How *dare* you? What in the world made you think that you had the right to call my friend and ask her to pick up my daughter without my permission?"

Alexei took a step backward, clearly shocked by her vehemence. "I was hoping that we might be able to extend our time together if you didn't have to pick up Jenna, so I called and asked Miss Bedford if she might do it for you. She was very accommodating."

"I'm sure she was," Natalie snapped. "She's a good friend and Jenna spends a lot of time with her, but that still didn't give you the right to go behind my back and call her."

"I'm sorry," Alexei said simply.

The ingenuousness of his expression was unmistakable and Natalie felt her anger evaporate. "Oh, it doesn't really matter," she admitted. "I have no qualms about Jenna being in Susan's care, so I suppose there's no harm done."

"I'm still sorry, though," Alexei repeated. "I wouldn't have called her if I'd known it would upset you."

"It's all right. Let's just forget it."

Alexei smiled encouragingly. "Agreed. Well, now that you know that you don't have to pick up Jenna, would you like to sit back down or maybe go somewhere and have a drink?"

Natalie shook her head. "No. I really think it's better if I leave now."

"Tasha . . ." he murmured, reaching out for her. "Don't go."

"I have to, Alex," she said, even as she allowed herself to be drawn into his embrace. "Please understand."

"Kiss me first."

"Alex . . ."

"Just once more, Tasha. Kiss me the way you used to."

Natalie gazed up into Alexei's dark eyes and felt herself drawn to him with the same magnetic power that had always existed between them. Succumbing to a desire far stronger than her resolve, she closed her eyes, sighing with pleasure as Alexei's warm, firm lips covered hers. This kiss, more leisurely and seductive than the quick one they had shared in his dressing room, was just as she remembered; full of passion and fire, yet romantic and caressing.

The kiss lasted a very long time as both of them drank in the sweetness of each other's lips. When finally Alexei raised his head, ending their embrace with a soft brush of his lips against her temple, Natalie slowly opened her eyes. "Oh, Alex," she whispered, her voice breathless from the passion they'd just shared, "I'm so sorry about everything."

Alexei looked at her for a long moment, as if memorizing her features in his mind. Then, in a voice so soft that she barely heard him, he murmured, "I will love you till the day I die."

And before she could respond, he turned and walked away.

TEN

Susan opened the door to the Louisburg Square town house to find a tearful Natalie standing on the stoop fumbling for her keys.

"Oh, my God." Susan groaned. "What happened? Was it awful?"

Natalie gave up her search and turned a plaintive look on her friend. "Yes, it was awful. I mean, no, it wasn't awful. In fact, it was wonderful. I mean, I don't know what it was. All I know is that I feel so sad that I want to curl up under my bed covers and never come out."

Susan reached out and pulled her sobbing friend into the house. "Oh, honey," she crooned, hugging Natalie to her like she was a small child, "don't cry. It'll be all right."

Natalie raised her head and shook it wildly. "No, it's not going to be all right. It's never going to be all right. What I did to that man is terrible and I'll never stop feeling guilty about it. He deserved much better than me."

Disentangling herself from Susan's embrace, Natalie lurched over to the sofa, throwing down her purse and collapsing into the luxurious cushions. "Where's Jenna?"

"Don't worry about Jenna," Susan answered. "She's next door playing with Robert and Lorelei Barnes's little girl, Emily."

Natalie nodded. "That's fine. The Barnes's are very nice people and Jenna just loves Emily. Robert has a Ph.D in Russian History. Maybe I should go over and talk to him about

Alexei. He probably understands the Russian mind far better than I do. After the way I've behaved toward Alexei, I certainly don't understand why he still seems willing to tolerate me." By now, Natalie's sobs had subsided into gulping little hiccoughs. "Anyway," she continued, "I'm glad Jenna is next door and not here. I don't want her to see me like this. I must look a fright."

"Well, let's just say that I've seen you looking better." Susan chuckled, walking over to an antique mahogany sideboard. "I'm going to pour us a glass of your excellent Bordeaux and then I want you to tell me everything; that is, if you can stop crucifying yourself long enough."

She poured the wine into exquisite Waterford crystal wineglasses and returned to the sofa, holding one out to Natalie. Sitting down, she took a sip of her wine, then turned her attention on her friend. "Okay, start at the beginning."

Natalie drew a shaky breath and began recounting her meeting with Alexei at the park, ending with their passionate kiss and her tearful walk back home.

"Well, what do you know?" Susan said as Natalie finished her story. "You *do* still love him, don't you? It's not just guilt that has you in such a state."

"I honestly don't know what I feel," Natalie responded. "That's my problem. I'm more confused than I've ever been in my life." She looked over at Susan with a tortured expression. "It's probably a moot point, anyway. After the way I left him today, I doubt I'll hear from him again."

"You may be right." Susan nodded. "A man is only going to take rejection from a woman so many times before he finally gives up and casts his nets elsewhere. I think if you want to see Mr. Alexei Romanov again, you're going to have to be the one to initiate it."

Natalie thought about this for a moment, then shook her head. "No, I think it's best if I leave things as they are. It's just that . . ."

"It's just that you don't want to, right?"

Natalie bit her lip, trying to quell the new rush of tears that threatened. "It's just that when I'm with him, I feel the same way I always did. There's something about the man that affects me differently than anyone else I've ever known."

"I think that something is called love, dearie," Susan noted wryly, "and it's obvious to me that you still feel it and so does he."

"I don't know if he does," Natalie said. "I think maybe he just wants to know why I broke off our relationship so he can find some kind of closure and move on."

"Oh, right"—Susan snorted—"and that's why he grabs you and kisses you every time he gets near you—so he can move on."

"Well, when you say it like that . . ."

Susan leaned back into the sofa cushions and contemplated her wine for a moment. "You know, I think you two are star-crossed. Destined for each other, like the great lovers in history and literature."

Despite her heartache, Natalie laughed. "Aren't you being just a little overly dramatic?"

"Maybe I am, but I honestly believe it's true."

"Well, if we are, indeed, star-crossed, then where is the sign?"

"Sign?"

"Yes, our sign. You know, star-crossed lovers always get some sort of sign from somewhere that proves to them that they are meant for each other. And, so far, I can assure you, I haven't gotten one."

"Give it time." Susan smiled. "You still have four days."

A quiet moment passed with each woman deep in her own thoughts. Then Natalie said, "Do you know what the last thing he said to me was?"

Susan turned toward her, curious. "What?"

"The last thing he said was, 'I will love you till the day I die.' "

"Oh, my God, Natalie," Susan moaned. "I can't even imagine a man saying that to me. No wonder you were sobbing."

" 'I will love you till the day I die'. . . ." Natalie repeated softly. "Somewhere I've heard those exact words before."

Susan looked at her in surprise. "Do you mean someone else has said that to you? My Lord, some women have all the luck."

Natalie shook her head. "No, not to me. But somewhere I've heard it."

"Maybe you read it in a book."

"No, it was more personal than a book. I wish I could remember . . ."

They lapsed back into silence until, suddenly, Natalie sat bolt upright and clutched Susan's arm, nearly spilling her wine. "My God, Susan, I just remembered. Come with me!"

"Where are we going?" Susan asked, hurriedly putting down her wineglass as Natalie dragged her off the sofa.

"To the attic."

"The attic! Whatever for?"

"Because I think I just received my sign."

Natalie bounded up the stairs with Susan trailing after her until they reached a door at the top of the third flight. "I haven't been up here in years, so it's probably really dusty," Natalie said as she opened the door and snapped on an overhead light.

Susan looked around the attic room, smiling at the accumulation of clutter piled up willy-nilly. "This room is so nice," she noted, reaching out to touch the wainscoted wall. "It looks finished—like someone could live up here."

"Someone did once," Natalie said. "Back when Stuart and Claire, my great-great-great-grandparents, lived here, this was where the servants stayed."

"What's this?" Susan asked, walking over and peeking around the corner into a small, separate chamber.

"A bathroom of sorts. Stuart Wellesley was very progressive and had plumbing installed in the house right after the Civil

War. And speaking of Stuart Wellesley, here's what I'm looking for." She knelt down in front of a large steamer trunk and lifted the heavy top.

Susan hurried over and dropped to her knees beside Natalie, her eyes widening as she stared down at the contents of the old trunk. "What are these things?" she asked, running her hand across an expanse of exquisite green silk material.

"Old clothes of Claire's, I guess." Natalie swept aside a green silk dress, uncovering a dark blue uniform. "Here is Stuart's Civil War uniform." Carefully, she lifted a faded military jacket out of the trunk and held it up for Susan's inspection.

"I can't believe you've saved all these things," Susan said, touching the uniform's rough material in fascination.

"My family keeps everything." Natalie laughed. Again, she turned back to the trunk, burrowing deeper into it. "Have I ever told you about the Wellesleys?"

"Only that they're that gorgeous couple in the portrait on the staircase and that she was southern and he was northern and they met during the Civil War."

"Actually, their story is much more interesting than just that," Natalie said. "Stuart Wellesley was a major in the Union army and Claire Boudreau was a nurse in Savannah, Georgia. From the stories I've been told, Stuart was shot by Confederate deserters while he was delivering secret documents to General Sherman. They took him to a hospital outside of Savannah and asked Claire to spy for the Confederacy by being his nurse and coercing him into telling her where the documents were. But before she could get him to confess, the Yankees overran the hospital, she was exposed as a spy, and Sherman decided to hang her."

"Sherman was always such a nice, compassionate guy," Susan commented wryly.

"Anyway, by this time Stuart was in love with Claire, and he convinced Sherman to let him marry her instead of hanging her."

"And, obviously, Sherman agreed."

"Yes"—Natalie laughed—"or I wouldn't be here."

"And they lived happily ever after?"

"Hardly," Natalie said, still feeling around the bottom of the trunk as she talked. "Stuart brought Claire back here to Boston and they lived in this very town house, but they weren't happy, at least at first. I don't know all the details, but it had something to do with some old southern boyfriend of hers and a lie that Stuart told her about the guy. Anyway . . ."

"Wait a minute," Susan interrupted, holding up her hand. "What was the lie?"

"I don't know all the particulars," Natalie said. "The story's gotten pretty convoluted over the years, but apparently, Stuart told Claire that her old boyfriend was dead when he knew he really wasn't."

"Ooh." Susan laughed. "Now, that's a *lie!*"

"Indeed, and the upshot of it was, they decided to get divorced."

"Divorced!" Susan cried. "In the 1860s? I didn't even know it was legal back then."

Natalie shrugged. "I guess it was legal, but certainly not common." Her hand closed around something at the bottom of the trunk and a smile lit her face. "Ah, here it is."

"Here *what* is?"

"What I've been looking for. My sign."

"Finish the story first," Susan said, entranced by the tale she was hearing.

"I will. The day that the divorce papers were being signed and Claire was to leave Boston to return to Savannah, Stuart sent her a bouquet of flowers with a note that made Claire realize how much he really loved her."

"And . . ." Susan prodded.

"And, they got back together, had about a dozen kids, including my great, great-grandmother, Savannah, and *then* they lived happily ever after."

Susan sat back on her heels, waiting for Natalie to say more, but she remained silent for so long that Susan nearly screamed in frustration. "Okay! So, it's a fabulous story. In fact, it's so good that somebody should probably write a book about it. But what the heck does it have to do with you and Alexei and your receiving a sign?"

"This." Natalie grinned, extracting her hand from the depths of the trunk and holding out a tiny antique picture frame.

Susan took the delicate wire lace frame out of Natalie's hand and studied it for a moment. "What *is* this?"

"It's the message that Stuart enclosed with the roses. Savannah's daughter, my great-grandmother Maureen, was still alive when I was a little girl, and she told me that this message meant so much to her grandmother, that she had it framed and kept it next to her bed.

Susan peered down at the cloudy old glass, barely able to make out the faded, handwritten message beneath it. When she finally realized what the bold, masculine scrawl said, she gasped and looked up at Natalie, her expression dumbstruck. 'I will love you till the day I die,' " she breathed.

Natalie nodded, her eyes welling with tears. "Think it's my sign?"

"You're darn right it's your sign, girl! Now, get on the phone and tell that man that you want to see him!"

Alexei set down the phone and stared blindly out the window of his hotel bedroom, still not quite able to believe the conversation he'd just had.

He'd been nursing a vodka when the telephone rang. He'd had no intention of answering it, but the ever vigilant Yuri had picked it up in the living room. When he'd heard the knock on his door, he hadn't even inquired as to whom was calling, knowing that in his current black mood, he didn't want to talk to anyone. Without even granting Yuri permission to enter the bedroom, he simply yelled, "Whoever it is, tell them I'm not available."

But when Yuri calmly responded, "It's Mrs. Saxon," Alexei quickly changed his mind.

"I'll take it in here," he amended, bolting out of the chair and lunging for the phone. His hand was about two inches away from the receiver when he drew it back, suddenly not sure that he could handle another conversation with Natalie. After the way they had parted in the park that afternoon, what could there possibly be left to say?

He opened his mouth to tell Yuri that he'd changed his mind about taking the call, then quickly closed it again, gritting his teeth and squeezing his eyes shut in indecision. On the one hand, he didn't know if his ego could stand any more blows, but on the other, he knew that if he refused to take her call, he would probably spend the rest of his life wondering what she'd wanted.

With a growl of frustration, he jerked the receiver off its cradle and snapped a terse, "Yes?"

"Alex?" came the surprised and slightly apprehensive reply from the other end of the line.

"Yes?"

"It's . . . Natalie."

"Yes?"

"Have I . . . caught you at a bad time? I mean, were you on your way out or something?"

"No. What can I do for you, Natalie?"

Sitting on the edge of her sofa, Natalie swallowed hard, suddenly realizing that she might be making a big mistake. After the way Alexei had walked away from her at the park that afternoon, perhaps he was so angry that he wouldn't want to see her again and she was going to do nothing more with this phone call than embarrass herself. For a moment, she considered just saying, "Good-bye," and hanging up, but then she caught sight of her great, great, great-grandmother's picture frame out of the corner of her eye. Pointedly ignoring the curt hostility in Alexei's voice, she plunged on. "I wondered if you're still available to have dinner tonight." When no response to this comment was immediately forthcoming, she quickly added, "I will certainly understand if you've already made other plans, but I thought if you hadn't . . ."

"I haven't made other plans," Alexei interrupted. "Where do you want to go?"

"I don't know," Natalie said, astonished by his sudden agreement. "Do you still want to go to Aujourd'hui?"

"That's fine."

"All right, then, what time?"

"I'll have the hotel send a car for you at about eight o'clock."

"Oh, that's not necessary," Natalie demurred. "I can drive. It's only a short distance."

"I'll send a car," Alexei repeated. "Eight o'clock."

"All right. I'll be ready. Until tonight, then . . ."

"Yes, until tonight. Good-bye."

After re-running their entire conversation through his mind, Alexei turned away from the window and walked out of the bedroom into the suite's living room. "I'm going out this evening, Yuri. Will you be sure that my dark blue suit is pressed? I don't think I've worn it since we've been here."

"Consider it done," the valet responded, careful to keep his tone dispassionate. "Would you like to wear your maroon tie with it?"

Alexei gave a dismissive shrug. "Whatever you think. Make reservations for two at eight-thirty at Aujourd'hui, will you?"

Yuri nodded and immediately headed for the phone. After speaking briefly with someone, he covered the receiver with his hand and turned back to Alexei. "The maître d' says that, regretfully, since tonight is Saturday, the restaurant is fully booked for the evening."

As Alexei's eyebrows rose imperiously, he quickly added, "He has offered you the use of one of the two private dining rooms at no extra charge. Will that be satisfactory?"

To Yuri's relief, Alexei's glowering expression immediately lightened. "Yes, that will be fine. And please tell him to be

sure that there are white roses on the table and a bottle of
their best champagne is chilling when we get there."

Yuri nodded and turned back to the telephone. A moment
later, he hung up. "Your reservation is confirmed for eight-
thirty and the maître d' assured me that there will be white
roses in the center of the table. Would you also like bouquets
on the mantel and coffee table? I can call him back and add
that if you do."

For the first time in several hours, Alexei's handsome features relaxed into a genuine smile. "No, I think a bouquet on
the table will be sufficient. I don't want the place to look like
a funeral parlor." He glanced at his watch. "It's five now. I
didn't sleep well last night and I'm tired, so I think I'll lie
down for a bit. If I go to sleep, please wake me by seven."

Yuri nodded his understanding and began to head toward
his bedroom. He had only taken a few steps, however, when
Alexei's voice stopped him.

"Yuri?"

The valet looked at his boss quizzically. "Yes?"

"Thank you."

Anya whirled on Yuri, her eyes blazing with anger. "What
do you mean, he's having dinner with her? Not two hours ago
you told me you thought they were finished for good."

Yuri shrugged sheepishly. "I did think that. As angry and
upset as Alexei was when he returned from their meeting in
the park, the last thing I expected was that they would be
dining together tonight."

"What did he do? Call her and beg?"

Yuri shook his head vehemently. "No, no. She called him."

"Damn her!" Anya cursed, flopping down on the sofa.
"Why can't she just leave him alone?"

"Calm down, Anya," Yuri soothed. "It's just dinner."

"Where are they eating? Here in the suite?"

"No, nothing like that. They're eating at the restaurant

downstairs." Purposely, he did not include the fact that the couple was dining in a private room.

A look of relief crossed Anya's face. "Well, that's a good sign, at least. I was afraid they were planning an intimate little soirée up here. Of course, even at the restaurant, they're still only an elevator ride away from a bedroom."

"Anya!" Yuri exclaimed, genuinely shocked by the young woman's bluntness.

"Well, it's true! You know it is. If that woman entices my brother into bed, then I shudder to think of what might happen to the future of this tour—and to Alexei's reputation, if he decides to cancel it so he can spend the summer here in Boston sleeping with her."

"Anya Romanova, your mother would faint if she could hear you."

"I don't care," Anya said petulantly. "I'm not a child any longer and I see what I see. Just the look that comes over Alexei's face when Natalie's name is mentioned is enough to make me blush. So, now they're planning dinner together and who knows what else afterward?"

"I really think it's just going to be dinner," Yuri said, trying to sound positive.

"Maybe, but they're still together. I just wish I could think of something—some way—to end this! I'm beginning to think that rather than try to keep Alexei from finding out about Jenna, maybe what we should do is tell him. Maybe if he knew how Natalie had lied to him all these years, it would turn him against her. I should go right now and tell him myself."

"That's not a good idea," Yuri said nervously.

"Well, we have to do something! He's becoming more smitten with her every minute."

Yuri stared off into space as a thought suddenly occurred to him. "You know, maybe the person you need to be talking to is Natalie."

Anya flipped her hand in the air dismissively. "I have nothing whatsoever to say to that woman."

Yuri ignored her dismissal as his plan began to solidify in his mind. With a smile, he sat down on the sofa next to Anya. "Now wait a minute. Don't be so hasty. What do you think Natalie's reaction would be if you confronted her with your knowledge that Jenna is Alexei's daughter?"

Anya looked at Yuri incredulously as the light of understanding suddenly lit her eyes. "Yuri, you're a genius! I think you just found the answer to our problems, and it's so obvious, I'm ashamed I didn't think of it myself." Impulsively, Anya leaned over and hugged him.

"All right, let's talk about this," she continued excitedly. "We know that for whatever reason, Natalie does not want Alexei to know that Jenna is his daughter, so if I went to her and told her that if she doesn't leave my brother alone, I'm going to tell him everything . . . Oh, Yuri, it's brilliant! Of *course* that would end it. She'd never see Alexei again!"

Although Yuri was delighted that his idea had met with such enthusiasm, he still held up a warning hand. "Not so fast now, Anya. We need to think this through completely."

"There's nothing else to think through," Anya protested. "It's the perfect answer."

"No, it's not perfect. There are still some things we need to figure out."

Anya looked at him, perplexed. "Like what?"

"Like, *why* has Natalie never wanted Alexei to know about Jenna?"

Anya's gleeful smile faded. "I don't know. I guess I've never thought about it. But you're right; there must be a reason."

Yuri stood up, rubbing his chin between his thumb and index finger as he began to pace. "There *is* a reason and I think I know what it is."

"You do?"

"I think so. It all goes back to what we were talking about the other day. Natalie comes from this fine old American family and she has a great deal of money and social prestige here in Boston."

"So?"

"So," Yuri continued, ceasing his pacing and turning back to face Anya, "she doesn't want to give that up. I always thought that was why she broke off with Alexei the first time. He asked her to marry him and she didn't want to give up her luxurious life here in America to become a Russian wife. It's my guess that she thinks if Alexei knew Jenna is his daughter, he might force her to make that decision."

Anya's brows drew together in bewilderment. "What decision?"

"The decision to either live in Russia or lose Jenna."

Anya shook her head in complete confusion. "Lose Jenna? How would she do that?"

"Custody, Anya, custody! Maybe Natalie doesn't want Alexei to know about Jenna because she's afraid he'd fight her for custody."

Anya tapped a long, tapered fingernail against her teeth, ruminating on all that Yuri had just said. "I don't think Alexei would do that, do you?"

"I honestly don't know." Yuri shrugged. "But the point is, neither does Natalie, and I doubt she wants to take the chance of finding out."

Anya began to nod very slowly. "I think I see now. What you're saying is that I should go to Natalie, tell her that I know about Jenna and that if she doesn't stop seeing Alexei, I will tell him what I know, which may cause him to decide he wants to fight her for custody of their daughter."

"Exactly." Yuri beamed. "So, what do you think?"

Anya jumped up and raced off in the direction of her bedroom. "I think it's inspired," she called back over her shoulder, "and I'm going to change my clothes and go see Mrs. Natalie Saxon right this minute!"

Throwing his hands in the air in exasperation, Yuri tore across the suite, catching Anya by the arm just as she reached out to open her bedroom door. "Anya, Anya! You are so impatient! Now is not the time to do this."

Anya looked down in irritation at Yuri's hand clamped around her arm. "Why not?"

Immediately, Yuri removed his hand, tossing her an apologetic smile. "It's too late to do this today. It's already close to seven, and they are having dinner at eight-thirty. There is nothing you can do to prevent them from seeing each other tonight."

"I guess you're right." Anya sighed. "Damn it!"

"Don't be upset. Who knows? Maybe after Alexei spends an entire evening with Natalie, he'll decide for himself that it's over between them. After all, they haven't spent an evening together in eight years, and people's feelings do change."

"Do you really believe that will happen?"

"No." Yuri chuckled. "But it's a possibility. What I do believe is that, even if their evening goes well tonight, tomorrow is soon enough for you to speak to Natalie. Unless, of course, they decide to run off to Las Vegas and get married tonight."

Anya's eyes widened with horror.

"I'm joking, little one"—Yuri chuckled—"just joking."

Anya threw him a jaundiced look. "I certainly hope so. And, as much as I hate to put off this confrontation, I guess you're right. It will just have to wait until tomorrow."

"If it's even necessary tomorrow," Yuri reminded her.

"Oh, I think it will be, but at least we have a real plan and that's a comfort. Now, if you'll excuse me, I think I'll go in my bedroom and think about exactly what I'm going to say to Natalie when I see her."

Yuri walked back into the living room and sank wearily into one of the overstuffed chairs. *Thank God this isn't the old days,* he told himself. *Alexei will probably fire me once he finds out that I had a hand in all this, but at least he can no longer have me banished to Siberia!*

ELEVEN

"How do I look?" Natalie turned away from the full-length mirror in her bedroom to face Susan, who was sitting on the edge of the bed.

Susan cocked her head and eyed Natalie speculatively. "Perfect little understated black dress, perfect two-inch black pumps, perfect single strand of pearls—real ones, I'm sure—perfect little black bag. I'd say you look like the perfect young Boston matron on her way to have dinner at Aujourd'hui."

Natalie looked down at herself, then back up at Susan. "Are you saying I look all right?"

Susan shook her head. "No, I'm saying you look perfect, and if perfect is what you're going for, then you've accomplished it."

"All right, Susan." Natalie sighed, throwing down her evening bag and planting her hands on her hips. "What's your point?"

Susan rose from the bed and headed for Natalie's massive walk-in closet. "My point is that if I had a dinner date with Alexei Romanov, I wouldn't want to blend into the woodwork."

"And that's what you think I'm going to do?"

"In that dress, yes. You're going to look like every other woman in the restaurant. That dress is like the Beacon Hill uniform."

"There's nothing wrong with this dress," Natalie called as Susan disappeared into the closet. "It's a Givenchy."

"I'm sure it is," Susan called back. "That's probably why

you remind me so much of Jackie Kennedy going out for dinner with a group of professional political fund-raisers—in 1962."

"Jackie usually wore Oleg Cassini," Natalie corrected.

"Whatever." Susan sighed. "It still looks like 1962."

"Well, thanks a lot." Angrily, Natalie kicked off her shoes and stomped over to the closet. "And just what do you suggest I wear?"

"This," Susan answered, whirling around and holding up a short black evening dress with a low-cut neckline.

"That? I can't wear that. It's much too provocative. I don't even know why I bought it."

"Probably because it's gorgeous," Susan said wryly, turning the dress around and gazing at it with a wistful expression. "And what's wrong with being a bit provocative?"

Natalie looked at the dress for a moment, then shook her head. "It would definitely send the wrong message."

"Yeah, you wouldn't want Alexei to catch a glimpse of those fabulous breasts of yours. He might get the wrong idea and think you're an alluring, sexy woman instead of a staid Boston matron fast approaching middle age."

Natalie's lips thinned with offense as she reached out and grabbed the dress from Susan. "All right, I'll wear it. But if it gets me into trouble tonight, it's going to be on your head."

Susan smiled in triumph. "I'll risk it. Besides, you're not going to get into any more trouble than you want to be in." She stepped back, watching Natalie as she pulled on the short, clingy dress, then nodded with satisfaction. "Much better. Now, loosen up that school-marm bun, put on your diamond necklace with the matching earrings and go knock the Brahmins dead."

The car from the hotel arrived promptly at eight.

"Your carriage awaits, madame." Susan laughed as she peeked out the window at the gleaming limo pulling up.

"This is utter nonsense," Natalie said, swirling a gauzy black shawl around her shoulders as she walked down the staircase. "The hotel is only a few blocks away. I certainly could have driven myself."

"Why drive yourself when you can go in a limo?"

"A limo? Alex just said he was sending a car."

Susan shrugged. "He did. A limo's a car. Just a very nice, very long one. Now quit complaining about the man wanting to spoil you a little and go have a good time."

Natalie nodded doubtfully. "I'll try. By the way, Robert Barnes said he'd walk Jenna home about eight-thirty, after she and Emily finish the video they're watching. She needs to go to bed by nine-thirty, so don't let her talk you into staying up any later."

"Aye, aye, Captain," Susan responded, saluting.

Natalie ignored her friend's playful mockery and added, "I should be home by eleven or so."

"Don't worry about it. I intend to spend the night, so it doesn't matter what time you come home . . . or if you come home at all, for that matter. Anytime tomorrow before noon will be fine."

"Susan, you don't need to feel that you have to spend the night. I'm sure I'll be home before midnight."

"I know I don't have to stay," Susan assured her, "but how often does a Wisconsin farm girl get the chance to sleep in a Louisburg Square town house? It'll give me something to write my mother about."

Natalie laughed and shook her head, then reached out and caught her friend's hands in her own. "Thank you for this, Sue. In fact, thanks for everything."

Susan waved at her dismissively. "I'm glad to do it. Now get going before your handsome Russian finds some other Givenchy-clad sophisticate to spend the evening with."

She watched the limo driver help Natalie into the car, then closed the town house's beautifully carved front door, hoping fervently that the mistress of the house would not open it again until well after sunrise tomorrow.

Natalie walked through the front doors of the hotel and was immediately approached by a tall, officious-looking man wearing a well-tailored tuxedo. "Mrs. Saxon?"

"Yes?" Natalie answered, looking at the man in surprise.

"Mr. Romanov is waiting for you at the restaurant." He stepped up next to Natalie and held out his arm politely. "If you'll just come with me . . ."

Natalie allowed the man to lead her into the restaurant, then looked around in bewilderment when she didn't see Alexei. "Is Mr. Romanov already at our table?" she asked softly.

"He's waiting for you in the private dining room."

Natalie's eyebrows rose sharply at this bit of information, but she said nothing. They reached a closed doorway on the west side of the restaurant and her escort knocked once, then released her arm and disappeared as Alexei answered the discreet summons and ushered her into a small, lavish room.

"Good evening, Tasha," he said softly as she set her purse and wrap down on the back of a tufted chair. "You look beautiful."

"Thank you," Natalie responded, finally allowing her gaze to settle on Alexei's handsome face. The mere sight of him sent a frisson of excitement skidding down her spine. He was dressed in an impeccably tailored dark blue suit with a tiny white rosebud stuck through the lapel. "So do you." As soon as her impulsive compliment was out of her mouth, she wished the words back.

How could I have said that? First I arrive in a skimpy dress, then I tell him he looks gorgeous. He's going to think I'm here for a quick romp. Her eyes quickly skimmed the intimate setting. *And this is just the place for it.*

Desperately, she tried to think of something to say that

would steer the conversation to a more impersonal subject. "This is a lovely room, Alex. It reminds me of *Funny Girl*."

Alexei looked up from the bottle of champagne he was un-corking and raised his eyebrows questioningly. *"Funny Girl?* What's that?"

"It's a movie with Barbra Streisand and Omar Sharif. He invites her to have dinner in the private dining room of a hotel in order to . . ." Her words trailed off, and again she wished she could drop through the floor. *What's wrong with me? You'd think I'd never been on a date before!*

Alexei held out a half-filled champagne flute to her. "In order to what?"

"Seduce her," Natalie mumbled, quickly raising the glass to her mouth and taking a strangled sip.

With a chuckle, Alexei took her by the hand and pulled her down next to him on a plush sofa. "Is that why you think I invited you here?" he asked, turning to face her. "To seduce you?"

"Oh course not," Natalie answered quickly. "I'm just saying that *Funny Girl* is the only time I've ever seen a private dining room like this."

"Well, I've never seen the movie, but I like Barbra Streisand, so maybe I'll have to."

"It's a good film. One of my mother's favorites."

Alexei smiled and set down his glass. "How are your parents? Are they still living here in Massachusetts?"

Natalie set her glass next to his and shook her head. "No. They sold the house in Marblehead. Now they spend their winters in Scottsdale, Arizona, and their summers in Colorado."

"In Durango?"

"Yes." She nodded, looking at him in surprise. "How did you know that?"

"I remember your telling me about your relatives who came from there, and that your family owned property in the town, so it was an obvious guess."

Good Lord, had the man forgotten nothing? Natalie didn't

have the slightest recollection of ever even mentioning her Wellesley ancestors to him, and yet he even remembered the name of the small town in Colorado where they had lived.

Leaning forward, Alexei picked up their flutes and handed Natalie's back to her. "Have you told your parents about seeing me again?"

"No," she answered hurriedly. "I . . . haven't talked to them in the last few days." *And even if I had, the last thing on earth I'd tell my mother is that you've reappeared in my life.*

"Well, be sure to give them my regards when you do."

"Yes, I'll do that," Natalie lied.

The conversation waned momentarily and Natalie again looked around the sumptuous room, her eyes settling on the exquisite bouquet of flowers in the center of the dining table. "White roses, Alex?"

He nodded. "I remembered that you liked them."

His simple admission caused Natalie's throat to tighten with emotion. She took another swallow of champagne and set her empty glass back on the coffee table. "Well, I'm flattered," she said honestly. "You seem to remember a great deal, considering it's been eight years since we last saw each other."

Slowly, Alexei leaned forward and traced his fingers gently down her cheek. "Did you really think I'd forget, *daragaya?* Aren't there things you remember about me, or did you so completely erase me from your life that all the memories are gone too?"

Unnerved by his touch, Natalie jumped up, turning away and unknowingly giving Alexei a seductive glimpse of her nearly nude back. "Of course the memories aren't all gone," she said, forcing herself to keep her voice casual. "I remember a lot of things about those days."

She heard him rise, then jumped as he came up behind her and began caressing her bare shoulders. "What do you remember, Tasha?" he whispered, his breath soft and warm against her ear. "Tell me what you think of when you remember those days."

"Oh, too many things to recount." She laughed nervously, ducking out from beneath his hands and turning to face him. "But it was so long ago, Alex, and I've never been a person who lived in the past."

"For some of us, the past is the only thing worth living in," he said, the unconcealed bitterness in his voice making Natalie wince.

Not knowing what to say in response to his heartbreaking admission, she again cast about for a change of topic. Walking over to the champagne bucket, she pulled the bottle out of the ice and refilled her glass. Then she lifted it and took a deep swallow before she spoke again. "So, Alex, have you eaten at Aujourd'hui before, or is tonight your first meal here?"

He ignored her inane question, staring at her intensely for a moment. "Do you always drink so much, Natalie, or do you just feel that you need to be drunk to get through this meal with me?"

Guiltily, Natalie set down her glass. "No, I usually don't drink much. I'm just . . ."

"Uncomfortable being alone with me?"

With a sigh, she nodded. "Yes. A little . . ."

Alex shook his head, his expression reflecting his disappointment. "I didn't have any underhanded reason for suggesting this dinner, Tasha, and you can quit worrying about my motives for booking this room. I'm not some actor in an old movie and I didn't bring you here to seduce you against your will."

"I know that."

He threw his hands wide in bewilderment. "Then why are you acting like you expect me to leap on you at any minute?"

"I don't know," she moaned, sitting down and dropping her head into her hands. "Everything has just been so strained between us these last few days. I was hoping that tonight we might be able to forget about the past and just have a pleasant meal together."

"And we will," he said positively. "When I originally asked

you out to supper, I promised you no strings. That hasn't changed, so why don't you stop worrying and just relax?"

Natalie raised her head and looked at him gratefully. "I'd like that, Alex. I really would."

"Then that's the way it will be." He walked over to a small table and picked up a menu, then again sat down beside Natalie on the sofa and opened it across both their laps. "What would you like to eat?"

Dinner was wonderful, the lobster was exquisite and the wine perfect. Natalie had forgotten how easy it was to talk to Alexei, but as they lingered over the lavish meal, their conversation ran the gamut from companionable chat about what kind of reception Alexei might expect from the various cities on his summer tour to a heated debate over the identity of the mysterious "immortal beloved" in Beethoven's life.

After Natalie had finally popped the last morsel of lobster into her mouth, she sat back and groaned pleasurably. "You know," she said, "people think that everyone who lives in Boston eats lobster three nights a week, but I can't remember the last time I had it."

Alexei smiled, and his dark eyes took on a faraway look. "Do you remember the time we rented a car and drove all the way to Gloucester because you were so hungry for lobster?"

Natalie laughed in fond remembrance. "Yes. We went to a lobster shack right on the wharf and ate it on newspapers with corn on the cob and potato chips. As I remember, it was absolutely wonderful."

Slowly, Alexei reached across the table and covered Natalie's hand with his. "As I remember, that whole day was wonderful."

Natalie gazed down at their clasped hands and all the long, lonely years spent apart seemed to melt away. "After we ate, we took a walk," she said softly. "We climbed up a hill and stood looking down over the bay . . ." Slowly, she raised her eyes to meet Alexei's. ". . . and you kissed me."

He nodded, his eyes drifting closed as the tender memory flooded his mind. "I remember that kiss—and everything that happened afterward." He opened his eyes and lifted Natalie's hand to his lips. "Tasha . . ."

The yearning in his voice sounded a warning bell in Natalie's mind and quickly she stood up, pulling her hand from his. "I should go," she whispered hoarsely. "It's getting late."

"Don't go yet," Alexei pleaded, again taking her hand and leading her over to the sofa. "Have one more glass of champagne."

Natalie hesitated for a long moment, then slowly nodded. She knew she should leave. It had been obvious since their intimate recollections at dinner that her relationship with Alexei was taking another turn—one that she wasn't sure she was prepared to handle. But still, she didn't want to go. There was something so right about being with him again that she was as reluctant to see the evening end as he.

They sat down on the sofa and Alexei handed her her champagne glass.

"Tonight has been wonderful." Natalie sighed, looking over at him and smiling.

Alexei picked up her hand and gave it a soft kiss. "It was always wonderful between us, Tasha."

Natalie nodded, biting her lip as she fought back the tears his softly spoken words had prompted. "I know. And I know I said I didn't want to talk about the past, but since it has seemed to come up, there's something I want to tell you."

Alexei gently pulled her to him, urging her head down on his shoulder. "What's that, sweetheart?"

"Sweetheart," she murmured. "You remembered that too."

"Barely." He chuckled. "It's been a very long time since I've said that word. Now, what is it that you want to say to me?"

Natalie blinked back the still threatening tears and said in a shaky voice, "Only that I'm sorry about everything. I treated you badly; I know I did. You deserved better from me than the way I handled our breakup, and I want you to know I'm sorry for the pain I know I must have caused you."

She expected him to say something in response to her apology, but he remained silent. Finally, she could stand it no longer. Lifting her head from the warm hollow of his shoulder, she looked at him beseechingly. "Alex, did you hear what I said?"

"I heard you, Tasha."

"Do you believe me?"

"Yes."

Again, she threw him a pleading look. "Are you still angry with me?"

"I was never angry with you. I was hurt when you stopped writing. I was confused because I didn't know what had happened between us. I was jealous of the man you married when you wouldn't marry me, but I was never really angry. And, whether you want to hear this or not, I never stopped loving you."

His quiet, heartfelt confession seemed to cause the dam of tortured emotions to suddenly break free from deep within Natalie. "Oh, Alex," she moaned, turning her face into his shoulder and letting loose the torrent of tears she had held back for so long. "I never stopped loving you either. You are the most wonderful, most incredible, most . . ."

She never finished her sentence, for the next thing she knew, she was being pulled up against Alexei's body and his lips were covering hers. His kiss was searing as his long-starved passion for her flared to life in an inferno of need.

Natalie's lips parted and she wrapped her arms around his neck, pulling him closer as their tongues entwined in an erotic reunion.

"I've missed you so much," he said hoarsely, gently swiping his thumbs against Natalie's cheeks to wipe away the last vestiges of her tears. "There was never a day that I didn't think about you . . . that I didn't want you."

Natalie looked up into his dark, somber eyes, seeing the truth of his anguished words in their fathomless depths. Threading her fingers in his soft hair, she again pulled his mouth down to hers, moaning softly when she felt his fingers caress her swelling breasts where the daring bodice of her dress left them bare.

Turning her in his arms, Alexei laid her back on the plush sofa, then stretched out beside her, one leg thrown over hers as he continued to kiss her. Finally, he lifted his mouth, leaving her feeling slightly abandoned until she realized that he was just moving lower along her body, tracing a path down her neck. She felt his mouth against her nipple through the thin material of her dress and in a breathless voice, whispered, "I can take this off."

To her surprise, Alexei suddenly stood up, raking his hand through his tousled hair. "No."

Natalie lifted herself on her elbow, looking at him in such bewilderment that he smiled, realizing she wanted him as badly as he wanted her. Reaching down, he offered her his hand, pulling her off the sofa and back into his embrace. "For eight years I've dreamed of making love to you again, but I want candles and a soft bed with clean sheets, not a narrow sofa in a room full of dirty dishes."

Natalie nodded, grateful that at least one of them was still showing a modicum of good sense despite the lust raging through them. "But didn't you say that you're staying in a suite with your sister and your valet?"

"Don't worry about that." Alex chuckled, reaching in his trouser pocket. He pulled his hand out and turned it palm upward, showing Natalie a room key. "I've arranged for us to have some privacy. Will you come?"

Natalie realized she should probably be offended that he had even considered that they might need a private room away from the other members of his entourage. But now, as she looked down at the key in his hand, she was grateful for his forethought.

This was Alex who was offering her this night of passion. Alex—the only man she had ever loved, the man whom she had just admitted she still loved—and regardless of the fact that this night might be all they would ever have, she could not deny him . . . or herself.

For his part, Alexei stood silently, looking at Natalie with his heart in his eyes as he waited for her to make up her mind.

Then, with a smile so hot that it nearly set his hair on fire, she put her hand in his. "Yes," she murmured, "I'll come."

TWELVE

The elevator seemed to take forever as it slowly crawled up toward the fifth floor. Alexei and Natalie were alone in the car, yet they said nothing, both of them too filled with nervous anticipation to talk.

When the doors finally opened, they stepped out of the elevator and walked down the quiet hotel corridor until Alexei found the room number matching the key he still held in his hand. He placed the key in the lock, then turned to give Natalie a look so full of sexual promise that she shivered.

"Are you cold?" he asked as he ushered her into the room and closed the door behind them.

The wine Natalie had drunk with dinner had done much to lower her inhibitions, and with sparkling eyes, she turned toward him and whispered, "No. In fact, I can't remember the last time I was so hot."

Alexei's eyes widened in pleased surprise at her provocative innuendo and he reached for her, wrapping his arm around her neck as he pulled her hard against him. "Come here, you gorgeous creature. I can't wait another second to kiss you."

Natalie melted against him, her eyes closing and her lips parting as he lowered his mouth in a devouring kiss. She welcomed his silky tongue with a little groan of pleasure, parrying his erotic thrusts and shuddering with excitement when he ran his hands seductively up her bare back. When they finally broke the fevered embrace, they were both breathless.

"I feel like a starving man who's being offered a feast,"

Alexei gasped, backing away and clenching his hands into fists to try to still his body's trembling.

"I know." Natalie nodded as she pressed her hands to her flaming cheeks. "I feel the same way."

Alexei looked down, noticing for the first time that he was still holding the room key. Absently, he tossed it on the dresser, then peeled off his suit jacket, stripped off his tie and unfastened the top two buttons of his dress shirt. "How long can you stay?" he asked softly.

Natalie threw him a wicked smile. "Susan Bedford is staying with Jenna, and she told me she planned to spend the night. . . ." Her words trailed off.

Alexei grinned, realizing that she was telling him she could stay till morning. "Remind me to send that lady a dozen roses tomorrow."

Turning, he walked over and opened the door, slipping the DO NOT DISTURB sign off the inside doorknob and placing it on the outside. When he turned back, Natalie was standing at the window, gazing out at the blazing panorama of lights below. "Oh, Alex, come look at the view," she beckoned. "The Public Gardens are an incredible sight from up here."

Alex came up behind her and began kissing her neck. "Incredible they might be, but there's only one sight I want to see tonight."

Natalie tilted her head back and closed her eyes as goosebumps rose all over her body. "What sight is that?" she asked throatily.

"The sight of you in my arms."

With a sigh, Natalie turned toward him, burying her fingers in his hair as they kissed.

"Is there anything I can get for you before we undress?" Alex asked as he dipped his head to kiss the upper swells of her breasts. "Anything you want?"

"Just you."

Alexei raised his eyes to hers, his expression serious. "You have me, Tasha. You've always had me."

His heartfelt words churned the sea of emotions already roiling within Natalie, and in a soft voice, she murmured, "Oh, Alex, I realize now that you've been right all along. There are a lot of things we need to talk about."

"I know," he rasped, continuing to kiss her, "but not tonight. Tonight I just want to make love to you. We'll talk tomorrow."

Natalie looked down at his dark head, contrasting so sharply against the pale skin of her breasts. She smiled, experiencing a moment of pleasure she'd never thought to know again—the joy of this one man intimately kissing her, the thrill of his warm lips on her body. Alex. *Her* Alex. Her one great love. Sophisticated, arrogant, demanding—he was all these things, and yet, at the core of his being, he was still just a man. A primitive, lusty, sexual man.

For four days now, he had driven her nearly mad with his relentless demands that she talk about their past relationship, explain her behavior, account for her actions so long ago. Now, tonight, when she finally understood that she needed to tell him the truth, that he deserved to know why she had acted as she had, he didn't want to hear it. He only wanted to make love.

Inwardly she chuckled. He was right. They could talk tomorrow. Tonight was for making love.

The sound of her zipper being slowly lowered brought Natalie back to the moment at hand. She smiled up at Alexei, helping him in his quest to disrobe her by shrugging her dress off her shoulders and skimming it down her hips till it fell in a soft pool at her feet. She was nude from the waist up, the garment's low-cut, tight bodice having left no room for a bra.

"My God," Alexei breathed, reaching out to stroke her naked breasts, "you're even more perfect than I remembered."

For a moment Natalie fought the urge to cover herself from his lustful gaze. It had been a long time since any man had looked at her nude body and eight years since a man had stared at her with the rapt masculine appreciation that Alexei was showing her right now.

But her brief moment of modesty passed as she felt his thumb graze the tip of her breast. Instinctively, she straightened her shoulders, pressing her taut, excited nipple against his hand, then sighing with pleasure when he drew his hand away and replaced it with his mouth.

His tongue erotically circled the sensitive little bud, causing something hot and liquid to unfurl deep inside her. Suddenly she felt as if her legs would no longer hold her up and she clutched at his shoulders.

Alexei splayed his hand against her bare back, pulling her to him. "Oh, God, Tasha," he whispered, holding her against his silk shirt, "I love the feel of you against me."

Natalie responded with a torrid look, then reached out and unfastened the rest of the buttons of his shirt, pushing it off his shoulders.

Alexei pulled her toward him again, intending to press her breasts against his naked chest, but, to his surprise, she pushed him away. Looking up into his startled face, she murmured, "I want to feel you against me too. All of you."

With deft hands, she unhooked his belt, then released his trousers, shimmying them down his lean hips. Dropping to her knees, she took off his shoes and socks, then stood again, catching her breath at the sight of his nakedness.

"I had forgotten how beautiful you are," she murmured. "Even more now than before."

It was true, she thought as she stared at him. The years had been kind to him. He had filled out; his shoulders were wider, his chest deeper. He was a man in his prime and she found the new maturity in his well-muscled body incredibly exciting. He reminded her of some ancient, dark god, fully aroused and splendid in his unashamed masculinity.

"I'm sure I would say the same about you, my love, if I could just see all of you."

Natalie looked down at herself, smiling as she realized that she was still wearing her sheer black panty hose. "Oh, I think that can be arranged." Hooking her thumbs in her waistband, she peeled the hosiery off. Then she reached up and pulled the pins out of her hair, her breasts lifting provocatively as she completed this most feminine of tasks. Shaking her head so that the thick blond tresses tumbled down to her shoulders, she faced Alexei squarely. "Is this better?"

In a heartbeat, he had her in his arms, pressing the entire length of her body against his as he feverishly kissed her. Finally, he lifted his lips from hers and, taking her face between his hands, stared down into the aquamarine depths of her eyes. "Every night when I went to bed, I dreamed about what you looked like, trying to remember every nuance of your body. But never, in all that imagining, did I ever have the good fortune to picture you as beautiful as you are tonight. You are like my dream come true, Tasha, and I can still hardly believe that I actually have you in my arms again."

"I had the same dreams about you, Alex," Natalie confessed shyly. "Always wondering what you looked like, where you were, remembering our nights together, wishing we could go back in time."

Alexei took a step back. "You thought about me too?"

"Of course." She nodded. "Every single day. There was never a time that you were far from my thoughts."

"But, Tasha, if you felt like that, then why . . ."

Gently, Natalie placed two fingers against his lips. "Not tonight, remember? Tomorrow. We'll talk about everything tomorrow."

Alexei blew out a long breath. "Yes. Tomorrow. Tonight is just for this." And gathering Natalie in his arms, he began kissing her again.

"Do you realize"—Natalie giggled when they finally stepped apart—"that you and I are standing here completely naked in front of this window? Anyone outside looking up can probably see us."

Alex threw a quick glance out the window, then grinned unrepentantly. "I don't care. Maybe some couple coming back to the hotel tonight saw us up here, and it will inspire them."

Natalie laughed and threw a playful look at Alexei's jutting erection. "Yes, Mr. Romanov, I'd say 'inspiring' is a perfect word to describe you."

"Come here," he said, taking her by the hand and leading her over to the bed, "and let me show you just how inspired you've made me."

Alexei lay back, pulling Natalie down on top of him and wrapping his arm around her neck as she lowered her head for his kiss. Her hair veiled his face like gold silk, and he threaded his long fingers through its softness, gently tilting her face as his lips reached for hers. Their mouths met and blended, tasting each other hungrily. "I'd forgotten what this was like." He groaned as he buried his face against the lushness of her full breasts.

Natalie smiled down at him disbelievingly. "Oh, come now, Alex. Surely you don't expect me to believe that you've been celibate for eight years."

"Not celibate," he said, rolling her over on her back and looking down at her with such honesty in his dark eyes that she could not doubt the truth of his words, "but it was never like this with anyone else."

A glad little cry tore from Natalie's throat and she reached up, urging Alexei's mouth down to hers. "I've missed you so."

"And I you," he answered hoarsely, his hand trailing down her stomach and abdomen until it came to rest at the juncture of her thighs. He paused, waiting for her to take the next step in their rediscovery of each other.

Natalie didn't disappoint him.

Subtly, she pressed upward against his hand, extending the ultimate invitation. His answer was immediate, and as she felt his hand move lower, she raised her hips, encouraging him to slip his fingers into her warm, welcoming body. She gasped with pleasure as he began to stroke her, then reached out and wrapped her hand around his hot, hard length, rubbing its moist, sensitive tip against her palm.

With a groan of primal sexual desire, Alexei rose to his knees, his handsome features hardened with lust.

Natalie answered his primitive call with a sigh of surrender, wrapping her legs around his lean flanks and guiding him into her.

Their union was sublime. All the pain of a tortured past, all the fears of a tenuous future were temporarily forgotten as they drowned themselves in the reality of what they were sharing. For both of them there was only this moment.

Alexei was careful to start slowly, not knowing and not wanting to know, how attuned Natalie was to frequent lovemaking. Gently, he began moving, but his thrusts quickly intensified in pace and strength as Natalie pressed her heels into his hips, subtly letting him know that she craved more from him. His long-starved desire for her made it nearly impossible to control his need, but he clamped down hard on his lust, not wanting her to feel that she was merely another conquest to him.

But Natalie was as excited by their lovemaking as he was, and it wasn't long before Alexei heard a low, throaty moan escape her. The provocative call was distinctly her own, and Alexei knew with the surety of keen remembrance that she was quickly approaching love's pinnacle. With a groan, he let himself go, his thrusts coming faster and faster until the erotic pressure building deep inside both of them exploded simultaneously in a climax filled with delight and exultation.

After a final thrust of completion, Alexei collapsed against her, his breath coming fast and his heart beating fiercely in his chest. "My sweet Tasha," he breathed, his mouth close to her ear, "what a wonder you are."

Natalie smiled in replete satisfaction. It had been eight long years since she had felt the sense of well-being she was now experiencing and she reveled in the sensation. It was staggering how right it seemed to be, making love to Alexei again. Her memory had always told her that no other man could equal his finesse, but she had often ridiculed her own thoughts, telling herself that it was just wistful recollection that made her feel that way. But tonight, as they had passionately reclaimed each other's bodies, she had discovered that her memories had been correct. Alexei truly was different—more passionate, more tender, and more skillful at bringing her pleasure than anyone she had ever known.

For several moments they continued to lie intimately joined as their hearts slowed and their breathing returned to normal. Finally, with a last gentle kiss to the soft skin under her earlobe, Alexei withdrew and turned on his back, pulling Natalie close until her head rested comfortably on his shoulder.

"It is just as I remember," he whispered. "Just as exciting, just as passionate, just as loving as it always was between us."

Natalie looked up at him with wide eyes, stunned to realize that his thoughts so closely paralleled her own. It had always been like that between them—their thoughts, their opinions, their passions so attuned to each other that it had seemed almost as if they shared two halves of the same soul.

And yet they had been lost to each other for so long that Natalie had nearly forgotten how complete she felt when she was with him. And now that he had suddenly reentered her life, she was not sure that she could face any more of her days without him.

"I love you, sweetheart," he whispered, kissing her gently. "I have loved you since the day I met you and I will love you till the day I die."

Those words. He had said those words again. *I will love you till the day I die.*

"I love you too," Natalie whispered back. "But Alex—"

"Shh," he soothed. "Nothing has to be decided tonight." Looking over at her, he smiled into her stricken eyes. "Don't look so worried, Tasha. We will figure something out. Now that I have you back, I know I cannot face living the rest of my life without you."

Gently, he pulled her back against his chest. "Sleep now,

daragaya," he whispered, burying his face in her hair. "When we wake up, we'll have plenty of time to talk."

Natalie nodded, drawing comfort from the fact that Alexei seemed so sure they would be able to work out their problems. For a few moments she lay thinking about the ecstasy they had just shared; then, with an impulsiveness that surprised even herself, she reached back with one hand and gently stroked him. "Alex?"

"Hmm?" he responded sleepily.

"Do you suppose we'll also have time to make love again?"

Alexei's eyes snapped open, and with a smile of astonished pleasure, he decided to play along with her provocative little game. Firmly removing her hand, he sighed dramatically. "I suppose, if we must."

"Oh, I definitely think we must," Natalie answered, again placing her hand over him and smiling with satisfaction as she felt him begin to harden.

"My God, but haven't you become the demanding vixen." Alexei chuckled, flipping her over on her back and lowering his mouth to her breast. "It must be true what they say about women reaching their sexual peak at thirty."

"And, lucky for me," Natalie purred, "it must *not* be true what they say about men over thirty needing to rest between encounters."

Alexei looked down at himself, then back at Natalie, his eyes full of laughter. "No, I guess not."

It was another full hour before they finally fell into an exhausted, blissful sleep.

THIRTEEN

Natalie couldn't think of a more perfect way to wake up than to find a gorgeous, naked man kneeling over her, raining kisses across her bare breasts. "Alex," she murmured, realizing that it must still be very early since she could barely see him in the shadowy darkness, "what are you doing?"

Alex lifted his head and smiled at her languidly. "Granting your wish, madame."

"My wish?" she asked, loving the sound of his deep voice and heavily accented English. "What wish?"

Alexei again lowered his head and began to swirl erotic little circles around her nipple with his tongue. "You said last night that you wanted to make love this morning. I'm just fulfilling your desire."

"Yes, you certainly are doing that." Natalie sighed. She reached down to stroke his tousled dark hair, then suddenly let out a little gasp of pleasure as he began moving down her body, his tongue tracing a molten path across her stomach and abdomen.

Understanding his intention, Natalie shivered with the first blush of ecstasy and instinctively drew up her knees.

Alexei smiled to himself, pleased with her reaction to his lovemaking. Placing his hands beneath her hips, he raised her, then lowered his head and began intimately stroking her with his tongue.

Natalie let out a little cry of ecstasy as the familiar pressure built inside her, until she felt she might explode. "Alex," she cried, her body writhing and squirming beneath his passionate assault, "My God, Alex!"

Alex glanced up into her flushed face and redoubled his efforts, tantalizing her senses until she finally convulsed against him as wave after wave of ecstasy washed over her.

When her body finally stilled and she relaxed, panting and sated, he straightened, sitting back on his heels and staring down at her in satisfaction. "I remembered that was one of your favorite ways to wake up."

Natalie smiled up at him, then lowered her eyes, staring in rapt fascination at his blatant arousal. "And I remember one of yours." With a lithe movement, she sat up and settled herself high on his thighs, wrapping her legs around his waist and positioning herself so that his erection slipped inside her.

With a groan of pleasure, Alexei grasped Natalie around the waist, pulling her more firmly against him as he filled her with his hardness.

Their union was quick, passionate, and carnal, with both of them so stimulated that barely a minute later they reached fulfillment and collapsed back into the pillows. After one last kiss, they separated and in a matter of seconds were both sound asleep.

Natalie woke an hour later to see that the sun was beginning to shed a soft, lemony light through the gauzy curtains of their room. She smiled, drifting in a happy, satisfied haze as she thought of the incredible night she and Alexei had just shared. Slowly turning her head, she gazed over at the sleeping man next to her.

I'll tell him this morning, she thought. *I'll tell him about Tom . . . and about Jenna. Susan's right: He's Jenna's father and he deserves to know about her. And surely, once he knows he has a daughter, he'll agree to stay in America with us.*

She closed her eyes for a moment, wondering where she was going to find the courage to carry out her resolve. It was going to be difficult to admit the truth, but after the night they had just spent, and especially since Alexei had told her that he wanted her in his life permanently, the time had come.

Natalie turned on her side, propping herself up on an elbow and looking down into Alexei's face. He looked younger when he was asleep, with his mouth relaxed and his long dark lashes casting shadows over the lean hollows of his cheeks. She reached out to gently brush back a lock of hair from his forehead, then blinked in surprise when he slowly opened his eyes and looked up at her.

"I didn't know you were awake," she whispered.

"I know." He smiled. "I've just been lying here enjoying having you ogle me."

"I wasn't ogling you!"

Alexei laughed and gave her a lusty kiss. "Yes, you were, and I love it. Anyway, you don't need to be embarrassed, because while you were still asleep, I was ogling you."

Natalie joined in his laughter at this confession. "Then you've been awake for awhile."

"Yes." He nodded, stretching luxuriously. "I've been thinking."

"Oh? About what?"

"Actually, about Jenna."

"Jenna?" Natalie blurted. "Whatever made you think of her?"

Alexei studied her closely for a moment, as if trying to determine whether he should tell her the truth. "Honestly, Tasha, I was lying here wishing that she were my child instead of your ex-husband's."

A little thrill of excitement skittered down Natalie's spine, and it was all she could do to keep her voice calm. "Why do you say that?"

"First of all, because she's wonderful and I would love to have a daughter exactly like her; secondly, because she's yours and, therefore, I wish she were also mine. And thirdly, because if she were my daughter, I could take her to Moscow to be educated at the Central School of Music, where she could truly realize her potential."

To Natalie, Alexei's last words had the same effect as someone throwing a bucket of ice water at her. "You'd want your child to be educated in Russia?" she asked softly.

Alexei looked at her solemnly. "Americans can say what they will about Russia, Natalie, but I don't think you can dispute the fact that my country has produced some great artists."

"But so have we."

"Yes," he conceded. "I'm not arguing that. All I am saying is that I think the Russian educational system for music students is superior to America's, and if I was blessed with a child with Jenna's talent, I'd want her to receive the finest instruction possible, no matter where in the world that happened to be."

Natalie quickly turned away, not at all sure that she could hide the surge of panic she was suddenly feeling. Without even realizing it, Alexei had just brought an end to all her hopes for a future with him by validating her worst fear.

If he knew Jenna was his daughter, he would want to take her to Russia, and there might be nothing she could do to stop him. The very thought made her queasy.

Without warning, Natalie threw back the covers and sprang out of bed, racing over to the closet and jerking a complimentary terry bathrobe off a hanger. Alexei gaped at her in astonishment as she pulled on the robe and cinched it tightly around her waist. "What are you doing?"

"I, ah, I think it's time I was getting home," she stammered, her eyes looking frantically around the room for her discarded clothes.

"Home?" Alexei exclaimed, his bewilderment with her sudden strange behavior obvious in his tone. "I thought we were going to spend the day together. I thought we were going to talk. . . ."

Natalie laughed nervously. "Yes, well, I know we said that last night, but it's Sunday and I really should . . ." Her voice trailed off as she tried to think of some reason that would compel her to leave.

A surge of anger suddenly replaced the confusion in Alexei's voice. "Should what?" he demanded. Whipping off the covers, he shot out of bed and strode toward her, seemingly totally oblivious to his nakedness.

"Should spend the day with Jenna," Natalie finished. Quickly she averted her eyes from the sight of his magnificent nude body coming toward her. She whirled around, pulling another bathrobe from the closet and blindly holding it out in his direction.

"I don't want that," he snapped, grabbing the bathrobe out of her hand and hurling it to the floor. "I want to know what's wrong. My God, Natalie, an hour ago we were making love, and now you won't even look at me. What happened?"

He paused, staring at her for a moment as a terrible thought struck him. "Oh, God," he whispered, his anger suddenly dissolving. "Please don't say that you regret what happened between us last night. Please don't tell me that . . ."

"No, that's not it," Natalie said quickly. Despite her desire to get away from Alexei before he read the truth in her eyes, she could not leave with him believing that she regretted what they had shared in the last twelve hours.

"Then, what is it?" he asked quietly. "Did I say something to offend you?"

Again she answered hurriedly, not wanting him to think back on their discussion and realize what had upset her. "No. You didn't say anything. I just think that I should get home before Jenna gets up and realizes that I've been gone all night." She forced what she hoped sounded like an embarrassed giggle. "That might be a bit hard to explain."

Alexei studied her averted face for another moment, then slowly bent over and scooped the bathrobe off the floor and put it on. "You can look at me now, Tasha. I'm decent."

Natalie swung around and stared at Alexei with stricken eyes. "You've never been anything but decent, Alex."

"Right," he said sarcastically. "So, then, why won't you look at me?" Walking over to the window, he plucked his trousers off the back of a chair and reached into a pocket, pulling out a pack of cigarettes and a lighter.

"Do you still smoke?" Natalie asked, aghast. "I thought you gave that up years ago."

"Only when I'm very, very upset," Alexei answered, lighting the cigarette and inhaling deeply. "It's a bad habit, but a hard one to break." He exhaled, staring at her for a long moment, then added, "Rather like you."

Natalie quickly turned away as she felt a knot of tears choking her throat. This was terrible. She loved this man with a passion she'd never felt for anyone else, but, as usual, she was causing him untold pain when he had done nothing to deserve it. Why did she always seem to hurt him when she loved him so much?

And yet, despite the remorse she was feeling, she knew there was nothing she could do to rectify this new rift between them. Alexei had admitted that if Jenna was his child, he'd want her raised in Russia, and regardless of how much Natalie loved him, she would not risk becoming involved in a battle with him over their daughter. She'd walk away from him first, just as she had eight years ago.

With slow steps, Natalie began gathering up her clothes. "I'm going to take a shower."

"Would you like some breakfast before you leave?" he asked tiredly. "I could order something from room service. It would probably be here by the time you're dressed."

"No, thanks," she answered, her heart breaking as she heard the resignation in his voice. He knew, as well as she did, that their time together was over. "I think the sooner I get home, the better."

He nodded curtly, then turned away, looking out the window as he took another drag on his cigarette.

Natalie walked into the bathroom and closed the door. When she came out again, he was gone.

FOURTEEN

Anya picked up her morning glass of orange juice and took a sip, then opened the Sunday edition of the *Boston Morning News*.

"Oh, no!" she cried, jumping up from the table as she stared in horror at the headline that jumped out at her from the middle of the front page.

COMRADES IN ARMS

Below the headline were three panels of pictures with a lengthy caption beneath. Anya grimaced as she rapidly read the caption.

Alexei Romanov, the famous Russian pianist currently performing at Symphony Hall, was seen in the Public Gardens yesterday in the company of a Boston woman identified as Natalie Worthington Saxon, daughter of Malcolm and Sarah Worthington and a descendent of Stuart Wellesley. Sources say the couple are longtime friends, a fact borne out by these amateur photographs snapped by a visiting Minnesota tourist.

"This is too much!" she snapped. "What in the world is Alexei thinking of, to be so obvious—and in public too!"

Again she looked at the pictures, which consisted of one of Alexei and Natalie seated on a park bench with their heads together, another of them walking along one of the garden's paths with his arm around her shoulder, and a final one of them sharing what appeared to be a passionate kiss next to the lagoon.

With a snort of disgust, Anya folded the paper and slapped it down on the table. Enough was enough. It was time to take matters into her own hands. Regardless of what had happened between Alexei and Natalie the previous evening, she was going to put Yuri's plan into action. Unfortunately, her meeting with Natalie would have to wait until this evening, since she had agreed to spend the day working as a celebrity judge at a local flower show. But even if she had to go to Natalie's house at midnight, she was determined to confront the hated woman before the day was over. It was time to end this misbegotten relationship before her brother became the laughing-stock of the entire country.

With a last furious glance at the embarrassing pictures, Anya stomped into her bedroom, slamming the door soundly behind her.

Alexei let himself into the suite, dropping his shoes, socks, jacket and tie in an untidy heap on the floor.

When Natalie had walked into the bathroom and closed the door against him, he was so furious that he had simply jerked on his underwear, trousers and shirt, then gathered the rest of his belongings and bolted out of the room.

He tore down the hall to the elevator in his bare feet, ignoring the stares he received from the guests who were waiting there, ready to go downstairs for an early breakfast.

When the elevator finally arrived, he stepped on last, punching the button for the penthouse and then standing in embarrassed silence as the elevator went down instead of up.

No one said a word for the entire five flights down to the lobby, but as the doors slid open, Alexei could almost feel the other occupants' curious stares boring into his back as they stepped around him to exit.

Now that he had finally reached the relative safety of his suite, overwhelming fatigue descended on him, the physical weariness from a nearly sleepless night spent making love coupled with emotional exhaustion as he tried to make sense of Natalie's unfathomable change of mood this morning.

Raking his hand through his already tousled hair, he trudged up the three steps to the suite's dining area and poured himself a cup of coffee, flipping open the folded newspaper that Anya had left on the table. What he saw caused him to suck in a shocked breath.

COMRADES IN ARMS

Alexei stared in appalled recognition at the pictures of himself and Natalie kissing in the park, then let out a groan of frustration and sank into a ladderback chair.

Who in the hell had taken these photos? He had been vaguely aware of the many camera-laden tourists surrounding them while he and Natalie had sat on the park bench and talked, but he hadn't paid enough attention to the milling strangers to notice if anyone was taking pictures of them. Obviously, some tourist from Minnesota had, and then must have run all the way downtown to the newspaper office to sell them.

Alexei looked more closely at the picture of himself kissing Natalie, realizing as he studied it that it was actually a very romantic portrait. The photographer had caught them at an angle that showed them in profile. Natalie's head was tilted back as Alexei bent over her, causing her beautiful blond hair to cascade over his arm while his lips covered hers in a passionate kiss. If the circumstances surrounding the taking of the picture had been different, he would have liked to have a copy of this photograph for himself.

For a moment, he wondered if maybe Natalie had seen these pictures and they were what had caused her unexpected flight this morning. But, no, she couldn't have. He was the first one to open the hotel room door and, even as upset as he had been when he charged out of the room, he remembered stepping over the unopened paper lying outside the door in the hallway.

Obviously, it was not these pictures that had caused her to leave so abruptly, but by now she surely must have seen them. Alexei frowned, thinking of how upset she must be, knowing that their public embrace had made the morning news and that the caption had included not only their names, but those of half of her famous family as well.

He had to talk to her. Natalie had always been a very private person, and if these photographs were an embarrassment to him, then he could only imagine how mortifying they must be to her. She had said that she was going home to spend the day with Jenna, so if that was where she was, then he was going over there, whether she wanted him to or not.

After all, the pictures would never have been taken if Natalie had been kissing some unknown man in the park. He was the cause of this embarrassing debacle, and he wanted to apologize to her in person.

With a decisive nod, Alexei headed toward his bedroom, intending to take a quick shower when, suddenly, Anya's bedroom door flew open and his sister stormed into the living room, her white satin bathrobe billowing out behind her.

Seeing him standing there holding the newspaper, she slammed her fists on her hips, her face red with anger. "How could you?" she demanded, sounding for all the world like a wronged wife. "It's bad enough that you're even associating with that woman after all the unhappiness she's caused you in the past, but to be pictured on the front page of the newspaper kissing her in public like some hormonally obsessed teenager is unconscionable! Why, these pictures will probably be in the Moscow papers by tomorrow, and everyone we know will find out what a fool you've made of yourself. How will I face people when we return home? I will *never* forgive you for this!"

Alexei glared at his overwrought sister and clenched his fists at his sides. This had already been a terrible morning and the last thing he needed was to have to deal with one of Anya's temper tantrums. There were a lot of people to whom he might have to explain himself, but his younger sister was not one of them.

As Anya opened her mouth to let loose another barrage of accusations, Alexei held up his hands, his eyes black with fury. "Anya, that is enough!" he bellowed. "This is not about you. The embarrassment caused by these pictures is mine and Natalie's to bear, not yours. You are always telling me that you are an adult and that I should respect that and not interfere with your life. Now, it is my turn to say the same to you. Stay out of my affairs. I do not want to hear another word from you or anyone else about Natalie Worthington, these pictures or anything else concerning my private life. Is that understood?"

Anya's fuming expression dissolved into one of stupefied astonishment. Rarely did she and Alexei quarrel, and never could she remember a time that he had ever spoken to her so angrily. "That woman is ruining you," she spat. "You are acting like a barbarian."

"I beg your pardon, little sister, but you are hardly in the position to call me a barbarian after shrieking at me like a Russian fishwife. And, just so you know, if I hear you call Natalie 'that woman' one more time, you will no longer be welcome in my company or in my suite. So, unless you have the financial wherewithal to pay for your own hotel room from now on, I'll thank you to watch your tongue!"

Anya sucked in her breath in outrage and lunged toward Alexei as if to slap him. But in her haste, she tripped over the shoes and jacket he had left on the floor, causing her to lose her balance and stumble into him, clutching at him frantically in an effort to regain her footing.

"What are those doing there?" she cried, wrenching away from him and staring down at the heap of clothing on the floor. Her eyes widened with shock as she realized that they were the clothes Alexei had been wearing the previous evening, and she spun around, flicking her gaze up and down his body as she noticed his unkempt appearance for the first time.

"You're just getting back from your dinner, aren't you?" she accused. "My God, Alexei, has she really brought you so low that you're sneaking around hotel corridors half dressed in yesterday's clothes? What has come over you?"

"Where I spend my nights and what time I get in is none of your damn business!" Alexei thundered.

Anya looked again at the clothes, then back at her brother. "I'm glad Mama and Papa are dead so they're not here to see this. You are a disgrace!"

"You're entitled to your opinion, Anya," Alexei said coldly, "but know this: I don't give a damn what you or anyone else thinks. Now, leave me alone!" Stepping over the pile of clothes, he flung open his bedroom door, then slammed it behind him.

With a tired sigh, Alexei stripped off his rumpled clothes and sat down on the edge of the bed, propping his elbows on his knees and lowering his aching head into his hands.

My God, how could such a beautiful night lead to such an awful morning? First, Natalie walked out on him for no reason he could fathom; next, he saw those embarrassing pictures in the newspaper and finally, he had the worst argument of his life with the sister he adored.

Absently, he looked down at his watch. Not even ten o'clock yet. Well, at least one thing was for sure: As bad as the morning had already been, the rest of the day had to get better. There was no other way it could go.

Natalie closed her eyes and leaned her head back against the plush cushions of her sitting room sofa. "I'll be lucky if I don't lose my job over this." She sighed.

"You're not going to lose your job," Susan said positively.

"Honestly, Nat, you're making way too much of this. It was only a kiss. To hear you talk, you'd think the paper was printing nude pictures of the two of you."

Natalie opened her eyes and frowned at her friend. "Susan, I'm a teacher. What kind of respect am I going to get from my students now?"

"Your students will probably think you're the coolest professor at the school. Or, at the very least, they'll just think you're human."

"I hope you're right."

"Of course I'm right! These are college students we're talking about, and I've never known a college kid in my life who would think there was anything wrong with two people kissing in the park on a beautiful spring afternoon."

"But still, it's so embarrassing. God, what a terrible morning this has been! Everything is such a mess." Miserably, Natalie dropped her head into her hands.

Susan watched in consternation as her friend's shoulders begin to shake, then reached over and threw an arm sympathetically around her. "What's wrong, honey? This is much more than just fear of losing your job, isn't it?"

Natalie lifted her head and nodded, her face wet with tears and her voice tremulous when she spoke. "Yes. My job is the least of my problems. What I'm really upset about is Alex."

"Alex?" Susan asked warily. "What about him?"

"It's over between us!" Natalie wailed.

"Oh, God, I was afraid that was what it was. Tell me what happened. Was last night terrible?"

"No! Last night was wonderful. It was this morning that it happened."

"That *what* happened?"

"Just a minute." Natalie stood up and walked over to a cherry wood candle table, opening a small drawer and extracting a travel-size package of tissues. Carrying the tissues back to the sofa, she sat down and loudly blew her nose. "What happened was that Alex finally said exactly what I've always been afraid he'd say."

"Which is . . ."

"That if he had a daughter like Jenna, he'd want her to be educated in Russia."

Susan grimaced. "Ouch. He really said that?"

"Yes."

"What did you say?"

"Nothing. Absolutely nothing . . . except that I told him I had to leave."

"And then?"

Natalie pulled another tissue out of the package and dabbed at her eyes. "You know, I've cried more in the past four days than I have in the last eight years. I guess that should tell me something, shouldn't it?"

"What it should tell you is that you're finally allowing yourself to get emotionally involved with someone again. There are a lot worse things than crying, Nat."

"Well, I don't know what." She sniffed.

"Being alone, for one thing." Susan sighed. "Now, never mind all that. Just tell me what happened after you told Alex you were going to leave."

"Nothing happened. I just got up, took a shower and left."

"Whoa!" Susan exclaimed, holding up her hands. "Wait a minute here. Are you saying that Alexei told you this while you two were in bed?"

"Yes."

Susan thumped the side of her head with the heel of her hand, as if trying to reposition her brain. "Pardon me for being dense, but how in the world did the subject of education come up while you two were . . . you know."

Natalie threw her friend a shaming frown. "For heaven's sake, Sue, we weren't 'you know.' We were just lying in bed, talking, and Alex said he wished he had a daughter like Jenna. . . ."

"He said that?" Susan gasped. "Talk about giving you an entree to tell him the truth!"

"I suppose so, but I'm glad I didn't because the next thing he said was that if he had a daughter with Jenna's talent, he'd want her educated at the Central Music School in Moscow, where she could, and I quote, 'realize her full potential.' "

Susan nodded slowly. "So at that point, you just got up, took a shower and left."

"Yes."

"Didn't Alex think that was a little strange?"

"Yes, but what else could I do? I couldn't stay there any longer. I had to get away. It doesn't matter anyway, because it's over between us."

"Okay, okay, now go back a little. What did you say to him after you came out of the shower?"

"Nothing, because when I came out, he was gone."

"He was gone . . ." Susan mused. "Think maybe he was a little put out with you, Nat?"

"Of course he was put out with me," Natalie cried, a new rush of tears coursing down her cheeks. "Why wouldn't he be?"

Susan thought for a moment, then shook her head. "I still don't understand him just walking out without even saying, 'good-bye' or, 'It's been fun,' or something. Even if you were acting like a deranged idiot, that seems a bit rude."

Natalie stiffened at Susan's description of her. "Excuse me, but I wasn't acting deranged."

Susan smiled inwardly, pleased that her insult had done what she intended. There was nothing like offending someone to pull them out of a crying jag. That tack might be a bit hard-hearted, but it almost always worked. "Okay, so you weren't acting deranged. Then Alex was just being a jerk."

"No, he wasn't. Actually, there was a little more to the situation than I've told you."

"I thought there might be," Susan said wryly. "Why don't you tell me the *whole* story this time?"

Natalie heaved a shuddering sigh. "Alex wanted to spend the day together today so we could talk about things."

"And you had agreed to that?"

"Last night, yes," Natalie admitted. "But then, after he said those things about Jenna this morning . . ."

"You just hopped out of bed and announced you were going home, right?"

"Well . . . yes."

Susan sat back and shot Natalie an exasperated look. "Then I take back all the nasty things I just said about him. Alex wasn't being rude. My take on this is that he probably felt like you were rejecting him *yet again,* and he decided to walk out on you before you walked out on him."

Natalie's face began to crumble again. "I think you're right. But it's probably for the best. At least this time, Alexei has the satisfaction of being the one to end it."

"End it! Who says he's ended it? The guy was mad, that's all. I bet you hear from him before the day is over."

"Oh, God, I hope not. I don't think I can face him again."

"Well, I think you're going to have to," Susan snapped, then instantly regretted her harsh tone when she saw Natalie's stricken expression. "Honey, you owe him that much. Alex has loved you for most of his adult life and you can't just end it with him without giving him some sort of explanation. You did that once and you know what it did to him. Do you really want to hurt him like that again?"

"Of course not! I don't want to hurt him at all."

"Well then, since you refuse to take my advice and tell the man the truth, you'd better start thinking of some other plausible explanation for your behavior because, unless I miss my guess, he's going to be around looking for one very, very soon."

"How can you still think that I should tell him the truth

after what he said about wanting his daughter educated in Russia?"

"My dear"—Susan smiled—"I have a lot of faults, but lying isn't one of them. I always think the truth is the best policy, and this situation is no different."

"I just can't do that," Natalie whispered, shredding the tissue she was holding in her agitation. "I know what you're saying is probably right, but I can't do it. Not now. Not after what he said. What if I told him and then he decided he wanted to take Jenna back to Russia with him?"

"Oh, Natalie, that's not going to happen. Alex loves you! Do you really think he'd try to take your daughter away from you?"

"I don't know what to think anymore." Natalie sighed despondently.

Susan reached over and squeezed her hand. "Well, it's your decision, Nat. You have to do what you think is best."

She glanced down at her watch and then got to her feet. "I'd better get going."

Natalie looked at her with pleading eyes. "Do you really have to leave?"

Susan nodded. "I'm sorry. I wish I could stay, but I absolutely have to go home and feed my poor cats. I'm sure they think I've abandoned them permanently. Right now, they're probably both in the kitchen trying to figure out how to use the electric can opener."

Despite how miserable she was feeling, Natalie smiled wanly. "I understand." She stood up and slowly walked toward the door with Susan.

"Call me later?" Susan asked.

Natalie nodded.

Impulsively, Susan reached out and gave her friend a warm hug. "Don't worry, sweetie. Things will work out. One way or another, they always do."

Natalie forced another smile, then softly closed the door. Leaning against it, she gave free rein to her misery, the sobs that shook her coming from the very depths of her soul.

Susan might believe that everything would work out, but Natalie knew better. In fact, right now she seriously doubted that anything would ever work out again.

FIFTEEN

Alexei stepped out of the bathroom and cocked his head toward the bedroom door. He could hear Anya talking to another woman in Russian, and although he couldn't clearly hear the second speaker's voice, he knew it was Sophie, his publicist's fat wife, come to gossip about the newspaper pictures and raid his honor bar of ten dollar jars of Macadamia nuts.

Alexei frowned as he dressed, wondering how he could get out of the suite without Sophie seeing him. All he wanted right now was to go to Natalie's house and talk to her. After the night they'd spent together, they couldn't leave things the way they were. He'd been hurt and angry this morning when she'd suddenly become so remote and distant, but now that he'd had a chance to cool off, he conceded that he was probably being overly sensitive and that, most likely, she really had felt that she should spend her Sunday with her daughter.

Whatever Natalie's reasons for her sudden haste to leave him earlier, they needed to put things back to rights between them, as well as discuss how to handle the newspaper pictures. And when all those issues were settled, he had to return to the hotel in time for a couple of hours of badly needed practice before his concert tonight.

With such a pressing time schedule, the last thing he needed right now was Sophie the Nosy grilling him unmercifully for the intimate details of his love life.

He opened the bedroom door a crack and peeked out, trying to ascertain where the women were sitting so he could figure out whether it was possible to get out of the suite unnoticed. Damn! They were both seated on the sofa with their profiles to him. There was no way he could escape without them seeing him.

"I agree with you completely, Sophie," he heard Anya say. "Alexei's behavior is an embarrassment to all of us."

He watched as Sophie leaned forward and picked up a raspberry tart from a silver platter sitting on the coffee table. "What I don't understand," she said as she popped the pastry into her mouth, "is why Alexei is carrying on with an American woman. Why can't he settle for a nice Russian girl? There must be dozens of them who would be happy to marry him. Just look at Margot Petrikova. Why, I bet she'd marry him in a minute if he'd ask her."

"I'm sure she would too," Anya agreed. "But despite how enamored Margot is with Alexei, I don't think he feels that there's the right chemistry between them for him to be really serious about her."

"Chemistry, bah!" Sophie said, gesturing with her third tart. "In the old days, our families decided who was a suitable match. Chemistry had nothing to do with it."

Alexei rolled his eyes at this archaic thought and glanced at his watch. It was already well after noon. Why couldn't the old bag just finish the plate of tarts and leave? If he didn't leave soon, he wasn't going to have time to get any practice in before his concert tonight. Gritting his teeth with impatience, Alexei again looked through the crack in the door, contemplating how much time he would lose if he just made an appearance and faced the barrage of questions Sophie was bound to hurl at him. Maybe not much. After all, how long would it take to tell her to mind her own business and walk out? He had just decided that this was probably the most expedient course of action when he saw Anya glance at the clock and stand up.

"I have to judge a flower show this afternoon," she told

Sophie, "and as much as I'd love to stay here and chat with you, I really must get ready to leave."

Alexei breathed a sigh of relief as he watched Sophie heft her considerable bulk off the sofa, pluck the last two tarts off the tray and head for the door. Finally, he was going to get out of here, and without having to face another scene with either Sophie or Anya.

Maybe things were looking up after all.

It took a half hour for Natalie to stop crying after Susan left, but, finally, the tears subsided. Wearily, she climbed the stairs to her bedroom and lay down on her antique four-poster bed, placing two chilled essence of cucumber pads over her eyes in the hope that the redness and swelling would disappear before Jenna saw her.

After what seemed like only a short time, she removed the pads and glanced at the clock on her bedside table, surprised to see that nearly an hour had passed. Quickly, she got up and walked over to check her appearance in the mirror. The rest, coupled with the cucumber, had done wonders. The swelling and redness were gone; the only visible traces left from her trying morning were mauve shadows under her eyes that could be easily concealed with makeup.

After changing into a pair of jeans and a beige sweater, she walked down the hall to Jenna's room, where she found her daughter engrossed in reading a Laura Ingalls Wilder book. "You know," she said, "those books were my favorites when I was a little girl."

"They're real good," Jenna agreed, laying the book aside. "It must have been fun to be a pioneer girl on the prairie."

Natalie looked at her doubtfully, unable to think of anything she would like less than living in a one-room sod hut or walking three miles to school, as the famous author had done during her youth.

"What would you like for supper?" she asked. "We'll have whatever you want."

"Hot dogs," Jenna answered instantly. "With lots of mustard and relish. And potato chips. And chocolate chocolate chip ice cream for dessert."

Natalie laughed and bent down to give her daughter a hug. "Then I guess we'll have to go to the market, because I'm fresh out of chocolate chocolate chip ice cream."

"Okay. We can stop there on our way back from the mall."

"The mall?"

Jenna wiggled out of her mother's arms and stood back, eyeing her warily. "You promised, Mommy. You said that if I was good and didn't cause Susan any trouble last night—and I didn't—that you'd take me to the mall today."

Natalie suddenly realized that there *was* something she'd like to do less than live in a sod hut—and that was spend the afternoon at the mall. But still, Jenna was right. She had promised. "Okay, pumpkin," she said, trying desperately to pump some enthusiasm into her voice, "the mall it is. And then to the market to get hot dogs and potato chips and ice cream."

"Yippee!" Jenna shouted. "The mall and then hot dogs. What a great day!"

Natalie sighed and closed her eyes in weary resignation. What a great day, indeed.

Susan sat down on the sofa in her tiny Back Bay apartment and flipped on the TV, surfing the cable channels until she found what she was looking for. "Ah." She sighed. "A four-hour miniseries with Jaclyn Smith. What better way to spend a lazy Sunday afternoon?" With a beatific smile, she picked up a single cigarette and the lighter that were lying on the coffee table. The very best thing about living alone was that there was no one to yell at her when she wanted to sneak a cigarette. Although her friends and family had talked her into giving up her "filthy habit" two years ago, there were still times when the craving became overwhelming, and occasionally, she allowed herself the guilty pleasure of just one.

"Oh, don't look at me like that," she said, glaring at her cat, who was staring up at her with baleful eyes. "After the morning I just spent with Natalie, I deserve this." Defiantly, she lit the cigarette and took a long puff, wondering when her cat had taken on the task of being her conscience.

Thinking of Natalie, she shook her head, then leaned down and picked up the cat, gently stroking her soft caramel-colored fur. "You know, Tallulah, if Natalie would just let her guard down a little and trust the man, I'm sure everything would work out fine between them." Laying the cigarette in the ashtray, she took the cat's head between her hands and gently scratched her behind her ears. "After all, he's gorgeous, he's famous, he's rich and he's obviously mad about her. So, why does she keep fighting it?"

Tallulah looked up at her mistress, purring ecstatically.

"I agree." Susan laughed. "If I had a man like that in my life, I'd be purring too, not scratching and clawing to keep my distance from him."

Still petting the cat, Susan reached over and picked up the cigarette, drawing on it thoughtfully. "Poor Natalie. She looked so sad when I left, I probably should have stayed with her. Maybe I should give her a call and make sure she's okay."

She stared at the TV for another few minutes, then stubbed at her cigarette and got to her feet. "Who am I kidding?" She sighed, clicking off the set and heading for the hall closet to get her jacket. "I can't just sit here and veg when I know Natalie's so miserable." With a last longing look at the comfortable sofa and the remote control, she picked up her purse and headed out the door.

Ten minutes later Susan was standing in front of Natalie's door, ringing the bell for the third time. "Where in the world could she be? I give up my Sunday afternoon movie to come over here and lend a comforting shoulder, and she's not even here. That's gratitude for you!"

After waiting another few seconds and still receiving no answer, Susan began to feel uneasy. It didn't make sense that Natalie was gone. She hadn't mentioned that she had any plans and, considering the emotional state she'd been in when Susan had left, she found it difficult to believe that Natalie would have made any new plans after that. Reaching into her purse, Susan fished out the duplicate house key Natalie had given her and inserted it into the lock.

"Yoo-hoo. Anybody home?" she called as she stepped into the foyer. She waited a moment and, receiving no answer, climbed the staircase to the second floor. "Natalie? Jenna? Is anybody home?"

After a quick search of both Natalie's and Jenna's bedrooms, she finally faced the fact that her friend and her daughter weren't there. "Just my luck," she groused as she walked back down the hallway. "I give up my movie, drive all the way over here and she doesn't even have the good grace to be home!"

Frowning, she started back down the staircase, reaching the bottom just as the doorbell rang.

Now, who can that be? she thought with annoyance. *It'd better not be a reporter from the* Morning News, *or they're going to receive a piece of my mind that they'll not soon forget!* Crossing the foyer, she pulled open the front door and found herself face to face with Alexei Romanov.

"Oh," Alexei said, obviously surprised to find Susan answering Natalie's door. "Miss Bedford, isn't it?"

"Yes," she answered, her heart catching in her throat as he flashed her a heart-stopping smile. "Ah . . . I bet you're here to see Natalie."

"Yes." Alexei nodded. "Is she home?"

"Apparently not. I just came over for a quick visit, but she and Jenna don't seem to be here."

Alexei's smile faded. "I see. Well, in that case . . ."

"Would you like to come in?" Susan asked, suddenly remembering her manners.

Alexei shook his head. "No, thank you. I'll just go back to the hotel. I need to practice before my concert tonight." He turned around just in time to see his limo pull away from the curb and head off down the street. Turning back to Susan, he threw her an embarrassed grin. "Well, maybe I'm not going back after all. Do you have any idea where Mrs. Saxon has gone, or when she might be returning?"

"I'm afraid not," Susan answered, "but I'm sure it would be all right if you wanted to stay here and wait for her."

Alexei opened his mouth to decline her invitation, then suddenly thought better of it. "That might not be a bad idea. I know Mrs. Saxon has a piano, and considering how many people have been in and out of my suite today since the debacle in the newspaper, I would appreciate having a chance to practice undisturbed."

"Why don't you come in?" Susan smiled. She opened the door wider, allowing Alexei to step into the marble-tiled foyer.

Slowly he turned in a circle, obviously impressed by the grandeur of Natalie's home. "What a beautiful old place."

"You've never been here?"

"No. When I knew Natalie before, she and I were in New York and her parents were still living here." He glanced down. "What a magnificent floor. The marble is exquisite."

Susan chuckled. "If you think that's beautiful, you should see the bathroom off the master bedroom. It has a marble bathtub!"

Alexei looked at her incredulously. "A marble bathtub? I've never heard of such a thing."

"Apparently it was all the rage among the American elite at the turn of the century. Of course, one of Natalie's ancestors had one installed."

Alexei smiled, his imagination painting him a delightfully arousing picture of Natalie reclining nude in a marble bathtub.

But his stirring thoughts were quickly banished by Susan's next words.

"I guess it's not quite as wonderful as it sounds, though." She chuckled. "Natalie told me the marble gets so cold in the winter that you have to fill the tub twice to use it—once to warm the marble and a second time to warm yourself. She says it's so inconvenient that she doesn't bother with it. She just takes a shower."

Now it was Alexei's turn to chuckle. "That sounds like my Tasha. Ever practical."

Susan did not miss his unconscious use of the possessive pronoun. She sighed enviously, then blushed with embarrassment as she noticed Alexei looking at her. "The piano is right in here," she said, gesturing toward the drawing room. "Before I go, is there anything I could get for you?"

Alexei smiled in appreciation. "No, nothing at all. But thank you for your offer."

Susan returned his smile, completely charmed by his unbelievable handsomeness and his romantic accent. "Well, then, I guess I'll be on my way."

At that moment, Alexei's eyes lit upon the beautiful Steinway grand piano sitting in the corner of the room and, for a moment, Susan caught a glimpse of what it must have been like for Natalie to be in love with a true artist. She felt as though he had probably forgotten she was even there. "Goodbye, Mr. Romanov," she called as he hurried over to the instrument.

"Good-bye, Miss Bedford," he answered, all of his attention focused on the piano, "and thank you again for your assistance."

Susan turned to leave as Alexei seated himself and began running his fingers lightly up and down the keyboard. She paused for a moment, enjoying the splendid cascade of notes that suddenly filled the huge room, then slowly retraced her steps. "Mr. Romanov, could I say something?"

Alexei looked up, as if surprised to find her still there. "Of course."

"I just want you to know how sorry I am about those pictures in the paper this morning. You probably remember that I work for that newspaper, but I knew nothing about those pictures. If I had, I would have done everything in my power to prevent them from being published."

"I appreciate that, Miss Bedford, although it never occurred to me that you had anything to do with their publication. Unfortunately, pictures like that are part of being a public person. An unfair part, but a part, nonetheless. My main concern is for Natalie. Was she terribly upset by them?"

"Yes," Susan admitted. "At first, anyway. But I think I convinced her that they wouldn't have any long-term effect on her life or her career, and she seemed to feel better."

"Well, thank you for that." Alexei paused for a moment, looking at Susan thoughtfully, then said, "You probably know, Miss Bedford, that Natalie and I have had some trouble in our relationship, but I hope you will believe me when I tell you that I have loved her for a very long time. It is my greatest wish that she and I find a way to work out our problems and build a future together."

Susan smiled, touched by his earnest confession. "I hope you get your wish, Mr. Romanov, because I believe you are just what Natalie needs. I knew that the moment you began playing the *Moonlight Sonata* at your concert last week. Natalie's reaction was very . . . telling."

"Her reaction?"

"Yes. When you started the piece, she closed her eyes, and there was an expression on her face that I have never seen before."

Alexei smiled. "That particular sonata meant a great deal to us. Beethoven may have had a lot of women in his life, but most historians believe that the woman for whom that piece was written was his one great love. That was the message I wanted to send to her by playing it."

"That she is your one great love?"

Alexei looked away for a moment, embarrassed that he had confessed so much to a near stranger. But when he spoke again, his voice was clear and his answer unflinching. "Yes. She is certainly that."

Impulsively, Susan leaned forward and placed her hand on his forearm. "I know things will work out between you. I just know it."

Bidding him a final farewell, Susan quietly left the room, stopping in the foyer to look at a photograph of Natalie and Jenna that sat on a small table. "Natalie Saxon," she whispered to the picture, "you are absolutely nuts, wacko, out of your mind crazy if you let that man get away!"

"Mommy, it sounds like someone is playing our piano," Jenna said as she and Natalie stood outside the front door of the town house.

Natalie stopped searching for her house keys and listened closely to the muted music wafting through the front door. "You're right, honey, it does."

"Is there somebody in the house?" Jenna asked.

Natalie drew in an alarmed breath but forced her voice to remain calm so as not to frighten her daughter. "There couldn't be. We locked the door when we left, and it's still locked. Maybe you left your radio on."

Jenna looked up at her mother with wide eyes, shaking her head. "No, I didn't."

"Well, then, let's just go in and see where the music is coming from. Maybe it's my clock radio."

Slowly, Natalie pushed open the front door and stepped into the foyer, looking immediately in the direction of the drawing room. "You're right," she whispered to Jenna. "Someone *is* playing our piano."

"I'll see who it is," Jenna declared, taking off at a run.

"Jenna! Come back here!" Natalie charged after her daughter, nearly running her down as Jenna did an unexpected about-face and raced back out of the drawing room.

"It's Mr. Romanov," she said excitedly.

"What?" Natalie gasped. "What is *he* doing here?"

"He's playing Chopin," Jenna answered, as if it was the most natural thing in the world for Alexei Romanov to be sitting at her piano, practicing.

Natalie peeked around the corner of the drawing room door and nodded. "So he is."

Alexei became aware of the commotion near the drawing room door and looked up. Immediately the music stopped. "Natalie," he said, rising and walking toward her.

"What are you doing here, Alexei? How did you get in?"

Alexei bent down and ruffled Jenna's blond hair, then said, "Miss Bedford let me in."

Natalie looked behind her. "Susan? Is she here?"

"No, she's gone now. I came over to see you and you were gone, but she was here. She suggested that I wait for you, so I decided to practice for awhile. I hope that was all right."

"Well, yes . . . of course it's all right," Natalie stammered. "I'm just surprised, that's all. I didn't expect . . ."

She never finished her sentence because at that moment, Alexei pulled her into his arms and kissed her, holding her tightly against his broad chest as if to protect her from all the outside forces that seemed to be conspiring against them. "Tasha, I'm sorry about those pictures," he whispered.

"It's not your fault," Natalie whispered back, her lips touching his as they talked. "It's just . . . unfortunate that someone saw us and decided to cash in on it."

"I know." He nodded. "It's one of the prices of celebrity that I hate." Reclaiming her lips, he began kissing her again.

During this entire exchange, Jenna had been staring up at the adults in astonishment. The only men she had ever seen her mother kiss were older male relatives who occasionally appeared at their house on Thanksgiving or Christmas, and those kisses were always brief little pecks on the cheek. She had never seen Natalie kiss anyone the way she was kissing Mr. Romanov. It looked like they were trying to eat each other. "You guys!" She giggled, planting her little hands on her hips and scrunching up her nose.

Guiltily, Alexei and Natalie broke apart, looking down at the momentarily forgotten child in embarrassment. Alexei was the first one to recover. Scooping Jenna up in his arms, he strode over to the piano, saying, "Come on, little one. Let's play something together."

Setting the little girl down on the bench, he sat down next to her and helped her sift through a stack of music until they found a piece adapted for four hands. "How about this one?" he suggested.

Jenna nodded enthusiastically. "Mommy and I play this sometimes."

"Good," he said. "Then you already know it. Let's you and I give it a try."

Alexei counted off a measure and, together, they began playing. It was soon obvious that Jenna did not know the piece as well as Alexei thought she did, but every time she fumbled, he paused, patiently explaining an intricate fingering pattern or demonstrating how to play a difficult section and then encouraging Jenna to try it until she had it mastered.

Finally, after struggling to reach an octave, Jenna stopped and shook her hand.

"What's wrong?" Alexei asked. "Does your hand hurt?"

"It's just my thumb," Jenna answered, trying the eight-note stretch again.

"Your thumb? Did you hurt it?"

"No, it's always like this. Show me this part again."

Natalie, who had witnessed this exchange with her heart in her throat, sighed with relief as Alexei and Jenna began playing again. She stood as if transfixed, watching the man she loved as he gently instructed their daughter on the nuances of the complex music. A half hour slipped by as Alexei worked with Jenna. Then, to Natalie's delight, they started at the beginning and played the piece all the way through in a nearly flawless performance. As they struck the last chord, Natalie broke into applause and ran forward, hugging Jenna to her.

"That was wonderful," she complimented. Looking at Alexei over Jenna's head, she mouthed a heartfelt, "Thank you."

"She's brilliant," he mouthed back, shaking his head in wonder as he stared down at the beautiful, golden-haired child.

Natalie looked at them again, as if trying to fix the moment in her mind forever. *They are so beautiful together,* she thought. Such kindred spirits. To her horror, she felt a familiar knot of tears building in her throat.

"You have a concert tonight, don't you?" she asked, trying to turn her thoughts away from the emotional tableau she'd just witnessed.

Alexei glanced down at his watch. "Yes, and I have less than an hour before I need to leave and go back to the hotel to dress." Looking down at Jenna, he asked, "Would you like to try another one before I go?"

"No," Jenna answered, jumping down from the bench. "I want to eat now."

Alexei looked at her in surprise. "Do you always stop in the middle of a practice session to eat?"

"Only when I'm hungry."

Natalie smiled at her daughter's frankness. "And especially when her mother wouldn't let her have any snacks at the mall because she promised to make her hot dogs as soon as they got home."

"Do you have one for me?" Alexei asked suddenly.

Jenna looked up at Natalie. "Do we, Mommy?"

Natalie hesitated before answering, not sure that she could handle having Alexei stay for dinner. But as she looked at his hopeful face, she realized that despite what had occurred between them that morning, she didn't want him to leave. "Do you really want a hot dog?"

"Sure." Alexei shrugged. "Why not? After all, this is America, and everyone eats hot dogs when they're in America."

"Then come on!" Jenna exclaimed, grabbing Alexei by the hand and pulling him off the piano bench. "Mommy can make the hot dogs, I'll get the mustard and pickles, and you can put the buns on the plates."

Alexei laughed and allowed Jenna to drag him off toward the kitchen. As they walked into the huge room, Alexei looked around, impressed by the hanging copper pots, the six-burner restaurant stove, and the huge, triple sink. "You could run a restaurant out of here." He chuckled.

Natalie opened the refrigerator door and pulled out a package of hot dogs. "Do you still like to cook?"

"Yes, and I'm even better than I used to be."

Again, Jenna looked at the adults in bewilderment, causing Natalie to say quickly, "Honey, before you start putting out the condiments, you need to go up to your room and wash your hands."

"I can wash them here in the sink."

"No," Natalie said firmly, wanting a private moment with Alexei. "Go up to your room, please."

Jenna frowned in annoyance but did as her mother bade.

Alexei watched Jenna disappear out the door, then walked over to Natalie, clasping her around her waist and kissing her with a passion that took her breath away. Finally, he lifted his head, staring down at her solemnly and saying, "Tasha, about this morning . . ."

Natalie quickly turned away, pulling an electric steamer out of a cupboard and setting it on the counter. "I know I owe you an explanation, Alex, but I can't talk about it now."

Quietly, he walked up behind her and wrapped his arms loosely around her slim waist. "You don't have to explain anything, *daragaya*. I think I know why you left."

Natalie's back stiffened. "You do?"

Stepping around her so he could see her face, he nodded. "It was because of what I said about Jenna, wasn't it? That if I had a daughter like her, I'd want her to be educated in Russia."

Playing for time, Natalie busied herself by filling the steamer with water and plugging it in. Then she slowly wiped her hands on a paper towel before looking up at Alexei, her expression riddled by indecision. "Yes, it was," she finally admitted. "This has always been a problem for us, Alex, and I just don't think we're ever going to be able to work it out."

"We have to work it out," Alexei said, pulling her to him and nestling her head against his shoulder.

Natalie released a dispirited sigh. "But how? I know your country means as much to you as mine does to me, so how can either one of us give up our homeland?"

"I don't know," he admitted. "I don't have any easy answers, Tasha, but I do know that now that I've found you again, I don't want to lose you."

Natalie looked up at him, tears welling in her eyes. "I don't want to lose you either, but . . ."

Gently, Alexei placed his fingers over her lips. "Don't say anything more. We'll talk about it later. I think Jenna is coming."

Natalie looked toward the doorway and, sure enough, Jenna was standing in the entrance to the kitchen, a look of concern on her little face.

"Mommy, what's wrong? You look like you're crying."

"It's nothing," Natalie said, quickly dashing the tears from her eyes. "I was just chopping onions for the hot dogs and they made me cry. You know how onions do that sometimes."

"Onions, ugh!" Jenna said, hopping up on a bar stool on the other side of the kitchen's center island. "Are the hot dogs ready yet?"

"Yes." Natalie nodded. "All ready."

As the three of them sat side by side at the counter and ate, Natalie couldn't help but think how right it seemed for them all to be together, sharing a simple family meal and talking of inconsequential things.

Too soon, Alexei scooped up the last bit of ice cream from his bowl and glanced down at his watch. "Look at the time.

I've got to go." Getting up from the counter, he walked over to the phone and called the hotel, asking them to send a limo for him.

Natalie and Jenna cleared the dishes away; then Jenna impulsively walked over to Alexei, who stood lounging against the counter, and beckoned to him to bend down.

Alexei smiled and leaned toward the little girl. His smile quickly turned into a grin as Jenna threw her arms around his neck and hugged him. "Thanks for playing the piano with me," she whispered. "You're better than Mommy."

Alexei laughed out loud at Jenna's traitorous compliment and returned her hug. "I liked playing with you too," he whispered back, "but you'd better not tell your mommy what you just told me. It might make her feel bad."

Jenna glanced over at her mother guiltily. "I won't," she promised. Then, after giving Alexei's cheek a smacking kiss, she released him and skipped out of the room.

Outside, a horn honked and Alexei reached for Natalie's hand, walking with her out to the foyer and picking up his jacket. "When will I see you again?" he asked quietly. "We need to have that talk."

Natalie gulped, knowing that her answer could change the entire course of her life. For the briefest moment, she pictured Jenna sitting at the piano with Alexei, spreading globs of mustard on his hot dog, and exuberantly hugging him and whispering in his ear. And in that infinitesimal speck of time, she knew she had only one choice. She had to tell him the truth, and she had to do it as soon as possible, while tonight's memories were fresh in her mind and before she lost her nerve. "Can you come back after your concert?" she asked softly. "There's something I need to tell you and I want to do it tonight."

Alexei nodded. "It'll be pretty late, but I'll get here as soon as I can."

With a last quick kiss, he hurried off toward the waiting

limo, leaving Natalie to stare after him and ponder the fact that she'd just made one of the most momentous decisions of her life based on how he and his daughter had looked eating hot dogs.

SIXTEEN

Natalie was just tucking Jenna into bed when she heard the doorbell ring downstairs.

"Who's here, Mommy?" Jenna asked sleepily.

"I don't know," Natalie replied, kissing her daughter's cheek and turning out the lamp by her bed. "Maybe it's Susan."

Jenna yawned and turned over on her side, gathering her favorite stuffed dog close to her. "Tell her good night."

"I will, sweetie. Now, go to sleep. You have school tomorrow."

Natalie left Jenna's room and hurried down the staircase, looking out through the peephole set into the heavy front door just as the bell sounded again.

Standing on her front porch was an attractive, dark-haired woman who looked vaguely familiar, although Natalie was sure she had never met her. Still, the woman did not appear to be at all menacing, so after slipping the security chain into its track, Natalie opened the door a crack. "May I help you?"

"Mrs. Saxon?" the other woman asked, her voice betraying a Russian accent.

"Yes?"

"I'm Anya Romanova, Alexei's sister. May I come in?"

Natalie felt her heart begin to beat wildly in her chest. She had no idea why Anya Romanova was at her front door, but she had a feeling that whatever the woman wanted to say to her, she wasn't going to want to hear it.

Forcing a smile, she unhooked the chain and opened the door. "Of course; come in."

Anya stepped into the house, her eyes sweeping around the foyer in a cursory appraisal. "I won't keep you long," she said, focusing her attention back on Natalie, "but there's something I would like to discuss with you."

"Certainly. Why don't we sit down?" Natalie ushered her uninvited guest into the sitting room, and the two of them sat down in chairs facing each other. "Would you like something to drink?" Natalie asked politely.

"No, thank you. This is not a social call."

Natalie's strained smile faded. "I see. Then, may I ask why you're here, Miss Romanova?"

Anya looked her adversary up and down, then drew a deep breath and got directly to the point. "I'm here to talk about Jenna."

Natalie could not conceal her surprise. In the past few minutes, a thousand reasons had crossed her mind for this unexpected call, but she had never considered that Anya had come to talk about Jenna. "My daughter?"

Anya's dark eyes narrowed. "Yes. Your daughter . . . and my brother's."

Natalie's gasp was audible in the quiet room. "Miss Romanova . . ." she began.

Anya held up a staying hand. "Don't bother to deny it, Mrs. Saxon. I have known for several days that Jenna is Alexei's daughter—ever since I saw her play the piano at the Schumann School last week."

Natalie exhaled a nervous little gust of breath and quickly got to her feet, walking over to the sideboard and pouring a splash of bourbon into a glass. "I'm dumbfounded, Miss Romanova," she said without turning around. "Whatever would make you think such a thing?"

"I think it because it's true, as you well know, but I will be happy to tell you just how I reached my conclusion. Jenna has an inherited deformity in the joint of her left thumb that in my country is commonly known as the Romanov Curse."

Natalie whirled around, her fingers gripping her glass so tightly that it shook in her hand. "The Romanov Curse? What a quaint name."

"Quaint it may be, but I can assure you, this family peculiarity is so well documented that there have been several cases of individuals of illegitimate birth successfully using the deformity to prove they are Romanovs."

Natalie set down the untouched glass of bourbon and locked her hands in front of her in an attempt to stop their trembling. "Tell me, Miss Romanova, since this curse, as you call it, seems to be so common in your family, why is it that Alexei doesn't have it and has never even mentioned it to me?"

Anya shrugged. "You're right; he doesn't have it, so why would he mention it? In fact, as far as I know, there is not a single member of my generation who suffers from it. But my grandfather had it, and so did his brother. In addition, in the past few years, three of our cousins' children have been diagnosed with it . . . and now, Jenna. Unfortunately, it appears that the gene that carries this trait has reappeared in the new generation of Romanov children."

"Well, this is all very interesting," Natalie said, again perching on the edge of the chair opposite Anya's, "but I am sure that there are any number of genetic problems that can affect the hand, and, although your family's particular deformity may look similar to the problem Jenna has, that is no reason to think that it is the same syndrome."

Anya looked away for a moment, as if contemplating her next statement, then turned back to Natalie, her eyes blazing with indignation. "Mrs. Saxon, I did not come here to argue with you. You and I both know that what I'm saying is true. Jenna is Alexei's daughter."

"Has Alex noticed Jenna's hand?" Natalie blurted. As soon as the hasty words were out of her mouth, she wanted to kick herself, knowing that her thoughtless blunder had as much as confirmed Anya's suspicions.

Anya did not miss Natalie's gaffe, and she smiled in satisfaction. "No, he has not noticed it, and I have not told him. Nor do I plan to, unless you leave me no other choice."

Natalie gasped. "Are you saying that you've come here to blackmail me?"

"I'm here, Mrs. Saxon, because I love my brother and I will not sit by and watch you destroy him for a second time. I saw what he went through when you played your cruel little game with him before. Now, against all advice, he has become involved with you again, and I am determined to do everything in my power to stop it. If that takes blackmail, then so be it."

"Do you realize that I could have you brought up on charges for what you've just said to me?" Natalie said, her tone threatening.

Anya shrugged. "You probably could, but you won't, because you just admitted that Alexei is Jenna's father and I am confident that you do not want to suffer the consequences of his finding out that fact."

Natalie again stood up and paced over to the window, leaning against the wide sill with her arms crossed over her chest. "Well, that's where you're wrong, Miss Romanova, because I have every intention of telling Alexei about Jenna. And, just so you're not shocked when he tells you, I plan to do so tonight."

"That would be a big mistake on your part," Anya warned. "Do you really believe that if you tell Alexei about Jenna he is going to immediately forgive you for eight years of deception? Because, if you believe that, then you don't know my brother as well as you seem to think you do."

"You have no way of knowing what his reaction will be," Natalie snapped.

"Oh, yes, I do," Anya shot back, "because Alexei is Russian. And Russian men have a great deal of pride. He will not forgive the woman who purposely deprived him of his child. My guess is that once he finds out, he will immediately take steps to gain custody of Jenna so he can take her back to Russia."

"He couldn't do that even if he wanted to," Natalie argued.

Anya laughed, a brittle, mirthless sound that made the hair on the back of Natalie's neck stand up. "You don't think so?

"Tom Saxon is her legal father."

"Until Alexei takes a paternity test." Anya raised her chin. "You seem to forget that Alexei is a very well-known and powerful international figure, not to mention that his talent is such a source of pride to the Russian people that he is considered a hero in our homeland. Do you really want to take on a man with that kind of status, when you will undoubtedly be portrayed as a liar and a whore?"

Natalie drew in an outraged breath, but even as angry as she was, she was terrified that there might be at least a modicum of truth in Anya's cruel words. "What is it that you want from me?"

Anya smiled, knowing that she was close to victory. She walked over to where Natalie still stood by the window, stepping in front of her, until Natalie felt as though she was being pinned. "I want you to break off your relationship with my brother and I want you to do it tonight. I don't care what excuse you give him; just end it. If I hear that you have done as I ask, I will not tell him what I know, and once we leave on Tuesday, your life can go back to being exactly what it was before we arrived in Boston last week."

Walking back over to the sofa, Anya gathered up her coat and purse, then turned back to Natalie. "Are we agreed?"

Despite how upset and frightened Natalie was, twenty generations of Wellesley and Worthington blood suddenly rose to the surface, and when she spoke again, her voice was strong and unwavering. "No, we are not agreed," she spat. "This is between Alexei and myself, and no one, not even you with your threats and your important Russian connections, is going to intimidate me."

"I'm sorry you feel that way," Anya said quietly. "I was

hoping that we could save Alexei, Jenna and even yourself the humiliation of this scandal being made public. But I see now that you are just as selfish as I've always suspected you were. You leave me no choice except to do what I have to do."

"That's right, Miss Romanova," Natalie nodded, walking out to the foyer and pulling open the front door. "You do what you have to do and I will do the same. Now, I would appreciate it if you would leave my house."

With a curt nod, Anya started out the door, then suddenly turned back. "Mrs. Saxon, may I ask you one question before I go?"

Natalie remained silent, which Anya interpreted to be an assent. "Why haven't you ever done anything to correct Jenna's thumb?" she asked. "Surely you must realize that it interferes with her ability to play the piano."

Natalie glared at the other woman in ill-concealed offense. "Not that it's any of your business, but I have taken Jenna to see several bone and joint specialists. Unfortunately, they have all said the same thing—that there is nothing that can be done surgically and our best hope is that Jenna will outgrow the problem as the muscles in her thumb strengthen with age."

Anya shook her head. "That's not going to happen. And there *is* something that can be done surgically. There is a doctor in Moscow who has made it his life's work to find a cure for the Romanov Curse. He has recently operated on several of my cousins' children with excellent results.

"Well, good for him," Natalie snapped. "I guess that just goes to show that your family's problem is not the same as Jenna's. If it was, I'm sure our American doctors would be using the same technique to treat her."

"Your American doctors probably aren't even aware that the procedure exists."

"Miss Romanova, I really do not want to discuss this any further."

"You mean you care so little for your daughter's welfare that you do not even want to know about a possible cure for her problem simply because it is a Russian doctor who discovered it?"

Natalie's eyes narrowed with anger at Anya's insinuation that she did not care about Jenna. "Good night, Miss Romanova," she said firmly.

Anya stared at her for a moment longer; then, with a look that was almost pitying, she turned and walked down the steps. "Good night, Mrs. Saxon."

Alexei let himself into the hotel suite and haphazardly threw his coat over one of the high-backed, upholstered chairs near the door. He glanced at the grandfather's clock in the corner and frowned. It was already eleven-forty.

Damn those reporters, he thought with irritation as he hurried toward his bedroom. He didn't think he was ever going to get out of Symphony Hall tonight. Because of the pictures of he and Natalie in the morning paper, there had been an even bigger, more aggressive swarm of them than usual waiting for him outside his dressing room. It wasn't until Sergei became downright insulting that they had finally backed off enough that he could escape.

He was just opening the bedroom door when he heard Anya's voice calling to him from somewhere deep in the shadows of the living room. "Alexei," she said, setting down the wineglass she was holding and walking toward him, "I want to talk to you."

"Can it wait until tomorrow, Anya? I'm in a hurry right now."

"No, it can't wait. I've been sitting here for over an hour waiting for you to get back from your concert, and I would hope that you would show me the courtesy of giving me a few minutes of your time."

Alexei blew out a frustrated breath but closed the bedroom door and turned toward his sister. "All right. What do you want to talk about?"

Anya did not equivocate. "I saw you hiding in the bedroom this morning so you wouldn't have to face Sophie Svetlanova. Are you so ashamed of what you're doing with Natalie Saxon that you can't even bring yourself to face the wife of one of your employees?"

Alexei rolled his eyes. The last thing he needed right now was to go ten rounds with Anya over a subject as inconsequential as Sophie Svetlanova. "Let's get a few things straight here," he said curtly. "First of all, I was not 'hiding.' I simply decided to wait it out in the bedroom while that fat old woman ate her way through a tray of tarts and bored you with her company, rather than face her prying. Frankly, I see nothing wrong with that decision, since I did not invite her to come here this morning and, therefore, did not feel it was my duty to entertain her."

"I didn't invite her, either," Anya said defensively. "She just showed up. Her arrival was as much a surprise to me as it was to you."

"My point exactly. I don't like surprises, and especially not one that is bound to cause me embarrassment."

"Be that as it may, your behavior was still rude. You know it was you she wanted to talk to."

"I couldn't care less whom she wanted to talk to. I didn't want to talk to her, and that was my choice. And as for you calling me to account yet again for my 'behavior,' I will tell you one more time what I told you before. My behavior is none of your damned business! Stay out of my private life, Anya, or I will send you back to Russia. And don't think for a minute I won't do it. You are here at my invitation, and I will not tolerate any more of your interference in my affairs or any more of your diatribes about my behavior. Now, if you will excuse me, I have plans and I am already late."

"Oh, I know all about your 'plans,' " Anya sneered. "You're on your way over to Natalie Saxon's, even though she's the one who's causing all this trouble between you and everyone who cares about you!" Impulsively, she raced over to where

Alexei was standing and gripped his arm in a desperate attempt to make him listen to her. "Don't you see what's happening, Alexei? Every time that woman enters your life, you completely fall to pieces. You and I almost never argue, and yet, since you've become involved with Natalie again, that's all we've been doing. Doesn't that tell you something?"

Alexei shook Anya's clutching hand off his arm, his eyes black with rage. "What it tells me," he growled, "is that you'd better change your attitude toward Natalie, and damn quickly. And you're right—I *am* on my way over to her house, and the reason I'm going there is to ask her to marry me. And since I'm quite sure she's going to say yes, you'd better start adjusting to her being a permanent part of my life."

Anya stepped back, clapping her hand against her chest. "Alexei, please tell me you're not going to do this."

"I am, so get used to it. There are still some details to work out, but it is my hope that we can be married as soon as possible, and then, when the school term ends, she and Jenna will join me for the remainder of the tour."

Anya sat down on one of the sofas, speechless with dismay. Alexei glared at her for a moment longer, then turned back toward the bedroom, muttering, "This discussion is over."

"Alexei!" Anya cried desperately, "please don't do this. You're making a terrible mistake. That woman doesn't care about you."

"Anya," Alexei thundered, "I'm warning you: not another word. You don't have any idea what you're talking about. Natalie and I have always loved each other, despite all the years we've been apart. Nothing you can say will make me believe differently, and you are risking alienating me permanently if you continue to try."

"But she doesn't love you, Alexei. She doesn't!" Leaping off the sofa, Anya raced over to Alexei and shook him desperately by the shoulders. "Listen to me!" Suddenly, the words with which that she'd threatened Natalie, but which she'd never really planned to say, were out of her mouth. "If Natalie loves you so much, then why hasn't she ever told you about your daughter?"

A deathly silence fell over the room as Alexei stared at his sister, his eyes narrowing dangerously. "What are you talking about?"

"Jenna! She's yours, Alexei. Haven't you realized that?"

Alexei felt the blood begin to drain out of his face, and for a moment, he felt as if the room were spinning. Grabbing onto the back of the sofa, he said quietly, "That's ridiculous, Anya. Jenna belongs to Natalie's ex-husband."

"Oh, Alexei, wake up! Jenna has the Curse, and that means she's your daughter."

"The curse?" Alexei asked dumbly. "What curse?"

"The Romanov Curse, for heaven's sake." Anya looked up into his stricken face and instantly regretted the careless way in which she had just told him this staggering news. Immediately her voice softened. "Alexei, I shouldn't be the one telling you this, but someone has to make you see the truth. Jenna Saxon has Romanov's Syndrome—the same deformity that Grandfather and Uncle Dimitri had. You must know what I'm talking about. That thumb that snaps out of its joint sometimes and makes it impossible to play the piano. The day that I went to Jenna's school to listen to her play, I saw it happen. I even asked her what was wrong, and she told me that she had been born with a 'funny' thumb. She has it, Alexei, and she inherited it from you."

In his mind's eye, Alexei saw Jenna as she'd been that afternoon, sitting next to him on the piano bench and shaking her hand as she told him about the problem she had with her "funny" thumb. But even with this overwhelming evidence placed before him, he could not believe that what Anya was saying was true. If Jenna was his daughter, Natalie would have told him. She couldn't have raised his child for seven years, passing her off to the world as Tom Saxon's daughter. She couldn't be that cruel. Anya had to be wrong. "This is all speculation on your part," he said slowly. "You don't know that anything you're saying is actually true."

Anya's eyes widened in astonishment. He didn't believe her! Despite all she'd just told him, he still didn't believe her. She drew a deep breath, knowing that she was going to have to tell him about her visit to Natalie. Alexei would probably hate her forever for interfering so seriously in his life, but even if he never spoke to her again, it would be worth it if admitting what she'd done prevented him from making the mistake of marrying Natalie Saxon.

"Whether you believe me or not, I know that everything I'm telling you is the truth, Alexei."

"How? How do you know?"

Anya closed her eyes, praying for the strength to get through the next few minutes. "Because Natalie told me it was."

The silence that met this statement was so complete that Anya could hear the clock ticking in the corner of the suite. "When?" Alexei finally asked.

"I . . . I went over to her house tonight after you left for the concert. I confronted her with what I suspected, and she admitted that Jenna was your daughter. She admitted it, Alexei!"

Alexei gripped the back of the sofa so tightly that his knuckles turned white. He wanted to scream, to cry, to hit something—anything to help alleviate the crushing weight that was bearing down on his soul. But he couldn't. The pain of what Anya had just told him was so terrible, so overwhelming in its intensity that he felt paralyzed, unable even to comfort himself with an explosion of anger.

"What happened then?"

"I . . . I just left," Anya lied. She lowered her head, too intimidated by the black expression on Alexei's face to tell him of her threats toward Natalie. When she finally looked up, she was surprised to see that he had turned away and was walking toward his bedroom.

Heedless of the consequences, she rushed after him, catching him by the arm. "Alexei, are you terribly angry with me?"

He looked down at her hand on his arm, then up at her face. Anya sucked in a startled breath, stunned by the flat, dead expression in his eyes. In a voice so quiet and devoid of emotion that she had to lean forward to hear him, he said, "Let go of me, Anya. Right now I am angrier than I've ever been in my life, and I don't want you near me."

"So you're blaming me for this," she cried. "Don't you think Natalie is the one you should be angry with? She's the one who's lied to you all these years."

"I am angry with Natalie," he admitted. "But mostly I'm just angry with myself for being such a damn fool."

Again, he turned toward his bedroom.

"Where are you going?" Anya cried.

"To see Natalie. One way or another, this charade ends tonight."

For what seemed like the hundredth time, Natalie peeked out the front window of her living room, her eyes scanning the length and breadth of Louisburg Square for signs of a car's headlights. There were none.

She glanced over at the clock in the foyer. It was very late, and time to face the fact that Alexei wasn't coming. She'd suspected it for nearly an hour, but now that it was after midnight, she knew it was true.

It was obvious that Anya had made good on her threats. She must have told Alexei everything as soon as he got back from his concert, and he must have decided that he never wanted to see her again.

Natalie sank down in a chair and covered her face with her hands. She couldn't cry anymore. Even though she knew it would probably make her feel better to do so, there were just no more tears left inside her.

She had lost him. Again. The pain that coiled up within her

as she contemplated living the rest of her life without Alexei was so intense that she didn't think she could bear it. And it was her own fault. She had had many opportunities to tell him the truth about Jenna. How could she have been such a fool as to believe that she could pick the moment without someone else learning of her deception and going to him first?

Now her life was ruined and there was no one to blame but herself. Her selfishness, her fear, her foolish belief that she could tell Alexei about Jenna when she was ready had cost her everything. Fate had given her the opportunity to set an old wrong to rights by bringing Alexei back into her life, and still she had let the opportunity slip away.

So, what was she to do now? Anya had said that once Alexei knew that Jenna was his daughter, he would undoubtedly take steps to gain custody of her. Although Natalie didn't really believe that any American court would wrest her daughter away from her and hand her over to a Russian father, the mere thought of the pain such a battle would cause was devastating.

She had to talk to Alex, had to try to make him see that Jenna was better off with her. Better off continuing to live the only life she'd ever known, with the only parent she'd ever known.

The first thing tomorrow, she would call Alex and ask him to meet with her. Surely he wouldn't refuse her that.

Natalie looked up at the clock one last time, then slowly stood up. She needed to get some sleep, and although she doubted that there was much chance for any real rest tonight, she had to try.

With weary steps, she climbed the stairs and walked into her bedroom, shedding her clothes and pulling on a soft, satin and lace nightgown. Walking over to the door, she snapped off the overhead light, then paused, cursing to herself when she noticed that the spectacular crystal chandelier in the foyer was still blazing. With a weary sigh, she pulled on the lace robe that matched her nightgown, slipped on a pair of satin mules, and walked back downstairs.

She had turned out the light and was headed back for the staircase when the headlights of an approaching car suddenly shone through the front curtains. Quickly, she ran over to the window and drew the drapes aside.

Dear God. He was here.

SEVENTEEN

Natalie watched through the window as Alexei stepped out of a taxi and paid the driver, surprised to see that he had taken a cab to her house rather than the hotel limo.

Maybe, she thought hopefully, he was just very late getting back from his concert, and rather than wait for the limo, he had taken a cab to get to her house as quickly as possible. Her heart leaped as she stretched that line of thought to include the possibility that, perhaps, he had been detained at his concert so long that he hadn't even returned to the hotel. Maybe he had come here directly from Symphony Hall and had not even seen Anya.

As Alexei walked up the sidewalk, Natalie realized that she was going to have to open the door without having any idea what his attitude toward her was going to be once she did. She squinted at his legs beneath his coat, trying to ascertain whether he was still wearing his silk tuxedo trousers, but it was too dark to tell. He'd have to take off his coat before she would know for sure if he'd returned to the hotel to change his clothes.

She heard his soft knock and drew a deep, calming breath, plastering what she hoped would pass for a welcoming smile on her face. She opened the door, and in the split second before Alexei stepped into the house, she studied him closely, hoping she could read something in his expression. But he merely looked tired.

"I'm sorry I'm so late," he said, slipping off his coat and draping it over a chair. "I was . . . detained."

"That's all right," Natalie responded, trying hard to conceal her profound relief when she saw that he was, indeed, still dressed in his formal evening wear.

He turned toward her, glancing at her speculatively when he saw that she was clad in nothing but a negligee. "Were you in bed?"

"No," she said quickly. "Would you like a drink?"

"Yes. I could use one."

Natalie felt a frisson of unease prickle at her neck. "Vodka?"

"Fine."

They walked over to the bar in the living room. Natalie took two highball glasses off the shelf, dropped a cube of ice into each and then poured the clear liquor over the cubes, all the while praying that Alexei would not notice how her hands were shaking.

She handed him his glass, then stared at him in astonishment as he downed nearly half of the contents in one long swallow. "Would you mind if I had a cigarette?" he asked.

Natalie's eyebrows rose with alarm at his unexpected question. "Is something the matter?"

"What makes you say that?"

"Well, you told me this morning that you only smoked when you were upset."

Alexei ignored her comment, merely drawing a cigarette out of his shirt pocket and holding it up. "Do you mind?"

Natalie shook her head, then reached up to the bar shelf and lifted down a crystal ashtray, which she held out to him.

Alexei took the ashtray and walked over to a chair, draining his glass as he went. "There's something I need to discuss with you," he said as he sat down and lit the cigarette.

Natalie swallowed. He must know, she thought, struggling to maintain a calm expression. Stiffly, she walked over and sat down on the edge of the sofa. "All right. What do you want to discuss?"

Alexei looked at her for a long moment, willing himself to keep his temper under control. "Based on the way you're dressed, I guess I can assume that you are enjoying the sex we've been having the last couple of days."

Natalie's eyes widened in astonishment at his coarse words. She'd had a difficult time reading his mood since he'd stepped into the house, and even as she'd agreed to this "discussion," she'd not been completely sure that Jenna was what he wanted to talk about. But it never occurred to her that he would begin by making a rude comment about her current state of dress.

Instinctively, she gathered the sheer lace robe more tightly around her and got to her feet. "I'm sorry if seeing me in my robe offends you. I'll go upstairs and get dressed."

Alexei shook his head. "Don't bother. I'm not going to be here that long. I just have one question to ask you, and then I'm leaving. With all the lovemaking we've been doing, what were you planning to do if you got pregnant?"

Natalie stared at him in complete bewilderment. "I . . . I hadn't really thought about it," she admitted. "You've used protection every time."

"You know very well that condoms aren't foolproof."

"But—"

"Let me phrase this another way," he interrupted. "If, in a month or two, you found that you were pregnant, would you tell me this time?"

Natalie closed her eyes as a tidal wave of guilt and despair crashed over her. So he did know. Slowly, she opened her eyes and forced herself to look into Alexei's hard, unyielding face. "I'm sorry," she whispered.

"Oh, Jesus." Alexei groaned, slamming the heels of his hands against his eyes. Even though he'd had no reason to believe that Anya was telling him anything but the truth, hearing Natalie confirm his sister's revelation was almost more than he could bear. "Then it *is* true. She's mine."

"Yes," Natalie choked, "she's yours."

Alexei lifted his head, his face a mask of hurt and betrayal.

"Why, Tasha? Why didn't you tell me? Did you think I didn't deserve to know, or did you hate me so much for going back to Russia that you thought this was a just punishment? Because if that's what you thought, you were right. Nothing you could have done would have hurt more than this."

With a strangled cry, Natalie dropped to her knees next to Alexei's chair, clutching his clenched fists in her hands and looking up at him with anguished eyes. "I never meant to hurt you, Alex, and I wasn't trying to punish you for anything. Please try to understand. I was so young, so scared, so alone. You were gone and I didn't know what to do."

"So you married someone else and passed my baby off as his!" Alexei shouted, his temper finally exploding. "And you told my daughter that her father was dead. My God, is there no end to your lies?"

"That wasn't really a lie," Natalie cried, her voice pleading for understanding. "Don't you see? Jenna has always thought that Tom was her father, and he *is* dead."

"But he's not her father! *I'm* her father and I am very much alive. But that doesn't seem to matter to you. You seem to think that because you've told me you were young and scared and alone, I should understand your decision to deny me my daughter and simply accept it. Well, I can't, Natalie. I can't and I won't. I wrote to you and asked you to marry me, for God's sake. Didn't you ever consider that to be an answer to your problem?" He paused, a bitter laugh escaping him. "Obviously not, since all I got in response to my proposal was a terse little note telling me that you were marrying someone else. And all the time you were carrying my baby. *My baby!*"

Natalie sat back on her heels, tears streaming down her face. "I'm sorry, Alex. I'm so very, very sorry. But please believe me, I was going to tell you tonight."

"Oh, of course you were." Alexei sneered. "That's why you're dressed the way you are . . . to have a serious discussion with me. Or maybe you just thought that if you were pressing that beautiful body of yours against me while you told me, I'd be too aroused to get angry. Well, your ploy didn't work, Natalie. I'm not aroused in the least!"

Natalie gasped at this insult and scrambled to her feet, stepping behind the sofa, as if by putting its bulky mass between them, she could fend off his cruel words. "How dare you say such a thing to me, as if I'm some groupie you picked up at the stage door after one of your concerts! Seducing you has nothing to do with the way I'm dressed. I was going to bed. You told me you were coming over right after your concert. Then your sister paid her little visit and threatened to tell you everything, so when it got so late and you still weren't here, I figured she had done just that and you weren't coming. I finally decided that I'd better get some rest. After all, it's one o'clock in the morning and I have to go to work tomorrow."

Alexei opened his mouth to say something, but Natalie was in no mood to let him interrupt. "And as for my telling you about Jenna, when you were leaving this afternoon, I said that when you came back I had something important to tell you. Don't you remember that?"

Alexei got to his feet and walked back to the bar, refilling his glass nearly to the brim with vodka before answering. "Of course I remember," he growled, turning back to face her, "and isn't it convenient for you to be able to say now that that's what you were going to tell me."

"Are you saying that you think I'm lying?" Natalie gasped.

Alexei skewered her with a withering look. "It wouldn't surprise me if you were."

All the anger on Natalie's face melted away, replaced by a look of defeated finality. "I don't think there's anything left for us to say to each other." With as much dignity as she could muster, she walked out to the foyer and picked up Alexei's coat.

Alexei set down his glass and followed her, his eyes narrowing when he saw her intention. "You are telling me to leave?"

"How astute of you," she answered, holding out his coat.

Alexei grabbed the coat out of her hand and threw it back over the chair. "I'm not leaving until we've finished talking."

"I just told you that we have nothing left to talk about."

"Oh, you're wrong about that, Natalie. We have plenty to talk about."

"Like what?"

"Like *our* daughter's future."

Natalie's eyes darkened with outrage. "How dare you?" she railed. "Who do you think you are to march into my house in the middle of the night and demand your parental rights?"

"I know who I am! I'm Jenna's father!"

"No, that's where *you're* wrong! Jenna isn't *our* daughter, Alexei, she's *my* daughter. You may have been present at her conception, but you have had nothing to do with raising her."

"And whose fault is that?" he shouted. "Don't you realize that if you had had the common decency to tell me you were pregnant, I would have come immediately?"

"To do what?" Natalie shouted back, as incensed now as he was. "To drag me off to Russia to live in some awful communal apartment and spend my days waiting on line for food?"

"Is that what you think I would have asked you to do?"

"Oh, come on, Alex, I watch the news. I know what living in Russia is like."

"Oh, I see." he snorted. "And that makes you an expert on living conditions in my country, right? How very . . . American of you, Natalie."

Natalie sighed and again bent to pick up his coat. "Please, let's stop this. I'm asking you politely, Alexei, to leave my house."

Alexei studied her for a moment, forcing himself to remain unmoved by the distraught, exhausted expression in her blue eyes. "As you wish," he said coldly. "But understand this:

Now that I know that Jenna is mine, I am not going to disappear for eight years as I did before."

"Oh? And just what is it that you think you're going to do? Sue for your paternal rights? Kidnap Jenna and take her back to Russia? What?"

Alexei blew out a long, tired breath. "Right now, I am going to go back to my hotel and think about the best course of action to take to try and mend the mess we have made of our lives. And while I think about that, I am also going to try very hard to find a way not to hate you for what you've done."

Natalie quickly turned her head away, knowing that if she looked Alexei in the face, she would burst into tears. Lunging toward the front door, she yanked it open. "Good night, Alexei."

Alexei shrugged on his coat and walked past her without so much as a sideward glance. "Good-bye, Natalie."

With a greater weariness than she had ever known in her life, Natalie closed the door and collapsed onto a hard chair. She had to go to bed. She was far too tired and far too upset to try to make any sense out of the events of this terrible day.

This terrible day. This terrible day. The phrase pounded through her head like a litany as, for some reason, she remembered a psychology professor she had had in college. He had once told her class of the old European proverb that a man on his deathbed who can remember no more than five terrible days has had a lucky life.

Well, Natalie thought, she was only twenty-nine years old and already she could remember four.

The first had been when she discovered she was pregnant; the second, the loss of her beloved grandmother; the third, the day that Tom had been killed; the fourth was today. Because today was the day that she heard directly from the lips of the only man she had ever loved that he hated her.

And no matter how tragic and sad her other terrible days

had been, nothing could be more devastating than knowing that through her own foolish mistakes, she had turned Alexei Romanov's love for her into loathing.

EIGHTEEN

The insistent sound of a telephone ringing close to her ear roused Natalie from a deep sleep. Without lifting her head off the pillow, she reached out a hand, groping along the top of her bedside table until her fingers closed around the receiver. "Hello?" she mumbled in a hoarse voice.

"Mrs. Saxon? Oh, thank God, you're all right."

"Who is this?"

"It's Marie Bennett at the conservatory. Are you ill, Mrs. Saxon?"

Natalie's eyes snapped open. The conservatory! Why would they be calling her at home? With eyes still blurred with sleep, she squinted at the clock. It was 10:05! My God, she must have turned off her alarm when it went off at seven and gone back to sleep . . . for three hours!

Jenna. Where was Jenna? Bolting upright in bed, Natalie looked around her room, as if expecting to see her daughter lurking somewhere in the shadows.

"Mrs. Saxon? Are you there?"

"Yes," Natalie answered, turning her attention back to the voice on the other end of the line. "I'm here, Marie."

"Are you ill, Mrs. Saxon? You missed your nine and ten o'clock classes. Are you not coming in today?"

Natalie thought fast. "No, I'm not coming in, Marie. I'm sorry that I didn't call earlier, but I'm . . . I'm feeling a bit under the weather. Will you please post a sign on my door?"

"Certainly," Marie answered. "Do you think you'll be well

enough to come in tomorrow, or should I cancel your Tuesday classes too?"

"No, don't do that," Natalie said quickly. "I'm sure I'll be fine by tomorrow."

"All right, Mrs. Saxon. You just rest now and feel better. I'll let your students know that you won't be here the rest of the day."

"Thank you, Marie. Good-bye."

Marie barely got the receiver back on its cradle before she bounded out of her chair and sped down the hall toward the teachers' lounge. Pushing open the door, she stuck her head in, grinning at the assembled throng of women seated inside. "Well, I got hold of her," she sang out, "and she's not coming in. She said she's sick and won't be in till tomorrow. I think she was still in bed when I called."

Most of the women in the room started to laugh, and several of them held out their hands while others slapped dollar bills into them.

"I knew she wouldn't dare show her face this morning," said one elderly professor through tightly pursed lips.

"Who can blame her?" said another, shaking her gray head disapprovingly. "If there were pictures of Alexei Romanov kissing me in the Public Garden on the front page of the Sunday paper, I don't think I could bring myself to face my associates the next day either."

Several of the younger women shot amused glances at each other at the thought of *anyone* kissing that particular lady in the Public Garden, much less Alexei Romanov.

"Oh, come on," said one of the teaching assistants, who was a friend of Natalie's. "It's not like they were doing anything wrong. They were just kissing."

The first woman who had spoken looked over the top of her glasses at Natalie's defender. "There's kissing, young lady, and then there's *kissing*, and what Natalie and that man were doing in that picture definitely falls into the second category."

"Yeah." Another younger woman sighed. "And I, for one, am incredibly jealous."

The younger teachers started to laugh again, causing the two spinsters to rise and glare at them all disapprovingly. "I just don't know about you young people these days," the second one said. "It's no wonder the world is in the state it is, when seemingly respectable young matrons from fine old Boston families cast all their manners and teaching aside and act in such a wanton manner . . . and in public too. It's positively disgraceful!"

Amid many groans and much rolling of eyes, the two old ladies took their leave.

"Do you suppose they *did* it?" one of the assistants asked another.

"Are you kidding?" Her companion laughed. "She probably had that gorgeous Russian lying right next to her when Marie called. I mean, if you had the chance and it was Alexei Romanov doing the asking, wouldn't you do it?"

Many hands were clapped over mouths in embarrassed glee as every head in the room nodded in agreement.

"Well, I wish her nothing but the best," the teacher who had defended Natalie said. "Natalie's one of the nicest people I've ever known, and after all she's been through, with her divorce and then her ex-husband being killed, and having to raise her little girl all by herself, she deserves some happiness."

"And if Alexei Romanov is half as good as he looks," piped up another, "then it's my guess that he's probably giving her plenty of happiness . . . maybe even as we speak!"

Another explosion of laughter rocked the room, and it was many minutes before the teaching staff of the staid Boston Conservatory went back to discussing Beethoven and Brahms.

* * *

Natalie jumped out of bed and rushed down the hall to Jenna's room. Just as she suspected, the child's bed was empty. With a guilty grimace, she flew down the stairs. "Jenna? Jenna, where are you?"

"In here, Mommy."

Natalie raced into the kitchen to find her daughter curled up in a chair in the informal eating area, still wearing her nightgown and watching a game show on TV.

"I'm so sorry, honey," Natalie said. "I overslept."

"I know." Jenna nodded happily. "I even tried to wake you up, but I couldn't."

"And now you're late for school."

"That's okay." Jenna smiled. "We aren't doing anything important today. I mean, it isn't like we have a field trip or anything."

As guilty as she felt, Natalie couldn't help but smile at her daughter's interpretation of "important." "Come on, now," she said, snapping off the television, "get your clothes on while I call your school and try to explain your tardiness."

"They already called," Jenna informed her.

"They did? What did you tell them?"

"That you were asleep and I couldn't wake you up."

"Oh, no." Natalie moaned. "They probably think I'm dead!"

"The secretary asked me if I wanted her to call nine-one-one, but I told her there wasn't anything wrong."

"And she believed you?"

Jenna nodded. "Especially after I told her about how loud you were snoring."

"Great," Natalie muttered. "Now that they know I'm not dead, they probably just think I'm sleeping off a drunk."

The morning had started so hectically that it wasn't until after Natalie called Jenna's school to apologize for her daughter's tardiness and was back upstairs taking a quick shower that she thought about Alexei and all that had transpired the night before.

Maybe I should call him this morning, she thought. *After all, he's leaving for New York tomorrow, and we can't leave things as they are now. I'll go crazy with worry if we can't get something settled between us.*

Briefly, she considered whether she should call her attorney and explain everything to him before calling Alexei, but she decided against it. After all, she reasoned, if she and Alexei could get past the hurtful words they'd exchanged last night and come to some sort of understanding in the more rational light of morning, there would be no need to get lawyers involved. And if they couldn't . . . well, she could always call her attorney after she talked to Alexei.

She drove Jenna to school, accompanying her into the office to get a pass and then suffering through the embarrassment of witnessing the school secretary's knowing smile as she tried to explain to the assistant principal why her daughter was late.

Returning home, she threw down her purse and poured herself a badly needed cup of coffee, drinking it greedily while she paced the length of the huge kitchen and tried to formulate what to say to Alexei when she called him.

She had just poured a second cup of coffee when the phone rang. Guessing that it was Susan, calling to berate her for not phoning her the previous night as she'd promised, Natalie picked up the phone.

"Hello?"

"Hello, Natalie. It's Alexei."

Natalie's breath caught in her throat, causing her to briefly wonder what it was about this man, that just hearing his voice always made her feel as if she couldn't breathe. "Good morning, Alexei." She paused, then added, "How are you?"

"I've been better," he answered curtly. "The reason I'm calling is that I've been talking to Anya this morning, and she mentioned that she told you last night about Dr. Serikoff's treatment for Romanov's Syndrome."

Natalie bit her lower lip as she guessed where this conversation was headed. "Yes, she did," she said warily.

"And what do you think about it?"

Natalie drew a shuddering breath, knowing how important it was that her answer to this question be as tactful as possible. "As I told your sister last night, Alexei, I'm sure that Dr. Serikoff is an excellent physician and I'm pleased to hear that he has developed a procedure to correct joint problems like Jenna's. I plan to tell her physician here in Boston about his research and suggest that maybe he could get in touch with Dr. Serikoff to see if this might be a viable treatment to consider for Jenna."

There was a long silence on the other end of the line; then in an icy voice, Alexei said, "So, what you're saying is that you would not consider letting Dr. Serikoff treat Jenna personally."

"He's in Moscow!" Natalie blurted.

"So? It's a twelve-hour flight from New York, and since Russia is now fully open for travel, there are American airlines making the trip every day."

"That may be," Natalie argued, "but I don't think it's necessary to fly halfway across the world to seek the advice of one particular doctor. After all, we have excellent bone and joint specialists here in America."

"Right," Alexei said sarcastically. "So excellent that all they've done so far to treat Jenna is tell her that she will probably outgrow the problem. Well, believe me, Natalie, she's not going to outgrow it. One of the most cruel aspects of Romanov's Syndrome is that, if left uncorrected, it only gets worse as time goes on. By the time Jenna is in her late thirties, the pain in her hand will probably be so bad that she won't be able to play the piano at all."

"Alexei, we don't even know for a fact that Jenna has Romanov's Syndrome. That's just your sister's guess."

Alexei laughed bitterly. "Well, considering what truths have been uncovered in the past few days, I'd say it's a pretty good one."

Natalie closed her eyes, hating the raw pain she heard in

his voice. "I just told you," she said with a sigh, "I have every intention of telling Jenna's physician about Dr. Serikoff. I'm sure that he will get in touch with him."

"Natalie, this isn't a problem that can be solved with a fax or an E-mail. Dr. Serikoff needs to see Jenna personally to make an accurate diagnosis."

"Well, I am not taking her to Russia," Natalie said with finality.

"All right. If that's your decision, then let me take her."

"Absolutely not."

When Alexei spoke again, all traces of polite civility had vanished from his voice. "She's my daughter too, Natalie," he gritted, "and if you don't care enough about her to want to see her get the treatment she needs, then the least you can do is let me handle it."

"Do you really think that I am going to let you take my daughter back to Russia with you?" Natalie gasped. "Why, once you got her back there, I'd probably never see her again." The second the rash words were out of her mouth, Natalie regretted them, and during the long silence that ensued, she realized that she had undoubtedly just destroyed any chance she would ever have of putting her relationship with Alexei back together. When he finally spoke again, the unconcealed loathing in his voice seemed to confirm her assumption.

"What a fool you are," he said, his voice flat and emotionless. "How could I ever have fallen in love with a woman like you? My daughter deserves better than to have been cursed with a mother who cares so little about her welfare."

"My God, Alexei," Natalie cried, her voice shaking with anger, "how can you say—"

"Let's not talk anymore, Natalie," he interrupted. "It's obvious that we're not going to come to any agreement about this, so let's just leave it to the lawyers. I'll get in touch with mine and I suggest you do the same."

And with that, he hung up.

* * *

"You know, Nat, maybe you *should* consider taking Jenna to Russia to see this doctor."

As always, the first person Natalie had called after her tumultuous conversation with Alexei was Susan. She was devastated to learn that her friend was out on an all-day assignment, but she left a message anyway, and promptly at six o'clock, Susan appeared at her front door, a pizza in one hand and a bottle of wine in the other. The women had eaten dinner with Jenna; then Natalie had sent her daughter upstairs to do her homework.

Now they were finally alone, seated in their favorite spot on Natalie's overstuffed sofa, sipping the excellent red that Susan had brought and discussing the ongoing soap opera that Natalie's life had, in the past week, become.

"After all, what do you have to lose by letting this Dr. Serikoff examine Jenna?" Susan continued. "If he really has spent his entire career perfecting a procedure to correct Jenna's problem, then he's probably the best in the world at it and he's the one she should see."

Natalie stared morosely into her glass of wine. "I'm not taking Jenna to Russia, Susan, and that's the end of it. As I told Alex on the phone, we don't even know for sure that this Romanov thing is what she has."

"Do you really believe that, Nat?"

Natalie shook her head. "No. I'm sure it's exactly what she has, but I still think there must be a doctor somewhere here in the United States who can correct it. I mean, if a Russian doctor could figure out a treatment, why couldn't an American doctor do the same?"

"I'm sure an American doctor could," Susan conceded, "given years of research time devoted exclusively to studying the syndrome."

"Well, for the right fee, Dr. Serikoff would probably be willing to share his expertise with a doctor here. That way, there wouldn't be any necessity for more research. The American doctor could immediately put Serikoff's findings into practice. That's the avenue I'm going to pursue."

"Just don't settle for second best," Susan advised. "If Serikoff is the best, don't let some American guy do the surgery just because his ego tells him that he's good enough to try it."

Natalie's head shot up and she threw Susan an offended glare. "Do you really think I'd settle for second best when it comes to Jenna? My Lord, Sue, you're beginning to sound like Alex! Does everyone think I'm that irresponsible?"

"Nobody thinks you're irresponsible, Nat," Susan soothed. "Not even Alexei, although he'd probably sooner die than admit that right now."

Natalie sighed, a long, defeated sound that was heartbreaking to hear. "I'm sure you're right about that. After our conversation this morning, I think the man truly hates me."

"He doesn't hate you! He's just mad and hurt and confused—just like you are. I still say that you should go over to his hotel tonight and try to work this thing out. I know you had a terrible confrontation this morning on the phone, but maybe if you were face to face . . ."

"We were face to face last night and that was terrible too," Natalie reminded her. "I'm not going over to his hotel and I wish you'd stop suggesting it. It's over between us and I just have to face it. Probably the only time I'll ever see the man again is if he actually makes good his threats and takes me to court over Jenna."

The corner of Susan's mouth pulled up into a wry twist. "I don't believe that. Call me an incurable romantic, but I still think you two were fated to be together, and somehow, some way, that's how you'll end up."

"You *are* an incurable romantic." Natalie smiled. "So, tell me, Miss Romance, how is your love life going these days? It seems like lately all we've talked about is mine."

"My love life?" Susan scoffed. "You mean with Larry the Uncommitted? How do you think it's going? Seven years I've been seeing that man, seven years of waiting for him to pop the question that has probably never entered his mind and probably never will."

"Well, what do you expect when you date an international photojournalist?" Natalie asked, happy to be discussing a subject other than herself for a change. "I mean, how often is he even in the country? Two weeks every three months or so? Would you really want to be married to a man who's gone that much?"

Susan shrugged. "A better question is, do I really want to be married at all? Actually, I think at my age, I'm so set in my ways that I'm probably better off just as I am."

"But don't you ever miss not having children?"

"Who needs children?" Susan chuckled. "After all, I have Tallulah and Egor, and once they actually learn how to run that can opener, I'm planning to take them on the road and make my fortune off them."

Natalie laughed at Susan's joke, then looked over at her friend, surprised to see Susan staring back at her with a serious expression on her face.

"What I would actually like," Susan said, her voice soft and wistful, "is to have what you have."

"What I have? And what's that? Single motherhood, a mediocre teaching career, or a lost love?"

"A great love." Susan sighed. "I'd give anything to be a strong man's one weakness, like you are to Alex."

Natalie shook her head sadly. "Maybe that was true once, but no more. Not after everything that's happened. You know, I should never have gone to his concert last week. I should have just left well enough alone. That way, at least I'd still have the memories of what we had together eight years ago."

"You'd also still have the guilt over Jenna that you've been carrying around for those eight years," Susan reminded her. "Admit it, Natalie: even if things don't work out between you and Alex, isn't it better to have that weight lifted off your shoulders?"

"I don't know," Natalie answered honestly. "Is it?"

"You're the only one who can answer that, sweetie." Susan paused for a moment, sipping her wine and desperately wishing for the comfort of a cigarette. Finally, she pushed away the fond thought of a Winston and turned back to Natalie. "Do you really wish that this past week had never happened?"

In her mind, Natalie saw Alexei as he had looked that day in the Public Gardens, his dark hair blowing in the wind and the laugh lines around his eyes crinkling with pleasure as he'd watched her walking toward him. Then she thought about how he'd looked that night at the hotel as he'd bent over her, his body hard and tanned after spending much of the winter on the beaches of the French Riviera and his mouth soft and seductive as he kissed her and murmured words of love to her in his deep, richly accented voice.

"No, I guess I don't wish it had never happened," she said quietly. "I just wish things could have worked out differently in the end."

Susan set down her empty wineglass and stood up, stretching her arms high over her tall, slender body. "Who knows? Maybe they still will."

Natalie shook her head. "No, they never will."

"Never say never, my dear," Susan advised with a wag of her finger. "As they say, it ain't over till the fat lady sings."

Together, the women walked to Natalie's front door. Susan pulled on her coat, shouted a farewell up the stairs to Jenna, then gave Natalie an affectionate hug.

"Unfortunately, I think I heard her this morning," Natalie whispered as they embraced.

Susan stepped back, looking at her in bewilderment. "Heard who?"

"The fat lady. Just before Alex hung up on me, I definitely heard her warbling in the background."

"Nonsense," Susan scoffed. "That wasn't the fat lady. That was probably just that fat Sophie you were telling me about, choking on one of Alexei's ten dollar Macadamia nuts!"

NINETEEN

Natalie had barely walked through the front doors of the Boston Conservatory of Music on Tuesday morning when Marianne Love, one of the teaching assistants, fell into step beside her.

"How are you feeling?" Marianne asked, her solicitous tone doing little to cover the devilish sparkle in her eyes.

"Better," Natalie answered. "I think it was just a twenty-four-hour bug of some kind."

"That's what I figured it must be." Marianne paused, but when her leading comment elicited no answer from Natalie, she added, "Since you didn't look sick at all when that photographer took those pictures of you at the public Gardens on Saturday."

Natalie stopped in the middle of the hallway and turned toward her friend, her lips pressed together in a tight line. "Marianne . . ."

Marianne reached out and gave Natalie's arm an excited shake, no longer able to control her curiosity. "Oh, come on, Natalie, tell! What's going on between you and Alexei Romanov? Everyone around here is just dying to know."

"There's nothing going on between Mr. Romanov and myself," Natalie said stiffly.

Marianne's heavily lashed brown eyes blinked disbelievingly behind her stylish wire-rimmed glasses.

"He was a professor of mine at Juilliard," Natalie continued. "We hadn't seen each other in years."

To Natalie's surprise, Marianne burst into laughter. "Oh, I see. Of course. That explains everything. I know whenever I happen to run into one of my old profs from B.U., they always greet me by bending me back over their arm and kissing me like Clark Gable in a Forties movie."

Natalie quickly began walking, trying to lose her inquisitive friend, but Marianne was not about to be shaken off so easily and, again, fell into step beside her.

"He didn't bend me back over his arm," Natalie muttered, "and I really don't want to discuss this anymore. I have a class to teach." Reaching her classroom, she raced through the door, saying, "Good-bye, Marianne," before closing it purposefully behind her.

Once she reached the sanctuary of her classroom, Natalie breathed a sigh of relief, figuring her ordeal with the Inquisition was over, but as she set her briefcase down on her desk and turned toward her students, she realized that it had only just begun. Even they were looking at her differently this morning, the boys' glances blatantly speculative and the girls' ranging from mildly amused to overtly envious.

The morning dragged on endlessly as Natalie tried to ignore the looks being thrown at her by each new class that entered her door. Finally, the bell rang signaling the end of the morning's sessions, and she grabbed her purse, hurrying over to the Student Union building to pick up a carton of yogurt for lunch.

As she stepped to the end of the long line for the cashier, she glanced up at one of several televisions positioned high in the corners of the room on triangular wooden shelves. The local noon news was on, and as the anchorman finished a story about the latest in a string of gang killings, the picture flipped to a scene at Logan Airport.

"On a lighter note," the announcer said, "famed Russian pianist Alexei Romanov left Boston this morning after a week of sold-out concerts at Symphony Hall. After a farewell breakfast at the Four Seasons Hotel attended by many local dignitaries, Mr. Romanov and his entourage boarded a jet for New

York, where he will continue his American tour with a series of concerts at Carnegie Hall."

Natalie stared at the television as it showed Alexei boarding the commuter plane, then pausing to wave at the small group of well-wishers who had gathered at the airport to see him off.

As the camera panned in for a last close-up of his handsome face, Natalie felt a now familiar knot of tears gather in her throat. Unable to tear her eyes away from the TV, she was not even aware how far the line had progressed in front of her until a finger stuck her rudely in the back and an impatient male voice said, "Hey, lady, move ahead, would you? I've got to eat and get to a class in twenty minutes."

Mumbling a flustered apology, Natalie took several quick steps to catch up with the end of the line. When she finally reached the cashier, she silently held out her cup of yogurt and a dollar bill.

The cashier, a friendly black woman who had worked at the school as long as anyone could remember, looked up at her, her broad smile fading when she saw Natalie's disconsolate expression and trembling lips. "Why, Ms. Saxon," she said, her lilting Louisiana accent still discernible despite all the years she'd lived in Boston, "what's the matter, honey? You look like you just lost your last friend."

"I'm fine, Patrice," Natalie sniffed, bravely attempting to smile. "It's just spring allergies."

Patrice looked at her doubtfully but did not press her further. Instead, she plucked the money from Natalie's outstretched hand and efficiently made change, handing several coins back to her. "Well, you enjoy that yogurt. Maybe it'll even help those allergies of yours. You know, they say that the bacteria they put in yogurt cures a whole lot of things."

Natalie nodded and moved on, staring at the cup of yogurt as she walked back to her classroom and wishing that its healing powers included the cure for a broken heart.

* * *

It was nearly ten after four by the time Natalie arrived at the Schumann School to pick Jenna up from her piano lesson. She glanced at her watch and frowned as she hurried down the narrow corridor leading to Penelope Pendergast's studio, silently cursing the traffic on Commonwealth Avenue.

When she finally reached Miss Pendergast's room, she was surprised to see that the door was shut. Leaning close, she listened for a moment, hearing the definite sounds of a lesson going on inside. She rapped softly on the door's frosted glass window, then smiled with embarrassment as Miss Pendergast opened it, her expression distinctly annoyed as she peered over the top of her half glasses at the intruder.

"Oh, Mrs. Saxon," Penelope said, her expression immediately changing to one of surprised curiosity. "What can I do for you?"

"I'm sorry I'm late," Natalie apologized, peeking over Penelope's shoulder to see if Jenna was still in the studio. "Is Jenna here?"

"Why, no, she's not," Penelope answered. She stepped aside, as if to prove to Natalie that the child seated at the piano wasn't hers. "We finished her lesson about fifteen minutes ago and I had another lesson starting at four, so when you weren't here, I suggested that she go down to the office to wait for you. I'm surprised you didn't see her there when you came in."

"I must have just missed her," Natalie said. "I'm sorry for interrupting you, Miss Pendergast."

Penelope smiled her forgiveness as Natalie turned and hurried back the way she had come. *How could Jenna have not seen me?* she thought, trying hard to tamp down the prickle of apprehension that was skittering up her spine. *I passed right by the office when I came in.*

Reaching her destination, Natalie pushed through the office's double doors and looked around anxiously for her daughter, but Jenna was nowhere in sight.

Llynwen Osborne, the school secretary, was on the telephone, but seeing Natalie's worried expression, she quickly said, "I'll have to call you back," and hung up.

"Mrs. Saxon," she said pleasantly, rising from her chair. "I didn't expect to see you here today."

"You didn't?" Natalie asked, her eyebrows rising. "I'm here to pick up Jenna. Miss Pendergast said she was waiting for me here."

Llynwen's eyes widened with surprise. "Jenna's not here. She left about fifteen minutes ago."

Natalie sucked in an alarmed breath. "What do you mean, she left? With whom?"

"Well, actually, I don't know who the lady was who picked her up," Llynwen admitted.

Natalie gripped the edge of the counter at which she stood, suddenly feeling light-headed with fear. "Are you saying that you allowed my daughter to leave here with a stranger?"

"I didn't allow anything," Llynwen countered defensively. "Jenna never came into the office. I saw her standing outside on the steps, then a limousine pulled up and a lady got out. She came up the walk and spoke to Jenna. I saw Jenna get into the car with her."

"What?" Natalie cried, her voice now nearly hysterical with terror. "What lady? What did she look like?"

Llynwen clapped her hands over her mouth as the enormity of the situation suddenly dawned on her. "She . . . she was older," she stammered. "Heavyset. Dark hair, I think, but it was hard to tell because she was wearing one of those babushkas."

"Jenna doesn't know anyone like that!"

"But she went with her!" Llynwen protested. "Jenna was . . . she was smiling. She didn't seem scared or anything. In fact, she even took the lady's hand, and they were talking as they walked to the car. I thought it was probably some relative of yours."

"In a limousine?" Natalie said, her eyes enormous in her

ashen face. "When have you ever seen anyone come to pick up Jenna in a limousine?"

"I'm sorry, Mrs. Saxon," Llynwen wailed, very close to tears. "I was busy and . . ."

"Oh, yes, I could see how busy you were when I came in here," Natalie sneered. "Never mind. Just hand me the phone. I have to call the police immediately."

Llynwen grabbed the phone off her desk, nearly wrenching the cord out of the wall in her haste to get it into Natalie's hands.

"Did you hear anything the woman said to Jenna?" Natalie asked as she lifted the receiver.

Llynwen shook her head. "No. I had the window open a little, since it's such a beautiful afternoon, but I couldn't hear their conversation. I did notice, though, that the lady sounded like she had a foreign accent."

Natalie paused with the phone halfway to her ear. "A foreign accent?" She gasped. "And she was wearing a babushka?"

Llynwen nodded eagerly. "Yes, I think that's what they're called. You know, one of those dowdy scarves that you see Russian women wearing." Suddenly her eyes widened. "That would account for her accent! I bet the lady was Russian!"

Very slowly, Natalie set the phone back on its cradle. "Alexei," she whispered.

Llynwen looked at her aghast. "Mrs. Saxon, do you think that Alexei Romanov has something to do with Jenna's disappearance?"

"I think he has everything to do with it!" Natalie cried. *"My God, he's kidnapped my daughter!"*

TWENTY

Natalie tore out the front doors of the Schumann School and headed for her car at a dead run. Awkwardly, she fumbled through her purse, finally pulling out her car keys and her cellular phone. She unlocked the car door with shaking fingers, then threw herself into the front seat, peeling out of the school's parking lot as she punched Susan's work number into the phone.

As usual, her friend was not at her desk, but after Natalie explained to the bored-sounding secretary that the call was an emergency, she finally agreed to track her down. After what seemed like an eternity, Susan came on the line.

"Susan Bedford."

"Alexei's taken Jenna!"

"What?"

"Today. He got to the Schumann School this afternoon before I did and he stole her."

"Slow down, Nat. You're babbling like a madwoman. You say Jenna's missing and you think Alexei took her?"

"Yes! Aren't you listening?"

There was a brief silence at the other end of the line as Susan digested this startling announcement; then in a calm, careful voice, she said, "Okay, start over, Natalie, and tell me everything that's happened."

As succinctly as her overwrought mind would allow, Natalie explained all that had transpired in the last hour, finishing with Llynwen Osborne's admission that Jenna had left the Schu-

mann School in a limousine with a woman wearing a babushka.

"Where are you now?" Susan asked.

"I'm in the car."

Susan shot out of her chair, her calm demeanor forgotten.
"Do you mean to tell me you're driving?"

The tenuous hold that Natalie had on her composure finally
broke and in a strangled voice she sobbed. "Yes, I'm driving.
Haven't you heard a word I've said? Alexei has stolen Jenna
and I have to find her!"

In as normal a tone as she could muster, Susan commanded,
"Natalie, I want you to pull off to the side of the road right
now. Do you understand me? You're too upset to be driving.
Now, pull off before you have an accident."

"All right," Natalie agreed, knowing her friend was right.
She signaled with her right blinker, then pulled off on to the
shoulder of the busy highway. "Okay, I'm over."

Susan exhaled a sigh of relief. "Good. Now, tell me, what
time do you think Alexei took Jenna?"

"This afternoon, right before four o'clock."

"Then it couldn't have been Alexei, Natalie, because he left
for New York this morning. I even saw a news item today that
showed him getting on the plane."

"I know that"—Natalie snorted—"but that doesn't mean
he's not at the bottom of this. He probably sent some emissary
of his to pick her up. Llynwen Osborne said it was an older,
fat woman. I'll bet it was Sophie."

"You mean the Macadamia nut thief?"

"Yes. As a matter of fact, now that I think about it, I'm
sure that's who it was."

"Why do you think it was her?"

"First of all, she always wears babushkas. Secondly, Llynwen said Jenna seemed to know the woman who came to get
her, and Jenna saw Sophie talking to me the night she and I
went to Alexei's concert. Sophie probably told her that she was
taking her to see Alexei, so Jenna went along without giving

it a second thought. I mean, I've talked and talked to Jenna about the importance of never speaking to strangers and especially never getting into a car with one. There was no force used to coerce her into the car, so Jenna must have known the woman. It had to be Sophie."

"Well, at least you know that Jenna isn't in any danger," Susan said, "although I still can't believe that Alexei had anything to do with this. He has to know that doing something as outrageous as kidnapping an American child could turn into a full-fledged international incident, even if she *is* his daughter."

"I think you just hit the nail on the head, Susan. It probably hasn't even occurred to Alexei that anyone would consider this a kidnapping. All he's thinking about is that he's Jenna's father and, therefore, he has a right to take her if he wants to."

"That's ridiculous, Natalie. Alexei's a sophisticated man. He knows that he doesn't have any legal rights as far as Jenna is concerned unless a court grants them. If he wasn't aware of that, then why would he have threatened you with court action the other day? He told you that he was going to get an attorney. Why would he have said that if he was planning to kidnap her?"

Natalie leaned her forehead against the steering wheel of her car, shaking her head in misery. "I don't know what he's thinking, Susan. All I know is that if Sophie took Jenna, she did it at Alexei's request. I'm wasting time sitting here talking about this. We know Alexei has left for New York, so if Sophie has Jenna, that must be where she's headed. I've got to get to the airport and catch a New York shuttle before my daughter thinks I've abandoned her to a bunch of strangers!"

Susan gritted her teeth, trying to think of anything she could say that would prevent Natalie from taking off on this wild-goose chase. "Where are you going once you get to New York?" she demanded. "Do you even know where Alexei is staying?"

"No," Natalie admitted. "I was hoping you could help me with that."

"Me?"

"Yes. You must know people in the New York press. Certainly somebody there will know where Alexei is staying. You knew where he was staying while he was in Boston, didn't you?"

"Well, yes."

"All right, then. Here's what we need to do. First, find out where Alexei is staying. Then, I'd appreciate it if you'd go over to my house, just in case the man comes to his senses and calls. Meanwhile, I'll fly to New York and call you as soon as I get there. With any luck, Jenna and I will be back late tonight."

"Natalie, are you sure you want to do this?"

"Of course I'm sure! If Jenna were your daughter, wouldn't you?"

Reluctantly, Susan nodded, knowing that as bizarre as Natalie's plans sounded, if she were in her place, she'd do exactly the same thing. "Okay." She sighed. "I'll go over to your house, but before I do, I think I'll stop at the Four Seasons and see if Sophie is still there. If she is, maybe somebody there has seen her with Jenna this afternoon. It's even possible that she's still in Boston."

"That's a good idea," Natalie agreed, "although I'm sure Sophie has left town by now. She probably figures that I'll view this as a simple kidnapping and will have the Boston authorities looking for Jenna here, so it would make sense that she would get her out of town as quickly as possible. Now, I've got to go. Wish me luck. I'll call you as soon as I land in New York."

Susan hung up the phone, then leaned back in her chair, shaking her head in disbelief at all that had happened during the past week in Natalie's normally humdrum life. She reached out and pulled her Rolodex toward her, looking for the name

of the music editor at the *New York Times,* all the while thinking that maybe unexciting old Larry wasn't so bad, after all.

Less than two hours later, Natalie's home phone rang. Susan,
who had spent a half hour pacing around the Louisburg Square
town house, dived to answer it.

"Okay, I'm here," Natalie said without preamble. "Did you
find out where Alexei is staying?"

"Yes," Susan answered. "He's at the Marriott Marquis in
Times Square. But he's probably not there now, because he
has a concert scheduled tonight at Carnegie Hall."

Natalie glanced at her watch and frowned. Susan was right.
It was seven-fifteen, and Alexei was undoubtedly at the concert
hall. "I guess I'll just go to the hotel and wait for him there.
Did you find out anything about Sophie?"

" 'Fraid not." Susan sighed. "The Four Seasons is very strict
about guest confidentiality. The front desk wouldn't even tell
me if she was still registered. I tried bribing a bellman, but
that didn't do any good either. I did find out one thing,
though."

"What's that?" Natalie asked hopefully.

"I called a friend of mine who works for one of the TV
stations here and asked him to look at the videotape they took
of Alexei's departure this morning. He says that from the foot-
age they shot, there's no sign of a fat older woman being
among Alexei's entourage."

"So, Sophie *did* stay in Boston after Alex left."

"Looks like it," Susan agreed. "And Natalie, there's one
more thing you should know."

"What?"

Susan swallowed hard, hating to have to tell Natalie the dis-
turbing news she'd learned from her housekeeper. "I called
Moira tonight and asked her if anything unusual happened today while she was here cleaning."

"Yes?" Natalie prodded, her voice suddenly heavy with dread.

"She said an older, foreign-sounding woman came to the door this morning and said that she was from Jenna's school and she had to pick up some clothes that Jenna was supposed to bring with her today for a field trip."

"Jenna didn't have a field trip today."

"Exactly," Susan answered. "Anyway, Moira said the woman went up to Jenna's room and came back a few minutes later carrying a small bag that appeared to have clothes in it."

"And Moira didn't call Jenna's school to confirm this? She just let this woman go into my daughter's room?"

"I guess so." Susan sighed.

"Well, she's fired."

"Natalie, I'm not finished."

"Oh, God, you mean there's more?"

"Yes. After I talked to Moira, I went up and looked around Jenna's room. It appears that the woman did take a bunch of her clothes, but I think she also took something else."

"What?" Natalie asked.

Susan drew a deep breath. "Her passport."

"Oh, my God!" Natalie cried. "Are you sure?"

"Don't you keep it in the farthest left pigeonhole in Jenna's desk?"

"Yes, always."

"Well, it's not there."

"He's going to take her to Russia!" Natalie shrieked, turning her back on the crowds of passengers walking down the busy concourse. "I swear, I'll kill him when I see him!"

"Now, Natalie, just settle down. You know Alexei is in New York, and if he's there, Jenna must be too. In the meantime, do you want me to call the Boston police? I haven't so far, but maybe we should notify them . . . you know, just in case Jenna isn't . . . where we think she is.

Natalie thought about this for a moment, then said, "No, don't call them yet. I want to talk to Alex first. I'm positive

Jenna's with him. There are just too many coincidences for it to be otherwise. And, if she is, then there's no reason to get the authorities involved. And, if she's not . . ."

"You're right, she is," Susan said positively. "Now, don't panic. Just go over to the Marriott and wait for Alexei. I'll stay here at your house till I hear from you, so call me as soon as you know anything."

"I will," Natalie promised."

She hung up, then slumped wearily against the wall next to the pay phone. How was she ever going to stand waiting for three hours until Alexei came back to the hotel from his concert? She thought briefly about going directly to Carnegie Hall, but she knew there was little chance that she would be allowed anywhere near Alexei's dressing room without a backstage pass. It didn't make sense that he would have Jenna at the concert with him anyway. If he had, indeed, kidnapped her, as she was sure he had, then, certainly, he wouldn't be foolish enough to parade her around in public.

Rubbing her forehead to try to alleviate the persistent ache that pounded there, Natalie pushed off from the wall and headed for the nearest taxi stand. One way or another, she was going to find her daughter, and then she was going to punish the man who had taken her, even if she had to go all the way to Moscow to do it.

Natalie saw Alexei before he saw her. Leaping up from the plush lobby chair on which she was sitting, she raced over to him as he headed for the elevators, grabbing him by the arm and spinning him around. "Where is my daughter?" she demanded, oblivious to the many heads that suddenly turned in their direction. "What have you done with her?"

"Natalie!" Alexei exclaimed, his face registering genuine surprise at seeing her. "What are you doing here?"

"What do you think I'm doing here? I've come to take Jenna home."

Alexei shook his head in bewilderment. "What are you talking about?"

"Did you really think I wouldn't figure it out, Alex? Did you really think you'd get away with it?" With a cry of rage, Natalie began pounding on his chest. "You arrogant, egotistical bastard! What have you done with my little girl?"

"Stop this!" Alexei commanded, trying to grab Natalie's wrists as she continued to rain blows on him. *"Natalie, stop this!"* Finally gaining control of her flailing arms, Alexei hauled her up against him. "What is the matter with you? Have you lost your mind?"

Natalie stepped back, wrenching her arms out of his grasp and then drawing back to slap him sharply across the face. "Don't touch me," she snarled. "Don't you ever touch me! Just give me my daughter back."

Alexei threw his arms wide in a gesture of confusion. "What are you talking about?" Then, as the accusations Natalie was hurling at him finally sank in, he gasped, his eyes widening with shock and distress. "My God, are you saying someone has taken Jenna?"

"You know very well that someone has taken Jenna because that someone is you!" Natalie railed.

"Me! I did not!"

"Maybe not directly, but you sent one of your Russian minions to do it for you, and don't try to deny it."

"Minions?" Alexei asked. "What is a minion?" Briefly, he glanced over at Yuri, who was watching the entire scene with openmouthed disbelief. Yuri looked back at him and shrugged, causing Alexei to again turn to Natalie.

"Oh, don't play that I-don't-understand-what-you're-saying game with me," Natalie shrieked. "You know very well that you sent Sophie to steal Jenna from her school this afternoon."

"Sophie!" Alexei gasped. "Sophie Svetlanova?"

"Of course, Sophie Svetlanova. How many other Sophies do you have in your little band of kidnappers?"

Alexei stared at Natalie for another moment; then he whirled around, his eyes scanning the ever-growing crowd around them until he found his publicist, Sergei Svetlanov, on the other side of the lobby. Striding over to Sergei, Alexei began speaking to him in rapid Russian, pointing at Natalie and then jabbing the older man's chest with his index finger.

Natalie watched closely as Alexei grilled Sergei, her eyes narrowing when she saw Sergei shake his head and shrug. She was just about ready to walk over and start accusing the man herself when Alexei suddenly turned on his heel and walked back to her. "He says he knows nothing about this," he said, "but we will get to the bottom of it, I promise you."

"You bet we will," Natalie gritted, "or the police will, and that I promise *you.*"

Alexei turned back to glance at Sergei again, seeming, for the first time, to notice the crowd that had gathered around them. Taking Natalie's arm, he began propelling her toward the elevators. "Come on; let's go upstairs to my suite. There's no sense in the entire New York press corps knowing about this."

"Let go of me!" Natalie spat, but she continued to walk next to him, knowing that what he said was true. It would only make matters worse if the press got wind of this debacle.

Alexei pressed the elevator button, then waited in silence until the glass-enclosed car arrived. He followed Natalie onto the elevator, then held up his hands as several other people sought to join them. "Please," he beseeched, "we have a problem here. If you could just wait for the next car . . ." Before anyone had time to protest, the doors closed and the elevator began to rise. Alexei pulled a coded card out of his pocket, then reached forward and pushed the button marked "45."

"How could you have done this?" Natalie asked suddenly.

"I'm not going to discuss this in a glass elevator with half of New York City staring up at us," he returned. "We'll talk once we get to the suite."

Natalie turned her back on him and crossed her arms over

her chest. They stood quietly for a few moments as the elevator continued its ascent; then, without turning around, she said, "Do you really expect me to believe that you had nothing to do with taking Jenna?"

"I didn't have anything to do with it," he answered flatly, "but I think I know who did."

Natalie whirled around to face him. "Who?"

"Anya."

"Anya! What would she want with my daughter?"

"It's what she wants with *my* daughter," Alexei answered.

"Are you saying that Anya took Jenna just because you're her father?"

Alexei held up his hands. "Natalie, please, just wait until we get upstairs. Then we'll sort all of this out."

Natalie turned back toward the front of the elevator, again presenting her back to Alexei. "Oh, we'll sort it out, all right. And once I call the authorities, your sister is going to spend the next ten years in an American prison."

Alexei's lips thinned at her rash threat, but he remained silent. He knew she was terrified about Jenna and furious with him since, despite his protestations, she undoubtedly still thought he was at the bottom of the abduction.

In truth, Alexei knew nothing about the child's disappearance. However, Natalie's description, coupled with Sergei's vague answers when asked about Sophie's whereabouts, presented strong evidence that Sophie had, indeed, been the one who had picked Jenna up from her school. If that was the case, then Anya was almost certainly at the bottom of this. As angry as Alexei was with his sister, he was nevertheless greatly relieved to think that Jenna was with her and, therefore, safe.

The elevator finally reached the forty-fifth floor of the huge hotel and Alexei stepped off, taking Natalie's elbow and ushering her down a long hallway toward his suite. Three times, Natalie tried to shake off his guiding hand, but Alexei refused

to free her. It wasn't until they were inside the luxurious room
that he finally released her.

"I have some calls to make," he said, and strode off into
one of the suite's two bedrooms, closing the door behind him.

Natalie started after him but then thought better of it. Let
him make his calls. If, by chance, he *was* telling her the truth
when he said he wasn't involved in Jenna's disappearance,
then, perhaps, the calls he was making would help to locate
her. She paced over to the suite's huge picture windows and
gazed out, but she was far too distraught to be able to appreciate the spectacular view of the brightly lit Chrysler and Em-
pire State buildings.

It seemed like an eternity that Alexei stayed in the bedroom.
Several times, Natalie walked over and pressed her ear against
the door, but every time she did, he was speaking in Russian
and she could understand nothing. It was apparent to her, however, that he was placing more than one call, since the inflec-
tions in his voice ranged from anger to impatience to an almost
diplomatic tone.

Finally, he reentered the suite's living room. Natalie whirled
around to face him as he stepped through the door, her eyes
questioning. "Well?"

"I was right. Anya has her."

Natalie threw her head back and blew out a long breath. "I
guess that's good news. At least she's not in the hands of some
terrorist or ransom-seeker. Did Anya tell you why she felt she
had the right to steal *my* daughter?"

Alexei ignored her accusatory tone and simply shook his
head. "I didn't speak to Anya."

Natalie's eyes widened. "You didn't? Then, how do you
know that she's the one . . ."

"I know," Alexei interrupted.

Natalie planted her hands on her hips and glared at him.
"Well, where are they? Do you know that?"

Alexei hesitated for a moment, then stepped forward until

he was standing directly in front of her. "They're on a plane, Natalie. On their way to Moscow."

Natalie's jaw dropped in stunned disbelief. "To Moscow! Oh, my God, I'll never see her again!"

"That's not true," Alexei said, reaching out to touch her face, then quickly changing his mind and dropping his hand to his side. "I've already made flight reservations for us. We leave for Moscow tomorrow morning."

"But how can I go to Moscow?" Natalie asked, throwing her arms wide. "I mean, I have my passport with me, but don't you need a visa or something?"

"Don't worry about that," Alexei answered. "I've made all the necessary arrangements."

"Moscow," Natalie moaned, sinking down onto a sofa. "My poor baby . . . she must be so scared, so confused."

Alexei sat down next to her and gently took her hands in his. "Jenna's fine, Tasha. She's not scared and she's not confused. As a matter of fact, she thinks this is all a great adventure."

Natalie wrenched her hands out of his, her eyes blazing. "Oh? And just how do you know that?"

"I talked to Sophie. She saw Anya and Jenna off at the airport, and she said that Jenna was very excited. Anya promised to take her to see all the sights, and Jenna couldn't wait to get on the plane."

"Sophie!" Natalie spat, pushing herself off the sofa, then turning to stare down at Alexei. "Just wait till I get my hands on that old cow. By the time I'm done with her, she'll rue the day she ever heard Jenna's name. And as for your sister . . ."

"Natalie, Natalie!" Alexei pleaded, standing up and cupping his hands firmly around her upper arms. "Listen to me. I know how angry and upset you are, and I realize there is probably nothing I can say to change your feelings, but now that I understand Anya's motive for doing what she did . . ."

"Motive!" Natalie cried, trying to twist out of his grasp. "She had a motive?"

"Yes."

Suddenly, Natalie stopped fighting and looked up at Alexei with beseeching eyes. "Then, tell me, Alex. Why would she do this? Why would she take my little girl?"

"To get her hand fixed," Alexei said quietly.

"What?"

"She took Jenna to Moscow to have Dr. Serikoff examine her thumb and see if his surgical procedure could correct her problem."

"But he can't do that!" Natalie protested. "Jenna's a minor. Doesn't there have to be parental consent in Russia before surgery is performed?"

"Ordinarily, yes." Alexei nodded. "But the Romanov family is very influential and sometimes . . . exceptions are made."

A look of startled horror crossed Natalie's face. "My God, Alex, are you saying that some foreign doctor whom I've never even met is going to put my daughter under the knife?"

"No, he's not," Alexei assured her. "I just talked to Serikoff, and he promised me that he would do nothing until we arrive."

"You did that? And he promised?"

Alexei nodded.

"Thank you," she croaked. "I appreciate your concern for Jenna . . . and for me."

Alexei stared at Natalie for a long moment, his heart feeling as if it was going to burst out of his chest. Never had his feelings for her been as profound as they were at this moment. Even after all she'd been through today, thinking that Jenna had been kidnapped, making the headlong flight to New York to confront him when she thought he was behind it, finding out that her daughter was halfway across the world—*still,* she had thanked him for helping her with a situation he had indirectly caused.

Alexei realized that he had never known a more noble or invincible woman and yet, as he gazed down into her exhausted eyes, there was a vulnerability in their sea blue depths that made him want to protect her—to prevent any harm or unhappiness from ever coming to her or to the beautiful child they had created together.

In that moment Alexei knew that despite everything that had happened between them—all the pain they had caused each other, all the harsh words they had exchanged, all the rash threats they had hurled at each other in the heat of anger— there would never be another woman for him.

He loved her. He had always loved her and he always would. All that remained now was to make Natalie believe that, and to pray that despite all the heartache they had shared, she still loved him in return.

To his surprise, Natalie's eyes suddenly filled with tears and with a long, shuddering sigh, she buried her face in his shoulder. "So, you're sure Jenna's all right?"

"Yes, darling," he murmured, "she's fine."

"I've been so worried," she sobbed. "So scared that something had happened to her."

Alexei wrapped his arms around Natalie's back, pulling her close. "Tasha, sweetheart, don't cry. Nothing has happened to Jenna, and nothing is going to. In a couple of hours, she'll be at my apartment in Moscow, safely tucked in bed and probably dreaming of concertos and rhapsodies." Gently, he kissed her soft, freesia-scented hair, then laid his cheek on the top of her head. *Daragaya,"* he crooned. "Please don't cry. We'll go get our little girl tomorrow and everything will be all right."

He led her back to the sofa and gently pulled her down next to him. "Tasha, look at me," he pleaded.

She looked up, sniffing loudly and wiping her eyes with the backs of her hands.

"There's one thing we have to get settled between us before any more time passes. I didn't know anything about what Anya was planning. Nothing. Please believe me. If I had known, I would have stopped her."

Natalie studied him for a long moment, knowing by the unflinching sincerity in his dark eyes that he was telling her the truth. "I believe you," she said softly.

With a groan of relief, Alexei pulled her to him, placing a finger under her chin and tilting her head back until their eyes met. "I love you," he whispered. "I'd never do anything to hurt either you or Jenna. Please believe that too."

"I do, Alex," Natalie whispered. "And . . . and despite all the cruel things we've said to each other and all the mistakes we've made, I love you too."

"Thank God," Alexei breathed; then, slowly, he lowered his mouth to cover hers. He felt Natalie's lips, still wet with tears, part beneath his, and with a moan of pleasure, he pulled her closer and deepened the kiss. Their lips caressed, their tongues entwined, and their breath mingled in a romantic, erotic blending that left them both shaking and breathless when they finally broke apart.

Alexei looked down into Natalie's upturned face, his eyes dark and serious. "Marry me, Tasha," he murmured. "I've loved you for as long as I can remember and I want to be your husband. I want you and Jenna and me to have a home together somewhere. I want to have more babies with you, and I want to grow old with you. Please, Natalie, say you'll marry me."

Another sob escaped from deep within Natalie. "There are still so many problems. . . ."

Gently, Alex laid two fingers across her lips. "Do you love me?" he asked.

Closing her eyes, Natalie nodded. "Yes. I've loved you since I was a girl. There's never been anyone else."

For the briefest moment, a smile lit Alexei's handsome face; then he sobered again. "Not even Tom?"

"He was a friend," Natalie whispered, staring into Alexei's dark eyes as hers pleaded for understanding. "A dear, dear friend, but that was all. You're the only man I've ever loved."

"Then, that's all that matters."

Natalie lowered her head. "Do you really think love is enough, Alex? There are so many other things between us. So much pain . . . so much heartache."

Again, he lifted her head until their eyes met. "Listen to me, *daragaya*. That's in the past. There is nothing between us now except our daughter and the fact that we love each other. I know you're worried about where we'll live, but, Natalie, I swear to you, I'd live in Timbuktu if you were there."

"Oh, Alex." Natalie sighed. "I do love you so . . ."

"Then you'll marry me?"

Natalie looked up into his handsome face, then threw her arms around his neck. "Yes." She nodded. "Yes, I'll marry you."

"Do you really mean it, Tasha?"

"Yes, I mean it." She laughed. "Yes, yes, *yes!*"

"Finally!" Alexei shouted. He jumped up and lifted Natalie off the sofa, swinging her around in huge circles as he laughed and kissed her in unabashed exultation.

Finally, they ceased their mad dance and collapsed back onto the sofa. Alexei looked down at his watch, then up at Natalie. "It's very late," he whispered, "and we've got a long, long flight ahead of us tomorrow. Don't you think we should probably go to bed?"

Natalie blushed at his suggestion but nodded. "You know what?" she whispered.

"What?"

"I don't have any clothes with me. I didn't even pack a bag before I left Boston, and the only thing I have with me is what I have on."

"Don't worry." Alexei grinned. "I have an extra toothbrush."

"Well, that's a start, but what am I going to wear tomorrow and the next day and the next?"

Alexei shrugged. "There are lots of shops in the hotel. Tomorrow morning before we leave, we'll stop and get you whatever you need. We're only going to be gone a few days, so we should be able to find enough things to tide you over."

"But what about tonight?" Natalie asked, trying hard to hold back a smile. "I don't have anything to wear tonight and it's so late, all the shops are closed. That's a problem."

Alexei reached over and pulled her unresisting body across his lap. "I don't call that a problem." He chuckled as he bent his head to kiss her. "I call that a dream come true."

TWENTY-ONE

Despite how anxious Alexei was to celebrate their engagement, Natalie insisted that he go sit on the other side of the room while she called Susan. The friends' conversation lasted only a few minutes, but to Alexei, it seemed as though they talked forever.

When Natalie finally put down the phone, he jumped up and grabbed her by the hand, heading straight for the bedroom. But they barely made it through the door before he turned and pulled her close, covering her mouth in a long, passionate kiss. "I cannot believe that after all these years, you are finally going to be my wife," he breathed, reluctant to lift his lips from hers even long enough to utter his feelings.

"And I can't believe that after all these years, I'm finally going to marry the man I've always loved," Natalie returned.

Alexei drew her lower lip into his mouth, teasing it with the tip of his tongue as he pulled her ivory silk blouse out of the waistband of her skirt and began sensuously rubbing his hands up her back. "I've waited so long for you," he whispered, beginning to kiss her again, "and now, finally, you're really mine."

Natalie sighed and arched her back as he stroked its sleek length, pressing her full breasts against his chest. "I've always been yours, Alex. Always yours."

As his excitement mounted, Alexei moved his hands forward under the blouse, cupping Natalie's breasts as he continued to kiss her.

"Let me take this off," Natalie pleaded, wanting to feel his hands against her bare skin. With trembling fingers, she unbuttoned her blouse and slid it off her shoulders, then reached behind her and unhooked her bra, lowering the satin straps until the delicate garment dropped to the floor.

Raising her eyes, she looked into Alexei's handsome, chiseled face, her breath coming fast and uneven as she stood before him, naked from the waist up.

Alexei stared back at her, hungrily drinking in the sight of her beautiful face, her blond hair brushing softly against her shoulders, and her luscious breasts. Lowering his head, he kissed her neck, then allowed his mouth to travel downward. Cupping her breasts in his hands, he teased a nipple with his tongue, causing it to harden and peak as Natalie moaned with pleasure.

Wanting to return his passionate caresses, Natalie reached up and unbuttoned his shirt, spreading it wide and then leaning forward to place nibbling little kisses on his chest.

As her tongue toyed provocatively with his sensitive, flat nipples, Alexei groaned and lowered his hands to her buttocks, pulling her hard against him so she could feel his arousal.

Natalie's reaction was immediate. She took a step back, hastily shedding her skirt, her hose, and her panties until all her clothes lay in a forgotten pool at her feet.

Alexei watched her disrobe, his eyes aflame and lusting; then, with a speed that would have done credit to a teenager, he divested himself of the rest of his clothes and pulled her back into his arms.

"You are the most beautiful woman on earth," he said, burying his face in her neck as he backed her up to the bed.

Natalie smiled at his compliment, then wrapped her arms around his neck as he lowered her to the soft mattress. They lay stretched out on the bed for several moments, the entire length of their bodies touching as they kissed and stroked each other. Then Alexei turned onto his back, pulling Natalie over on top of him. Placing his hands under her arms, he lifted her until her breasts hovered tantalizingly just above his mouth.

"You haven't changed a bit." She laughed, rubbing the tips of her breasts across his soft lips. "You always were a breast man."

He smiled. "And yours are even more beautiful now than they used to be."

"Just a little bigger," she whispered. "I've had a baby, remember?"

Alexei closed his eyes and nodded. "Our baby. Our daughter. Now that I know that, I can't wait to see her again."

Natalie smiled, sublimely happy in the knowledge that she, Alexei, and Jenna were finally going to be together, as fate had intended them to be.

Bracing her hands on either side of his hips, she began moving down the length of his body, her lips and tongue trailing down his chest, past the firm muscles of his stomach and tightly ribbed abdomen until she reached his thick, hard length. She stroked him seductively, smiling with feminine satisfaction when he sighed with pleasure. Then she lowered her head and drew him into her mouth, her tongue and lips erotically swirling and caressing him.

"Oh, God, Tasha, what you do to me," he panted. The last few words of his hoarse cry were uttered in Russian, causing Natalie to look up at him.

"Now I know I'm doing something right," she murmured, crawling up the bed and crouching over him.

"How do you know that?" Alexei asked, punctuating each word with a fiery kiss.

"Because you're speaking Russian, and you always did that when you were really excited." She reached down to fondle him again.

"That's because," he gasped, "when you're doing—this—I can't think enough to—speak English!"

Natalie laughed, a sexy, throaty sound that, coupled with her stroking fingers, nearly pushed Alexei past the brink of his control. "And how about when I do this?" she asked. Throwing her leg over his hips, she sat down on him.

Alexei's eyes flew open as he plunged deep into her satiny warmth, his expression betraying his surprise at her boldness. Natalie answered by tightening her muscles around him and throwing him a smile that was so hot and eager that he felt like he might explode.

With a groan of surrender, he gave himself over to her, totally captivated by her unexpected, passionate assault. They came together with a shout of joy; then Natalie collapsed on his chest, happy and exhausted.

Alexei ran his hand over her silky hair, his eyes closed, a relaxed, contented smile on his face. "You've learned a lot about lovemaking in the last eight years," he murmured.

"Not really." She smiled. "You taught me all this a long, long time ago. I was just too shy back then to put your lessons to use."

"Well, I'm certainly glad you've gotten over your shyness."

Slowly, Natalie raised herself to her knees, breaking their intimate contact and lying down beside him with her head on his shoulder. "So am I."

They slept for several hours, then woke just before dawn to make love again. This time their encounter was slow and romantic as they exchanged whispered words of love and promised each other never to part again.

When love's storm had again abated, they lay in companionable silence, each lost in their own thoughts until, finally, Alexei spoke. "Tasha, there are a few things we need to talk about before we leave for Moscow today."

Natalie raised limpid eyes to his. "Yes?"

"I have to know . . ." He paused, hesitating so long that Natalie's eyebrows drew together in consternation.

"Have to know what?" she asked softly.

Alexei drew a deep breath. "Are you planning to bring charges against Anya for kidnapping Jenna?"

Natalie slid out of his embrace so that she could clearly see his eyes as she spoke. "I've been lying here thinking about that."

"And have you made a decision?"

"Yes. As long is Jenna is all right, I'm not going to press charges."

Alexei closed his eyes, profound relief obvious on his face. "Thank you."

Natalie propped herself up on an elbow, staring down at him with a serious expression. "Don't get me wrong, Alex: What Anya did was wrong, very wrong, and I haven't forgiven her. In fact, I don't know if I ever can. But I do understand that she thought she was doing the right thing in trying to get Jenna the medical help she thinks she needs."

Alexei looked up at her, his expression as serious as her own. "I agree with you. Anya was wrong to take Jenna, and I understand if you aren't able to forgive her, but I appreciate you not taking legal action against her."

Natalie drew a slow, lazy circle on his chest with her fingernail. "I don't want to start our marriage with a legal hassle between us. The most important thing right now is that you and Jenna and I work toward becoming a family."

Alexei lifted himself up on his elbows and kissed her lovingly. "You have the most generous spirit of anyone I've ever known."

Natalie turned her face away, and he noticed her chin begin to tremble. "You're wrong about that. If that was true, you and I would have been married a long time ago. Anya's not the only one guilty of poor decisions."

"Shh," he soothed, touching her cheek with his finger to encourage her to face him again. "That's all behind us now. What is it that you Americans say? Better late than never?"

Natalie looked over at him, her eyes swimming with grateful

tears. "Alex, can you ever forgive me for not telling you about Jenna?"

"I've already done that," he answered softly, pulling her back into his arms and holding her close. "Anyway, it's as much my fault as it is yours. I should never have gone back to Russia without you."

"I don't recall that I left you much choice."

"I should have tied you up and stuffed you into one of my trunks. Of course, you might have been a little angry with me if I'd made you arrive in Moscow inside my luggage, but at least I would have had you there."

Natalie giggled and planted a quick kiss on the soft skin beneath Alexei's ear. "You have me now, and this time, I promise to sit willingly on the plane with you."

They shared a quiet laugh; then Natalie turned and glanced at the clock on the bedside table. "Shouldn't we be getting up? It's already after six."

"In a minute," Alexei hedged. "There's one more thing we need to talk about."

Natalie looked over at him and nodded. "I know what you're going to say. You're going to ask me if Jenna can see Dr. Serikoff while we're in Moscow, aren't you?"

Alexei looked at her in surprise. "Well, no, that wasn't what I was going to say, but now that you mention it . . ."

"I want her to see him," Natalie said firmly. "If he feels that what Jenna has is the Romanov Curse, and you say he is the foremost expert in the world concerning the syndrome, then I would be a fool not to have him treat Jenna."

"I'm glad you feel that way"—Alexei nodded—"but I want you to know that I won't pressure you about it. You're her mother and it's your decision."

"No, Alex," Natalie whispered. "It's not just my decision anymore. It's *our* decision. I may be her mother, but you're her father, and we need to start making decisions about Jenna together."

Alexei flashed her a grin so devastatingly handsome that

Natalie caught her breath, awed, as always, by the chiseled perfection of his features. "You don't know how happy that makes me," he said, "and it also brings me back to the question I was intending to ask you."

He looked away, the words he was going to say so important to him that he needed to take a minute to phrase them exactly right. "After we're married," he began slowly, "if it's all right with you and with Jenna, I would like to adopt her. And if she agrees to that, then I'd like her to know who I really am."

Natalie studied him thoughtfully for a moment, nodding slowly. "Jenna has always wanted a father and I've always felt guilty for depriving her of you. If you and she decide that you want to legalize your relationship, then I will do whatever I can to help."

"And what about telling her that I'm her father?" Alexei asked carefully.

Natalie pursed her mouth. "That's a much harder decision, Alex. It's only fair to both of you that she eventually know, but I'm afraid she's too young to be able to understand why I made the decisions I did. Maybe when she's a little older . . . ten or eleven or so."

Alexei tried hard to hide his disappointment, but Natalie could see it in his eyes. Still, when he again spoke, there was no resentment in his voice, only quiet resignation. "I'll go along with whatever you think is best for her," he said.

"Thank you for understanding." Snuggling closer to him, she laid her head back on his shoulder and again began to lightly caress his chest. "I suppose we'd better get up now." She sighed.

Alexei's only response was to put his hand over hers and guide it downward. As soon as Natalie touched him, her eyes widened and she looked up at him, astonished to find that he was again fully aroused. "Do we have to?" He chuckled. "Don't you think we could stay in bed just a few minutes more?"

Natalie smiled and ran her tongue suggestively over her lips. "Well, maybe just a few minutes more."

It was another half hour before they finally got up.

TWENTY-TWO

It was raining when they arrived in Moscow, but despite the inclement weather, Natalie was impressed by the beauty of the great old city.

Alexei had made several calls before they left New York, and when they stepped out of the airport doorway onto the wet pavement, a man hurried over, clapping Alexei on the back and holding an umbrella solicitously over her head. After sharing several quiet words in Russian with Alexei, he led them to a large car and held the door as they climbed into the backseat.

It was the middle of the afternoon and traffic was heavy, causing them to inch slowly forward through the glut of cars, but despite her impatience to see Jenna, Natalie found herself enjoying their slow trip through the city. As they made their way past Red Square, she stared in awe at the onion-shaped domes atop St. Basil's Cathedral, the extraordinary sixteenth-century creation of Ivan the Terrible. Alexei explained to her that, according to legend, Ivan commissioned two architects to build his masterpiece and, once they were finished, had them blinded so they could never again create such a beautiful church.

"I guess Ivan came by his title honestly, didn't he?" Natalie chuckled, then turned her attention back to the window as they passed another towering structure built high above the banks of the Moskva River.

"What building is that?"

"The Kremlin."

"Really? I had no idea it was so beautiful."

Alexei looked at the ancient fort, trying to see it through Natalie's eyes. "It *is* beautiful, isn't it? I think most people from the West think of the Kremlin as some sort of cement bunker that served only as the headquarters for the Communist Party. They don't realize that it was here seven hundred years before the Communists took power and will probably be here for seven hundred more."

"You love this city, don't you?" Natalie asked softly.

Alexei shrugged. "Of course. It's my home."

They drove slowly on, but the time passed quickly as Alexei pointed out other spots of historical significance along their route. They were just passing Pushkin Square when, suddenly, Natalie began to laugh.

"What's so funny?"

"The Golden Arches." Natalie giggled. "What a sight. McDonald's in the middle of Moscow."

"Capitalism at its best." Alexei nodded, delighted that Natalie seemed to be enjoying their drive. "We also have Pizza Hut and Baskin-Robbins ice cream now, so if you get a craving . . ."

"Oh, I think I can do without a Big Mac for a couple of days," Natalie assured him.

As they left the historical area of the city behind, Natalie became restless, shifting on the seat and glancing at her watch several times.

"We're almost there." Alexei smiled, reaching over and squeezing her hand. "Just a little longer and you'll see your baby."

"I can't wait," Natalie admitted. "I've only been away from her for a couple of days, but it seems like an eternity."

"Believe me," Alexei said wryly, "I understand what eternity seems like."

Natalie threw him a guilty look, but before she could think of a suitable response, they pulled up in front of a large, well-

kept apartment building. "Here we are," Alexei said, opening
his door and bounding out of the car before the driver even
turned the engine off. Racing around the back of the vehicle,
he opened Natalie's door, taking her hand and helping her out
of the car. "Come on. I want you to see my 'awful communal
apartment.' "

Natalie grimaced, mortified that Alexei remembered her
cruel words from their argument a few days before. "I'm sorry
I said that," she mumbled, dropping her head in embarrassment.

"Forget it." He laughed and gave her a quick kiss. "I'm just
anxious for you to see it." Together, they entered the building
and took an elevator to the top floor. They stepped out into a
long hall and walked to the end, stopping in front of a pair of
double doors.

Alexei fished a set of keys out of his pocket and inserted
one into the lock, then opened the door. "Welcome to my
home, Tasha."

Natalie stepped into Alexei's apartment, then froze, looking
around in stunned amazement. "Alex, it's beautiful," she
breathed. Her eyes scanned the foyer, marveling at the stone
floor, the forest green wallpaper, and a highly polished oak
breakfront. There was a large living room off to the left, its
hardwood floor covered by a magnificent Aubusson rug. From
where she stood, Natalie could see that the room was decorated
in muted tones of mauve and gray, lending it a lovely air of
understated elegance. To her right, a hall led off in another
direction, and she looked down its shadowy length curiously.
"The bedrooms?" she asked.

Alexei laughed and leered at her openly. "My, my, Ms.
Saxon, you don't even have your coat off yet and already you
want to know where my bedroom is? What would your high-
society friends in Boston say if they could hear you?"

Natalie was saved the embarrassment of having to try to
explain her comment when suddenly Jenna came hurtling
down the hall, bursting into the foyer and throwing her arms

around Natalie with such enthusiasm that she nearly knocked her mother off her feet. "Mommy! Mommy, you're here!"

"Oh, baby!" Natalie cried, dropping to her knees and wrapping her arms so tightly around the little girl that Jenna let out a little grunt of surprise. "I'm so glad to see you. I've miss you so much!"

"I missed you too, Mommy." Jenna grinned, quickly extricating herself from her mother's crushing hug. "Auntie Anya said that you were coming today, but she didn't know what time. I'm glad you're finally here. I've been waiting all day."

Natalie flicked a quick glance at Alexei. "*Auntie* Anya?" she repeated.

"Uh-huh," Jenna confirmed. "She told me I could call her that."

Natalie drew a deep breath, incensed that Anya was already asserting herself as Jenna's aunt, but knowing that now was the not the time to deal with the woman's presumption. "Are you all right, sweetie?" she asked, again turning to look at Jenna. "Did you enjoy your plane ride?"

"No," Jenna said bluntly. "It was boring. They only showed one movie, and the rest of the time we just had to sit there."

"It *is* a very long trip," Natalie agreed, taking off her coat and laying it over the back of a chair.

"Moscow's fun, though," Jenna continued. "I've been having a real good time. Come and see my bedroom. It has two beds in it, so you can sleep in there with me."

"That sounds fine." Natalie nodded, then grinned when she noticed Alexei's dismayed expression. "That is, if it's all right with Mr. Romanov, of course. After all, it's his house, so he should probably be the one to decide where we're all going to sleep."

"You're going to have to sleep with me, Mommy, " Jenna said positively. "There are only three bedrooms. Auntie Anya has one and Mr. Romanov has the other, so that only leaves mine."

"Yes, I guess it does only leave yours. Well, let's not worry about it now. Why don't you show me where the bathroom is so I can freshen up a little?"

Jenna took her mother by the hand and eagerly led her down the hall. "The bathroom's funny," she informed her. "The bathtub has feet on it, and there's a chain you pull to flush the toilet."

Smiling, Alexei watched Natalie and Jenna disappear down the hall; then he strolled into the living room to fix himself a drink. Immediately he noticed Anya standing against a far wall, her face shrouded in shadow.

"Anya?"

"Hello, Alexei," she murmured, her voice laced with trepidation. "Welcome home."

"Come over here," he demanded, immediately switching from English to Russian. "We need to talk. Right now."

Slowly, Anya pushed away from the wall and approached her brother. "You're very angry with me, aren't you?"

"Yes," Alexei answered bluntly. "Words can't even express how furious I am with you. Do you have any idea what a serious crime you've committed? You have kidnapped a minor child and taken her into a foreign country. Surely you must realize that if Natalie decides to press charges against you, you could go to prison for the rest of your life."

"Is she going to do that?" Anya gasped.

Although Alexei knew full well that Natalie was not intending to press charges, he was not about to let his sister off the hook so easily. "I would not blame her if she did," he retorted. "What in hell were you thinking to do such an outrageous thing?"

"I just wanted to see that Jenna's hand got fixed properly, and her mother refused to listen to me. . . ."

"Anya!" Alexei warned, his voice rising angrily. "Refer to Natalie in that tone of voice again and you will leave my house. Do you understand?"

Reluctantly, Anya nodded. Then, clamping her hand on her brother's arm, she looked up at him with pleading eyes. "Alexei, please try to understand why I did what I did. Jenna is so talented that she deserves a chance to develop her gift, and if she doesn't have that thumb corrected, you know what will happen."

Impatiently, Alexei shook off her hand. "I agree that Jenna is talented," he gritted, "but it is not your decision to make whether or not she will have her thumb corrected."

"I just wanted to make sure that she got the attention she needed," Anya said, her voice beginning to tremble and tears gathering in her eyes. "After all, I'm her aunt . . ."

"And I'm her father!" Alexei shouted, his temper again flaring. "And Natalie is her mother and we will make the decisions, not you!"

Suddenly, Anya drew in a sharp breath, her eyes sliding over to the living room doorway. "Jenna! I didn't see you standing there, darling. Where is your mother?"

"She's in the bathroom," Jenna said, walking into the room and looking up at Alexei warily. "Why are you shouting?"

Alexei blew out a long breath and clapped his hand to his chest. "I'm sorry, Jenna," he said, his voice contrite. "Did I scare you?"

Jenna shrugged. "You were pretty loud. I know you were talking in Russian, but I heard you say my name and Mommy's. Are you fighting about us?"

"No," Alexei said quickly, squatting down and holding his hands out toward his daughter. "Anya and I were just having a little disagreement. Come here, sweetheart."

Jenna stepped forward and allowed Alexei to give her a hug; then she pulled away and walked over to Anya, reaching up and taking her hand. "Please don't yell at Auntie Anya, Mr. Romanov. You made her cry, and that makes me sad since she's my friend."

Natalie hurried into the room just as this exchange was taking place. She had heard the raised voices from the bathroom, but she had no idea that Jenna was involved in whatever altercation Alexei was having with Anya. Now, her jaw dropped

in disbelief as she watched Jenna clasp Anya's hand, then fear-
lessly take Alexei to task for shouting at her.

Anya looked down lovingly at her little defender, then
dropped to her knees and pulled Jenna into her arms. "You
are so wonderful," she crooned. "I simply adore you." Then,
getting back to her feet, she looked into Natalie's stunned face
and entreated, "Please forgive me. I know what I did was
wrong and I'm very, very sorry. I think Jenna is the most
precious child in the world, and I would never do anything to
harm her."

Natalie nodded curtly, still not ready to forgive Anya but
knowing, as she watched Jenna take her aunt's hand again, that
she would have to find it in her heart to do so.

Alexei shot Natalie a meaningful look, and at her answering
nod, said, "Anya, there are some things that Natalie and I need
to discuss with Jenna. Would you excuse us, please?"

Anya nodded and bent down to give the top of Jenna's head
a last kiss. Alexei watched her leave the room, then walked
over to a beautiful Louis Quatorze-style couch as Natalie held
her hand out to Jenna. Jenna followed her mother over to the
sofa, crawling up in her lap and laying her head against her
shoulder as Alexei began speaking.

"Jenna, what I'm going to say is very important, so please
listen carefully." He hesitated, then smiled when Jenna nodded
soberly, thinking how much her expression resembled
Natalie's. "Your mommy and I love each other very much,
Jenna, and we would like to get married, but before we do,
we want to know if it would be all right with you."

Jenna immediately sat up, a grin lighting her face. "Sure. I
think you *should* marry Mommy, since you're my daddy. All
my friends' daddies are married to their mommies."

Simultaneously, Natalie's and Alexei's mouths dropped open.
"Jenna!" Natalie gasped. "How do you know that Mr. Romanov is your daddy? Did someone tell you that?"

"No," Jenna shrugged. "I figured it out all by myself. When
Auntie Anya told me she was my aunt, I remembered what

my teacher said when we were learning about families in school."

"And what was that?" Natalie prompted.

"She said that your aunt is your mommy or your daddy's sister, and since Auntie Anya is Mr. Romanov's sister, then he must be my daddy."

For an endless moment, Natalie and Alexei stared at each other in speechless amazement till, finally, Jenna again broke the silence. "Isn't that right?"

Natalie nodded dumbly. "Yes, that's right."

"Oh, Jenna." Alexei laughed, pulling her over onto his lap and kissing her on her cheek. "Anya is right. You are wonderful. And do you know what?"

"What?" Jenna asked, rubbing her cheek where his day's growth of beard had rasped against it.

"I promise that I will try to be the very best daddy I can."

"Can we play the piano together?" Jenna asked.

"Anytime you want to, darling."

"And can I call you 'daddy' instead of 'Mr. Romanov'?"

When he answered, Alexei's voice was thick with emotion. "Jenna, there is nothing in the world that would make me happier."

Jenna smiled in satisfaction, then suddenly turned back to her mother, her little brow wrinkling. "But what about my daddy in heaven, Mommy? Wasn't he my daddy too?"

Natalie hesitated for a moment, trying to decide what to tell Jenna about Tom, but as she looked at her daughter's upturned face, she realized that this was no time for half-truths. Jenna was asking her a straightforward question and she deserved a straightforward answer. "Sweetie, your daddy in heaven was your daddy because he was married to me when you were born. But Mr. Romanov is your real daddy. He and I made you together, but then he had to come back here to Russia and I married Tom Saxon. That made him your stepfather. Do you know what a stepfather is?"

Jenna nodded. "We learned about step families in school

too. Lots of my friends have stepfathers or mothers or sisters and brothers." She looked over at Alexei, grinning up at him as though they shared a special secret. "But you're not my stepfather, are you? You're my real daddy."

"Yes, Jenna." Alexei nodded. "I'm your real daddy."

"And your name is Alexei."

"Yes."

"And one of my names is Alexandra." Suddenly she turned back toward Natalie, her eyes wide with revelation. "Is that why my middle name is Alexandra, Mommy? Because it sounds like my real daddy's name?"

Natalie blushed as she suddenly felt Alexei's eyes on her. "Yes, Jenna." She nodded, relieved that all the truths were finally out in the open. "That's why your middle name is Alexandra."

"Cool!" Jenna grinned. "Can I go have a cookie now?"

"*May* I have a cookie," Natalie corrected.

Jenna sighed. "*May* I?"

"Yes, you may."

As the little girl skipped happily out of the room, Alexei reached over and took Natalie's hand, pressing it to his cheek. "You named her after me?" he whispered.

Natalie nodded, her heart in her eyes. "It seemed like an appropriate thing to do. I've been trying to find the right time to tell you, but I guess Jenna solved that problem for me."

Alexei leaned forward and gave her a soft, lingering kiss. "It seems like little Jenna has solved a lot of problems for us in the past half hour."

"She has, hasn't she?" Natalie smiled, throwing her head back as Alexei started kissing her neck.

"She's a wonderful child," Alexei said between kisses, "and I love her more every minute I spend with her."

Natalie tipped her head down to kiss Alexei on the lips, her heart overflowing with happiness that he and Jenna were establishing such a close relationship so quickly. "I'm so glad," she murmured, their kiss deepening as he pulled her closer.

"I am too," he rasped, "but there's just one more thing I want to know about her."

Reluctantly, Natalie pulled away, looking at him curiously. "What's that?"

Smiling, Alexei drew her back into his arms. "What time does she go to bed?"

Natalie giggled and playfully pushed him away. "Eight-thirty, but she's always sound asleep by nine, and she never wakes up before seven in the morning."

Alexei grinned and began nibbling on Natalie's ear. "Oh, I do love that child."

Early the next morning, Natalie and Jenna sat in the cozy little kitchen in Alexei's apartment, eating toast and talking about their plans for the day.

"Is today the day I'm going to the doctor?" Jenna asked.

Natalie looked at her in surprise. "Did Auntie Anya tell you about that?"

Jenna nodded. "She told me on the plane that's why she was bringing me to Moscow. Because she knows a doctor who can fix my thumb so it won't hurt anymore when I reach for an octave."

"And you want to see this doctor?"

"I guess so." Jenna took another bite of toast, then looked up at her mother with hopeful eyes. "It's not going to hurt when he fixes it, is it, Mommy?"

"Maybe just a little," Natalie answered. "If the problem you have with your thumb is what Daddy and Auntie Anya think it is, then you'll have to have an operation to fix it. Do you know what an operation is?"

Jenna nodded. "Brittany Schuler at my school had to have an operation to get her tonsils out. She said it hurt her throat, but it was okay because she got to eat all the ice cream she wanted. Can I have ice cream if I have to get an operation?"

"Sure you can, sweetie. Baskin-Robbins too."

"All thirty-one flavors?"

"All thirty-one."

"Okay, then I'll do it. I know I can't play when my thumb hurts, and I want to play as well as Daddy . . . and, of course, you too, Mommy."

Natalie looked at her daughter and broke up laughing. "Of course, me too."

EPILOGUE

"Is she asleep?"

Natalie walked into the living room of Alexei's Moscow apartment and nodded. "Sound asleep. She told me just before she went to bed that her hand hardly hurts at all."

Alexei smiled. "Serikoff's a good doctor, and after he said that we'd caught Jenna's condition at such an early stage that it was still minor, I suspected it wouldn't take long for her to heal."

"Still," Natalie mused, "I never expected her to be this well recovered after only five days."

"Well, maybe now you'll believe me when I tell you that Russian doctors know what they're doing," Alexei teased.

Natalie sank down on the sofa next to him, tucking her feet up under her and laying her head on his shoulder. "Yes, comrade, you've definitely made a believer out of me. And speaking of Dr. Serikoff, there's something I've been meaning to ask you."

"What's that?"

"The day of Jenna's surgery, when he came into the waiting room to tell us that everything had gone well, he said something to you that made you get a really strange look on your face."

"Oh? What kind of look?"

Natalie lifted her head off Alexei's shoulder and sat up. "I don't know, but your eyes widened like he'd said something you found surprising. Don't you remember?"

Alexei grinned. "Yes, I remember."

Natalie waited a moment for him to elaborate and when he didn't, she gave him a playful punch on the arm. "Well, come on. What did he say?"

"He said that Jenna's surgery had been such a success that in twenty years or so, he expected to read in the papers that she is as great a pianist as her papa."

Natalie drew in a breath. Her papa . . . meaning you?"

"Yes."

"So he knows."

Alexei shrugged. "I'm sure he never had a doubt as to Jenna's paternity. After all, the name of the ailment is Romanov's Syndrome, and if Jenna weren't a Romanov, she wouldn't have it." He paused, looking at Natalie closely for a moment, then said, "Do you mind if people find out that Jenna is my daughter?"

Natalie settled her head back on Alexei's shoulder. "No, not anymore. I'll admit, there was a time when I didn't want anyone to know because I was afraid it would bring disgrace to the Worthington name if people found out that I'd gotten pregnant when I wasn't married."

Alexei chuckled wryly. "I'm sure after we get married and I adopt Jenna, a lot of people are going to at least suspect it."

"I hope so." Natalie smiled. "I want the whole world to know that I am the woman who was lucky enough to be the mother of Alexei Romanov's beautiful, brilliant daughter, Jenna Alexandra."

Alexei looked down at Natalie, all the love and passion he felt for her shining in his dark eyes. "I love you, Tasha," he whispered. "You and Jenna mean everything in the world to me and I will love you both till the day I die."

Natalie smiled at his words, thinking of her great, great, great-grandparents and the note she had found in the attic at Louisburg Square. Casting a grateful glance up at the heavens, she whispered, "Thank you, Grandma Claire. Thank you for helping make all my dreams come true."

BOOK YOUR PLACE ON OUR WEBSITE AND MAKE THE READING CONNECTION!

We've created a customized website just for our very special readers, where you can get the inside scoop on everything that's going on with Zebra, Pinnacle and Kensington books.

When you come online, you'll have the exciting opportunity to:

- View covers of upcoming books
- Read sample chapters
- Learn about our future publishing schedule (listed by publication month *and author*)
- Find out when your favorite authors will be visiting a city near you
- Search for and order backlist books from our online catalog
- Check out author bios and background information
- Send e-mail to your favorite authors
- Meet the Kensington staff online
- Join us in weekly chats with authors, readers and other guests
- Get writing guidelines
- AND MUCH MORE!

Visit our website at
http://www.zebrabooks.com

Put a Little Romance in Your Life With
Fern Michaels

__Dear Emily	0-8217-5676-1	$6.99US/$8.50CAN
__Sara's Song	0-8217-5856-X	$6.99US/$8.50CAN
__Wish List	0-8217-5228-6	$6.99US/$7.99CAN
__Vegas Rich	0-8217-5594-3	$6.99US/$8.50CAN
__Vegas Heat	0-8217-5758-X	$6.99US/$8.50CAN
__Vegas Sunrise	1-55817-5983-3	$6.99US/$8.50CAN
__Whitefire	0-8217-5638-9	$6.99US/$8.50CAN

Put a Little Romance in Your Life With
Janelle Taylor

__Anything for Love	0-8217-4992-7	$5.99US/$6.99CAN
__Forever Ecstasy	0-8217-5241-3	$5.99US/$6.99CAN
__Fortune's Flames	0-8217-5450-5	$5.99US/$6.99CAN
__Destiny's Temptress	0-8217-5448-3	$5.99US/$6.99CAN
__Love Me With Fury	0-8217-5452-1	$5.99US/$6.99CAN
__First Love, Wild Love	0-8217-5277-4	$5.99US/$6.99CAN
__Kiss of the Night Wind	0-8217-5279-0	$5.99US/$6.99CAN
__Love With a Stranger	0-8217-5416-5	$6.99US/$8.50CAN
__Forbidden Ecstasy	0-8217-5278-2	$5.99US/$6.99CAN
__Defiant Ecstasy	0-8217-5447-5	$5.99US/$6.99CAN
__Follow the Wind	0-8217-5449-1	$5.99US/$6.99CAN
__Wild Winds	0-8217-6026-2	$6.99US/$8.50CAN
__Defiant Hearts	0-8217-5563-3	$6.50US/$8.00CAN
__Golden Torment	0-8217-5451-3	$5.99US/$6.99CAN
__Bittersweet Ecstasy	0-8217-5445-9	$5.99US/$6.99CAN
__Taking Chances	0-8217-4259-0	$4.50US/$5.50CAN
__By Candlelight	0-8217-5703-2	$6.99US/$8.50CAN
__Chase the Wind	0-8217-4740-1	$5.99US/$6.99CAN
__Destiny Mine	0-8217-5185-9	$5.99US/$6.99CAN
__Midnight Secrets	0-8217-5280-4	$5.99US/$6.99CAN
__Sweet Savage Heart	0-8217-5276-6	$5.99US/$6.99CAN
__Moonbeams and Magic	0-7860-0184-4	$5.99US/$6.99CAN
__Brazen Ecstasy	0-8217-5446-7	$5.99US/$6.99CAN

Celebrate Romance With Two of Today's Hottest Authors

Meagan McKinney

__The Fortune Hunter	$6.50US/$8.00CAN	0-8217-6037-8
__Gentle from the Night	$5.99US/$7.50CAN	0-8217-5803-9
__A Man to Slay Dragons	$5.99US/$6.99CAN	0-8217-5345-2
__My Wicked Enchantress	$5.99US/$7.50CAN	0-8217-5661-3
__No Choice but Surrender	$5.99US/$7.50CAN	0-8217-5859-4

Meryl Sawyer

__Half Moon Bay	$6.50US/$8.00CAN	0-8217-6144-7
__The Hideaway	$5.99US/$7.50CAN	0-8217-5780-6
__Tempting Fate	$6.50US/$8.00CAN	0-8217-5858-6
__Unforgettable	$6.50US/$8.00CAN	0-8217-5564-1
